EBURY PRESS

SIVAKAMI'S VOW: BOOK III
THE BIKSHU'S LOVE

Ramaswamy Krishnamurthy (1899–1954), better known by his pen name Kalki, was an editor, writer, journalist, poet, critic and activist for Indian independence. Kalki's expansive body of work includes editorials, short stories, film and music reviews, and historical and social novels. His stories have been made into films, such as *Thyaga Bhoomi* (Land of Sacrifice, 1939), the M.S. Subbulakshmi-starrer *Meera* (1945), *Kalvanin Kadhali* (The Thief's Lover, 1955), *Parthiban Kanavu* (Parthiban's Dream, 1960) and, most recently, the Mani Ratnam-directed *Ponniyin Selvan* (Ponni's Beloved, 2022). One of the most renowned names in Tamil literature, Kalki was awarded the Sahitya Akademi Award for his novel *Alai Osai* (The Sound of Waves).

Nandini Vijayaraghavan, born and raised in Chennai, is a director and head of research at the Singapore office of Korea Development Bank as of 2023. Her translation of Kalki's *Parthiban Kanavu* (*Pratibhan's Dream* 2021) was shortlisted for the Valley of Words Awards in 2022. Nandini's columns on finance and economy have appeared in *BusinessLine*, *The Hindu*, *Economic & Political Weekly* and *Financial Express*. *Unfinished Business* (Penguin Random House India, 2023) is her first India-centric business book. Nandini co-authored a non-fiction book, *The Singapore Blue Chips* (2017), with Umesh Desai. Nandini blogs at www.litintrans.com.

SIVAKAMI'S VOW

BOOK III

THE BIKSHU'S LOVE

KALKI

Translated from the Tamil by
NANDINI VIJAYARAGHAVAN

EBURY
PRESS

An imprint of Penguin Random House

EBURY PRESS

USA | Canada | UK | Ireland | Australia
New Zealand | India | South Africa | China | Singapore

Ebury Press is part of the Penguin Random House group of companies
whose addresses can be found at global.penguinrandomhouse.com

Published by Penguin Random House India Pvt. Ltd
4th Floor, Capital Tower 1, MG Road,
Gurugram 122 002, Haryana, India

Penguin
Random House
India

First published in Ebury Press by Penguin Random House India 2023

Translation copyright © Nandini Vijayaraghavan 2023

All rights reserved

10 9 8 7 6 5 4 3 2

This is a work of fiction. Names, characters, places and incidents
are either the product of the author's imagination or are used fictitiously,
and any resemblance to any actual person, living or dead, events or
locales is entirely coincidental.

ISBN 9780143460046

Typeset in Adobe Caslon Pro by MAP Systems, Bengaluru, India
Printed at Replika Press Pvt. Ltd, India

www.penguin.co.in

MIX
Paper from
responsible sources
FSC® C016779

Contents

Characters

Pallava Dynasty

Mahendra Varma Pallavar	Emperor of the Pallava kingdom
Bhuvana Mahadevi	Queen consort of Mahendra Varma Pallavar
Narasimha Varma Pallavar aka Mamallar	Mahendra Varma Pallavar's only son and the crown prince of the Pallava kingdom

Chalukya Dynasty

Satyasrarya Pulikesi	Emperor of the Chalukya kingdom
Vishnuvardhanan	Pulikesi's younger brother and the king of Vengi

Other Royalty

Jayanta Varma Pandian	King of the Pandya kingdom
Durvineethan	King of Ganga Nadu

Monks

Thirunavukkarasar	A Saivite monk
Naganandi adigal	A bikshu

Commoners/civilians

Aayanar	A renowned sculptor of the Pallava kingdom
Sivakami	Aayanar's daughter and a talented danseuse
Paranjyothi	A rustic youth from Thirusengattankudi in Chola Nadu
Kalipahayar	Commander of the Pallava army
Shatrugnan	Head of the espionage force of the Pallava kingdom
Gundodharan	A Pallava spy
Kannabiran	Mahendra Varma Pallavar's charioteer
Kamali	Kannabiran's wife and Sivakami's friend
Ashwabalar	Kannabiran's father
Rudrachariar	An exponent of music and Mahendra Pallavar's music teacher
Namasivaya vaidhyar	A renowned physician and Paranjyothi's maternal uncle
Vajrabahu	Paranjyothi's co-traveller

Foreword

Kalki Krishnamurthy's numerous books, especially those belonging to the historical fiction genre, are very famous. The kings of the Pallava and Chola dynasties became household names after the publication of his *Parthiban Kanavu, Sivakamiyin Sabadham* and *Ponniyin Selvan*—all in the category of historical fiction. His avid readers went to the extent of believing that all the characters in these novels were historical, so powerful was his word picture.

Kalki's books are an enormous contribution to the history, heritage and culture of Tamil Nadu. I wonder if many of his readers would have known about the Cholas and Pallavas in such great detail if not for his writings. *Sivakamiyin Sabadham* has brought out the glory and greatness of the Pallavas in minute detail, highlighting the political, economic, social and cultural history of this dynasty.

Students of history know well the rivalry between the two important political powers of South India—the Chalukyas and the Pallavas—in the seventh and eighth centuries C.E. Many a war was fought between the rulers of these two dynasties, spanning many centuries. A famous war among them was fought between the famous ruler Chalukya Pulakesi and his equally illustrious adversary, Pallava Mahendravarman, in the seventh century CE. The opening paragraph of the third volume of Nandini Vijayaraghavan's translation immediately captures the attention of the reader. The war between the Pallavas and their arch-enemies, the Chalukyas, is on and the Chalukya ruler, Pulikesi has entered the Pallava country and laid siege to Kanchipuram, the Pallava capital. Mahendravarman, the Pallava king, is ably trying to defend his famous capital against the formidable adversary. The details, presented in a graphic manner, highlight the plight of the Chalukya army, which ran short of food and water supplies and eventually had to retreat.

Other than the historical personages in this book, the characters conjured by Kalki's imagination have caught the fancy of his readers. The famous sculptor Aayanar and his daughter, the immensely gifted dancer Sivakami, are important characters in this book. In fact, readers have often asked historians where Aayanar lived in Mamallapuram (the port city of the Pallavas) and where Sivakami danced. When told that they were not there in flesh and blood in the Pallava times, the expression of these readers is difficult to put into words! The Pallavas were known for their contribution to temple architecture and sculpture. Their cave temples, monolithic shrines and structural stone temples in many places in north Tamil Nadu stand testimony to this. There must have been numerous extraordinary architects and sculptors in the Pallava times like Kalki's Aayanar. It is true that the Pallavas encouraged the performing arts in their land and honoured these artistes as seen from inscriptions and sculptures, and this had been highlighted in Kalki's word picture. A touch of romance is also there—the crown prince Mamallar and the danseuse, Sivakami, are in love with each other. What eventually happens to their mutual affection is to be seen at the end of the book.

The paintings of Ajanta are world famous. The frescoes which were painted in the time of earlier dynasties, like the Satavahanas and Vakatakas, had been known to the Pallavas also. It is possible that, but for Kalki's book, many readers may not have, in times before the internet, even heard of the greatness of the murals of Ajanta. His descriptions have kindled their curiosity to know about the same and even to visit this remote place, for sure.

Kalki, in *Sivakamiyin Sabadham*, also highlights the importance of ministers, army generals like Paranjyoti and spies. Military tactics, administration, treachery, anxiety, love . . . *Sivakamiyin Sabadham* has it all. Those who have read the original Tamil work of Kalki will know that this book is an addiction—a tome that needs to be read time and again. The reader knows the story after the first reading but feels compelled to read it repeatedly. I, for one, have done this several times and will do so again in future.

It is no easy task to translate *Sivakamiyin Sabadham*—it needs a person with a knowledge and love for history, and a good grip over both Tamil and English to be able to do so. Nandini Vijayaraghavan has very ably captured the essence. It is important that books like *Sivakamiyin Sabadham* are translated into English so a wider audience can get to know about the glory of dynasties like the Pallavas, which were regional powers. School textbooks in India seldom focus on the rich history of such dynasties. It is essential that readers not conversant with regional languages have access to English translations of such historical novels. I wish

Nandini Vijayaraghavan many more such translations in the future. Her passion for history and her ability to ably translate from Tamil to English will bring the grandeur of India's heritage to the forefront.

Chithra Madhavan
(Historian and author)
Chennai

The Story Thus Far

Paranjyothi, a brave youth from Thirusengattankudi, a village in Chola Nadu, walks to Kanchi, Pallava Nadu's capital, to enrol himself as a student at saint Thirunavukkarasar's monastery. He befriends Naganandi bikshu on the way.

On reaching the Kanchi fort, the duo learns that the arangetram of danseuse Sivakami, the renowned sculptor and painter Aayanar's daughter, had ended abruptly that evening. The Pallava emperor, Mahendra Pallavar (aka Mahendrar), had ordered the fort gates to be sealed. Speculation that the Chalukya emperor, Pulikesi, plans to invade Kanchi is rife. Naganandi and Paranjyothi part ways. Naganandi heads to a viharam. Paranjyothi strolls around Kanchi looking for Thirunavukkarasar's monastery.

A temple elephant runs amok and charges towards Aayanar and Sivakami, who are returning to their forest residence in a palanquin. Paranjyothi, who fortuitously arrives there, wields his spear at the elephant, which chases him. Aayanar and Sivakami are rescued. Paranjyothi escapes unhurt too.

Due to the imminent war, Mahendrar imposes a night curfew. The city guards, who find Paranjyothi loitering, imprison him. Naganandi helps Paranjyothi escape from prison and introduces him to Aayanar, who agrees to educate the youth. Meanwhile, Sivakami clandestinely meets her lover, the crown prince Narasimha Pallavar (aka Mamallar), Mahendrar's only son.

Naganandi persuades Aayanar to send Paranjyothi to Nagarjuna mountain to learn the secret of the indelible paints used in the Ajantha caves. Aayanar, who is keen to unravel the mystery, secures a steed and travel permit for Paranjyothi. Naganandi gives Paranjyothi an epistle to carry.

En route to Nagarjuna mountain, Paranjyothi befriends Vajrabahu, a warrior. That night, Vajrabahu drugs Paranjyothi to sleep and replaces the message the youth is carrying with one penned by him. Paranjyothi continues his journey the following morning and stops at a monastery, as instructed by Naganandi. The senior bikshu of that monastery sends Paranjyothi with six horsemen, who are supposedly heading to Nagarjuna mountain. Paranjyothi, sensing the horsemen are heading elsewhere, tries to escape. The horsemen imprison Paranjyothi and take him to the Chalukya encampment, where he runs into Vajrabahu. Paranjyothi is produced before Pulikesi, who confiscates the message. Pulikesi is unable to comprehend the message. He solicits Vajrabahu's assistance, who states that the message may be for Pulikesi's brother and the ruler of Vengi, Vishnuvardhanan.

Pulikesi commands nine horsemen to escort Paranjyothi to Vengi and kill the youth if Vishnuvardhanan is unable to decipher the message. Vajrabahu promises to meet Paranjyothi en route to Vengi. The following night, Vajrabahu helps Paranjyothi escape. The duo kills the horsemen. As they ride to the Pallava encampment, their friendship grows. Vajrabahu promises to help Paranjyothi, who is keen to join the Pallava army.

On reaching the camp, Vajrabahu asks Paranjyothi to wait outside till he secures Mahendrar's permission. As Paranjyothi is waiting, the Pallava army suddenly turns jubilant. He learns that Mahendrar has reached the encampment.

Paranjyothi enlists with the Pallava army and meteorically rises to lead its cavalry. Mahendrar appoints him commander of the Kanchi fort, where he befriends Mamallar.

By making his son promise to remain confined within the fort, Mahendrar separates Mamallar and Sivakami. Mamallar's charioteer, Kannabiran, acts as the go-between helping the lovers exchange epistles. Naganandi accuses Mamallar of being a coward and a womanizer. Dejected by the separation, Sivakami believes Naganandi's allegations. She ignores Mamallar's missive asking her to remain at her forest residence. Naganandi, Aayanar, Sivakami and her aunt leave for Nagapattinam, where the bikshu promises to arrange for Sivakami to perform before an august audience.

En route they meet Gundodharan, a Pallava spy masquerading as Aayanar's apprentice. Gundodharan disabuses Sivakami of her misconceptions about Mamallar. He delivers to Naganandi a message which states that King Durvineethan of Ganga Nadu, as instructed by the bikshu, is invading Kanchi. Naganandi, who gave no such instruction, realizes treachery is afoot. He asks Aayanar and his family to stay in a viharam at Ashokapuram and rushes to meet Durvineethan. Gundodharan disappears too.

A few days later, Aayanar and Sivakami observe the Pallava warriors chasing the Ganga Nadu soldiers. Mamallar and Paranjyothi pass by the viharam while pursuing Durvineethan.

Mamallar sees Sivakami standing outside the viharam but does not speak to her. Kannabiran informs Sivakami of Mamallar vanquishing Durvineethan at the Pullalur battle and promises to convey her apology to him.

Gundodharan returns to Ashokapuram and shadows Naganandi. But he is unable to stop the bikshu from breaching a dam amidst a cyclone. Gundodharan, however, pushes Naganandi into the dam and hastens to Ashokapuram.

The flood waters reach Ashokapuram ahead of Gundodharan, who manages to procure a boat. Mamallar leaves his army behind and reaches Ashokapuram to rescue Sivakami. He and Gundodharan row Aayanar and his family to a village named Mandapapattu. During their stay at Mandapapattu, Mamallar promises Sivakami that she will be his queen-consort when he ascends the throne.

Meanwhile, Mahendrar and the spymaster, Shatrugnan, search for Mamallar. So does Paranjyothi, who traces Mamallar to Mandapapattu. They receive Mahendrar's missive instructing them to hasten to Kanchi, which they comply with.

Mahendrar and Shatrugnan reach Mandapapattu and meet Gundodharan, who informs them of Naganandi's attempts to kill Mamallar. Gundodharan accompanies Mahendrar and Shatrugnan to the guest house where Aayanar and Sivakami are staying. Mahendrar guesses that Naganandi is hiding there and hands over to Aayanar the lion insignia, which would give the bearer instant access to the kingdom's senior-most officials. As expected, Naganandi appropriates the insignia.

Mahendrar isolates Sivakami. He urges her to free Mamallar from her love so that he can solemnize Mamallar's wedding with the Pandya princess, thereby incentivizing the Pandyas to help him win Pulikesi. Sivakami refuses.

Naganandi disguised as a Pallava spy enters the ministers' council at Kanchi and announces that the Chalukyas have imprisoned Mahendrar. Mamallar prepares to attack the Chalukyas and liberate his father.

Unfortunately for Naganandi, Mahendrar returns and imprisons him. The emperor gives a rousing speech to the ministers' council. A guard rushes in and reports that the Chalukya army was approaching Kanchi. Mahendrar commands Paranjyothi to demolish the last surviving moat. The siege of Kanchi begins.

Chapter 1

Indestructible Ramparts

The Vatapi emperor Pulikesi laid siege to the Kanchi fort during Mahendra Pallavar's reign. This is a well-known incident in the annals of Dakshina Bharata.

The siege lasted about eight months, during which time the ramparts of the Kanchi fort stood tall and undamaged. Not even one soldier of the Vatapi army was able to enter the Kanchi fort.

The Vatapi forces surrounded the Kanchi fort and used aggressive means to capture it in one go as they had done in Vyjayanthi Pattinam. Swarms of foot soldiers simultaneously tried to swim across the moat from all four sides. The arrows the Pallava soldiers showered on the invaders from hidden locations in the fort walls and the crocodiles in the moat sent them to Yama Loka. Those soldiers who managed to reach the opposite bank were caught in the concealed traps that had been set up adjacent to the fort walls. The elephants that entered the moat combatted fiercely with the crocodiles, turning the waters of the moat red.

Having failed in their first attempt, the Vatapi army tried to bridge the moat and get the elephants to batter down the fort gates. The intoxicated elephants uprooted the large trees that surrounded Kanchi and laid them across the moat. But this task could not be executed smoothly. The Pallava soldiers hiding in the upper storeys of the fort entrance flung spears at the elephants in rapid succession. The spears found their mark in the elephants' eyes and other parts of their bodies. The injured elephants were forced to beat a retreat and they attacked the Chalukya soldiers instead.

The Chalukya army exercised great effort in building a bridge across the moat directly to the fort entrance. When the elephants rammed into the fort gates, the outer gates gave way. But a shock lay in store for the elephants. Embedded in the newly erected inner fort gates were hundreds of spear tips, which pierced the pachyderms. The beasts shrieked in pain, trampled the Chalukya foot soldiers who were following them, and fled. Chalukya soldiers broke down the door fitted with spear tips using massive logs of wood. There stood a sturdy inner wall constructed with hard stone and lime.

Even though these attempts, which lasted a month, did not succeed, Pulikesi decided to continue with the siege. His intention was to starve those within the fort and force them to surrender. The Vatapi army hoisted its flag and set up its camp in a large area surrounding Kanchi.

Six months after the siege began, the Vatapi army was facing the danger that Pulikesi had expected to befall those inside the fort. They ran short of food. How could food be procured for the lakhs of soldiers and thousands of elephants and bullocks that were used to draw carts if they were stationed at the same place? The Vatapi forces were unable to procure food in the area that spanned the banks of the North Pennai River and Kanchi. This was because the Pallava army that had gradually retreated from the banks of the North Pennai had taken all the food supplies with them, ensuring that the Vatapi army would have no access to food. The villages that surrounded Kanchi had also been evacuated, making it impossible for the invaders to procure food.

For two to three months, the elephants destroyed the forests and groves around Kanchi and consumed whatever was available. After this, it was necessary to travel several kaadam to procure food for the elephants. Even then it was difficult to spot greenery in the severe summer that year.

The Vatapi army faced another disaster during peak summer. There was an acute shortage of drinking water.

That year, miracles occurred in the area that spanned seven to eight kaadam around Kanchi. The dams that used to overflow in the months of Karthikai and Markazhi unexpectedly breached the embankments in the Thai and Masi months and flooded the surrounding areas. On account of this, there was not a drop of water during the month of Cittirai.

All the wells and ponds were filled with the flood waters from the breached dams. Even if a little water was found somewhere, it was stale and stinking, rendering it unfit to drink.

In those days, dams were constructed at three locations across the Palar River. Only a small quantity of water was let out of the dams during spring. But that year, during summer, even the Palar ran dry due to the breaches in the embankments that had occurred earlier in the year. As the Palar was dry, the canal that connected Kanchi to the sea also ran dry. The water in the moat surrounding the Kanchi fort turned into a marshy swamp of blood and flesh.

So wells were dug in the Palar riverbed to provide water to the lakhs of soldiers, elephants, horses and bullocks in the Vatapi army.

Several elephants ran amok due to hunger and thirst, causing a stampede. These elephants crushed many soldiers under their feet and dispatched them to Yama Loka.

One day in the month of Ani, Pulikesi's war-time ministers' council assembled in a tent atop which the varaha flag was fluttering. The seven to eight army chiefs, who had previously been with the Vatapi king on the banks of the North Pennai, were seated on a carpet, while the monarch was regally seated on an ivory throne.

Pulikesi's face was angrier and crueller than it had been earlier. He told the army chiefs: 'Mahendra Varman's father's name is Simha Vishnu and his son's name is Narasimhan. But Mahendran is like a fox. He is hiding inside the fort like a fox that hides in its hole. How long can we wait for the fox to emerge from its hole? Do any of you have any idea?'

The army chiefs kept quiet. No one dared to speak.

'Why are you all silent?! When we won successive victories, all of you were eager to offer suggestions. When we are in need of ideas, all of you keep mum. Ah! If only our bikshu were here now . . . !' lamented Pulikesi and sighed.

One of those assembled asked, 'Prabhu, is there any news about the bikshu?'

'The bikshu has not sent a message for a long time. There has been no message from him since the one he sent through a Kallapal chieftain named Vajrabahu when we had camped on the banks of North Pennai. I wonder what happened to him when he went to meet the Pandya king at Madurai. If only the bikshu were here now, he wouldn't be blinking like you. Chief of the Spies! I had asked you to trace the whereabouts of the bikshu eight months ago. Is there any news?' asked Pulikesi. The chief of the spies hung his head.

Then Pulikesi asked the leader of those assembled, 'Commander, what do you think? Do we have to continue with the siege? How much longer do you think Mahendra Pallavan will take to surrender?'

The Vatapi commander responded, 'There is no trace of fatigue or hunger amongst the Pallava soldiers stationed on the fort walls. But our soldiers get food enough to fill only half their stomachs. In another month, we will not be able to provide even that. There is not a single morsel of food in the ten kaadam surrounding the fort!'

Pulikesi, boiling with anger on hearing this, questioned, 'Oh yes! You always whine about the food scarcity! Is there no one here who can suggest something useful instead of complaining like this?'

One of the army chiefs suggested, 'Prabhu, the Pandya king has been waiting on the banks of the Kaveri River for six months. There was a bumper harvest in Chola Nadu last year. If we send a message to Jayanta Varma Pandian, he may send us food.'

Hearing this, Pulikesi remained immersed in thought for some time. He suddenly stood up, looked around at everyone, and declared, 'I have made up my mind. If I continue sitting idle here, I will go mad. Commander! You retain a large part of the army and continue with the siege here. I will head south to visit the Pandya king accompanied by one lakh soldiers. Ah! Our elephants that were so well fed when they left Vatapi are now so emaciated. Won't there be ample food for our elephants on the banks of the Kaveri River?'

The chief of spies observed, 'Prabhu, is it right for you to go with a small force? I'm not sure what the Pandya king's motives are.'

Pulikesi responded, 'I don't care what the Pandya king's motives are! He will not dare wage war with us. Even if he has treacherous motives, what can he do? There are no forts to hide in on the banks of the Kaveri. I have no fear as long as our foes wage a war on the battlefield.'

Chapter 2

Elephant Bridge

That year, the Kaveri and the Kollidam were flooded by the end of the month of Ani itself. When the Vatapi emperor and his army reached the banks of the Kollidam after travelling for two weeks, the river was in spate.

Senthan Jayanta Varma Pandian had pitched his army camp on the opposite bank of the Kollidam. His vassals, Kadumbalur Madhava Kallapallan and the Chera king, Illancheralathan, had accompanied him.

The Pandian was enraged with the Pallavas, as they had turned down his proposal to solemnize the wedding of his sister with Mamallar. A few days after the siege of the Kanchi fort had begun, the Pandya army had reached the area between the Kaveri and Kollidam rivers. The Pandya king had commanded Kadumbalur Madhava Kallapallan and Cheran Illancheralathan to bring their small armies along. Those days, all the Tamil kings who ruled the area to the south of the Kollidam were adversarial to the Pallavas. So, Jayanta Varman along with the two vassal kings decided to join hands with the Vatapi emperor and settle scores with the Pallava dynasty. However, Parthiba Cholan, who had recently ascended the Uraiyur throne, did not follow suit. Though Parthiba Cholan also resented the supremacy of the Pallavas, he was unwilling to align with the invaders from Utthara Bharata, or to seek their assistance.

The Chola kingdom, which was located to the south of Thondaimandalam, had been under the reign of the Pallavas since the time of Mahendra Pallavar's father, Simha Vishnu. Jayanta Varman had decided to use this opportunity to annex the Chola kingdom to the Pandya kingdom.

But the citizens of the Chola kingdom were opposed to this. They had been followers of Saivism for several generations. Ever since Mahendra Pallavar had embraced Saivism under the influence of Thirunavukkarasar, the citizens of Chola Nadu had become even more loyal to him. So, the citizens of Chola Nadu disappointed Jayanta Varman by not according him an enthusiastic welcome. On account of this, and also because he had been waiting on the banks of the Kollidam River for several months, Jayanta Varman was irritated. As the siege of the Kanchi fort continued for a long time, his respect for the Vatapi emperor also waned. Thus, despite being aware of Pulikesi's arrival on the opposite bank of the Kollidam River, Jayanta Varman took no initiative to visit him. Instead, he sent a message to Pulikesi, citing the flooded Kollidam River and inadequate boats to transport him and his retinue across the river as reasons for his not meeting the emperor.

Pulikesi responded by saying that he would build a bridge across the Kollidam River and cross it to meet the Pandian. Hearing this, the Pandian was initially amused. He laughingly wondered, 'How can a bridge be built across the Kollidam? What madness is this?'

But the following day, the Pandian witnessed an amazing sight while standing in his army camp. There was actually a bridge across the Kollidam River. And it was no ordinary bridge. Elephants were standing across the river with wooden planks placed on their backs! Seeing this wondrous sight, the Pandya king regained his respect for the Vatapi emperor.

When Pulikesi and key members of his retinue travelled across that bridge, the Pandian and his vassals welcomed him and accorded him the respect due to an emperor.

Over the next three days, the two kings conversed freely and amicably. They were in complete agreement that the Pallavas ought to be humbled. They decided to obliterate the Pallava dynasty, and to annex the region up to Kanchi to the Pandya kingdom and the region to the north of Kanchi to the Chalukya kingdom.

When Jayanta Varman offered to march up to Kanchi along with his army, Pulikesi insisted that the honour of capturing Kanchi ought to rest solely with him. Pulikesi invited the Pandian to Kanchi once the Chalukyas had captured the Kanchi fort, and it would suffice if Jayanta Varman sent food supplies to the Vatapi army. The Pandian agreed, and offered to send the food supplies he had accumulated for his army to the Chalukyas.

Chapter 3

Treaty

The Vatapi emperor and the Pandya king soon became intimate friends. Pulikesi invited Jayanta Varman to visit the northern banks of the Kollidam and be his guest for some time. Jayanta Varman accepted the invitation and visited the Chalukya army camp with his key ministers. Pulikesi not only showered lavish hospitality on Jayanta Varman, but also impressed him by showing him the four divisions of his army. After an extravagant feast, archers, swordsmen and wrestlers of the Vatapi army demonstrated their skills before the two kings.

Then, Vatapi's court poet sang laudatory verses that he had composed specially for the occasion. The Pandya king and the other vassals seemed mesmerized when the Vatapi court poet described the march of the ocean-like Vatapi army to the south, a scared Mahendra Pallavan hiding with his pond-like army within the Kanchi fort, the Vatapi emperor marching further south to see the beautiful Kaveri River, the immense joy the Vatapi emperor had felt on meeting the Pandya emperor, how the flow of the Kaveri River had been interrupted when the elephants stood across the river to form a bridge and how the water levels in the Kaveri had risen when the frenzied elephants had fallen into the river. Finally, it was time for Jayanta Varma Pandian to bid farewell to Pulikesi. He remarked, 'Satyasraya, after defeating the Pallavan and capturing Kanchi, you should not return directly to Vatapi. You must visit Madurai before you return!' In those days, Madurai was the most famous city after Kanchi in Dakshina Bharata. It was Jayanta Varman's intention to showcase Madurai's glory and impress Pulikesi.

Hearing this, Pulikesi sighed. 'Yes, I have been yearning to see Madurai for a long time. The bikshu who had written about Kanchi had also described Madurai. But—'

The Pandya king interrupted him, saying, 'I meant to ask you about the bikshu. Where is he? I expected him to accompany you.'

'We have no news about the bikshu! I wanted to ask *you* about him. Didn't he visit Madurai? What happened there? What did he tell you before leaving? Where did he say he was headed to?' asked the Vatapi king.

Jayanta Varman revealed that the bikshu's visit to Madurai had coincided with his father's demise, and the bikshu had been imprisoned in the confusion that had prevailed at the time. Jayanta Varman had released the bikshu after his coronation. Jayanta Varman further stated, 'As soon as the bikshu was released, he asked me if the Vatapi army had reached Kanchi. He was greatly shocked when I informed him that the Vatapi army was still on the banks of the North Pennai. He asked me to come along with my army to the banks of the Kollidam

River and said that he would proceed ahead of me. Didn't he meet you after he was freed?'

'No, I find that surprising. I wonder if, on account of that fool, Durvineethan, both of them met with a mishap. There is no news. I feel handicapped without the bikshu,' acknowledged Pulikesi.

The Pandian responded, 'Yes. I developed immense respect for the bikshu after having known him for just a few days. But why did that Ganga Nadu king rush towards Kanchi and get captured? Durvineethan's actions were in complete contradiction to what the bikshu told me. The bikshu insisted that I ought to be present on the banks of the Kollidam River should Mahendra Pallavan try to escape southwards, and that he had made arrangements for Durvineethan to act likewise should Mahendra Pallavan flee westwards. Why did Durvineethan have to march towards Kanchi in a rush? By doing that, he gave the Pallavan the opportunity to trumpet his victory at the Pullalur battle as though it was a significant achievement. It is because of this that the citizens of the Pallava and Chola kingdoms are feeling so proud!'

'Durvineethan's behaviour is a big mystery! We don't know for certain whether he is alive or dead. If we can find out what became of him, we may also be able to trace the bikshu's whereabouts. But all the despicable villagers of the Pallava kingdom claim to know nothing. This enrages me so much that I feel like torching all the villages in Thondaimandalam and reducing them to ashes!' When Pulikesi seethed thus, his already red eyes emitted sparks of fire.

'Yes, I too heard about everything. It seems that the citizens of the Pallava kingdom broke down all the dams and did not cultivate any crops during summer this year. They complain of famine in all the villages. It seems that they have hidden all the grains and complain of food scarcity and hunger! Wicked people!' exclaimed the Pandian. 'I know how to counter their wickedness. I also know how to extract the grains out of them. I don't want to engage in such acts now.'

'I ought to teach a lesson to the haughty citizens of Chola Nadu too one day. I am waiting for the Kanchi fort to fall . . . Never mind! Weren't you enquiring about Durvineethan? I recollect my spies telling me something. I will ask them right away,' remarked Jayanta Varman, and summoned the chief of his spy force.

The chief of the Pandya spies reported: 'When our army crossed the Kaveri and was approaching the Kollidam, we heard about the Pullalur battle. I immediately dispatched a few spies to find out more about it. It seems that the defeated Ganga Nadu king fled southwards. The breach in the Thirupaar Kadal Dam prevented Mamallar from advancing further. So, the Ganga Nadu king was able to cross the South Pennai River and seek refuge in the Jain seminary at Patalipuram. We don't know exactly what happened after that. A few people said that the chief of the Thirukovalur Kottam attacked the Jain seminary, razed it to the ground and imprisoned the Ganga Nadu king. I also heard that he is imprisoned in the mountains to the south of Thirukovalur.'

Both the kings then held discussions and formulated the following strategy. Pulikesi agreed to return to Kanchi and intensify the siege of the Kanchi fort. The Pandya king agreed to supply the necessary food to the Vatapi army for as long as the siege lasted. Once the water levels in Kollidam receded, the Pandian would cross the river with his army and capture the area up to the South Pennai River. They agreed to apprehend the chief of the Thirukovalur Kottam, accord harsh punishment to him, free Durvineethan if he was imprisoned in the mountains there and send the Ganga Nadu king back. If Jayanta Varman offered all this assistance, Pulikesi would acknowledge him as the emperor of the region stretching from Kanyakumari to the South Pennai River. After having concluded a treaty that was satisfactory to both parties, Jayanta Varman took leave of the Vatapi emperor and returned to the southern banks of the Kollidam.

Chapter 4

The Envoy from Vengi

After Jayanta Varman's departure, Pulikesi looked at his commanders and quipped, 'Fortune favours not only the mighty but also the meek! Ever since that Pallava fox hid himself inside the fort, this Pandya cat has become very ambitious! The Pandian wants to become the emperor of Dakshina Bharata on a par with the emperor of Utthara Bharata, Harshavardhana and me, the emperor of Madhya Bharata! His avarice is unbelievable! Let us first capture the Kanchi fort. Then we will teach this weakling a lesson before returning to Vatapi!'

Just as Pulikesi finished speaking, the sound of horses swiftly approaching the army camp was heard. The Chalukya commander who was leading the siege of the Kanchi fort had sent an urgent message through emissaries, who were accompanied by an envoy from Vengi. Pulikesi commanded that they be brought to him immediately. The leader of the emissaries and the Vengi envoy were produced before Pulikesi.

The envoy from Vengi had sustained heavy injuries and sported several bandages. Both the messengers prostrated before the emperor. The commander's messenger stated, 'Prabhu, he is carrying an important message from Vengi. Apparently, some people tried to waylay him en route to Kanchi. He fought with them and escaped. To ensure that he faced no danger while coming here, the commander ordered seven warriors to escort him.' Then the envoy from Vengi took out the message he had carefully placed in the sheath of his sword and deferentially handed it over to the emperor.

Pulikesi accepted the message and looked at the interpreter present in his assembly. The interpreter quickly stepped forward, deferentially received the message and read as follows:

> 'Respectful greetings to the emperor of the three realms, King Satyasraya Pulikesi, from your brother, Vishnuvardhanan. I have received no news from you ever since you reached Kanchi. Neither has there been any response to the several messages I sent. I wonder whether my messages reached you at all.
>
> 'As commanded by you, my coronation was held under the auspices of Guru Pujya Pathar. However, our difficulties are not yet over. The Vengi army is hiding in the mountains and is troubling us. There is discontentment amongst the citizens. There's another amazing piece of news! Buddha Varman, the son of Mahendra Varmar's uncle, has cropped up from nowhere with a large army. It seems that he is threatening to stop me if I cross the southern banks of the Krishna River and come to assist you.
>
> 'I have not yet fully recovered from the injuries I sustained during the Vengi battle. I am becoming progressively weaker and am unable even to mount a horse. There's a more important

piece of information than all this. Before hiding himself in the fort, Mahendra Pallavan apparently sent a message seeking the assistance of the emperor of Utthara Bharata. There is a rumour that Harshavardhanar is planning to invade Asalapuram and Vatapi since you and I are stuck in Kanchi and Vengi respectively. A traveller who was headed to the Nagarjuna mountain from Kanyakubja said so. The rumour is that Harshavardhanar is planning to invade us as he is keen to view the paintings in the Ajantha caves.

'In this situation, I want to know what your orders for me are. If you were to order me to come immediately along with my army, I am prepared to do so. You are a loving brother, father, guru, king, and a dear friend to me. Your decree is of greater importance to me than God's command. My body and soul are ready to be of service to you at any moment. I beseech you not to let me languish in doubt and confusion for a long time and to unequivocally command me to do something definitive.'

Pulikesi's eyes emitted sparks of anger when the interpreter began to read the message. Then he heaved a deep sigh like a spellbound cobra. When he listened to the concluding part of the message, he shed copious tears. He cried, 'I wonder when I'm going to see my dear brother Vishnuvardhanan again!' None of the commanders seated in the assembly attempted to console him. They were too terrified to say anything; lest their words had unintended consequences.

Suddenly Pulikesi stopped muttering aloud, wiped away his tears and roared like a lion, 'Who is the astrologer who computed the auspicious day to embark on this invasion? Has he come with us?'

One of the commanders replied, 'He has not come with us. He stayed back in Vatapi.'

'In that case, do remember this. Our first task when we return to Vatapi is to get an elephant to trample the astrologer!' commanded Pulikesi.

Just at that moment, a man bound with ropes was brought before Pulikesi. It seemed as though he had been brought in for the express purpose of becoming a victim of Pulikesi's anger. Pulikesi roared, 'Who is he? Who is he?'

The leader of the messengers who had come from Kanchi stated, 'Prabhu, he is a spy from Kanchi. We met him on the way here. We tied him up and brought him along.'

'Ah! It seems as though this cursed Pallava kingdom is inhabited by just spies. Good! Get an elephant to trample him instead of the astrologer!' commanded Pulikesi.

The man sentenced to such a harsh punishment was none other than Gundodharan. But he was not the rustic Gundodharan of the past. He was wearing fashionable clothes. And it seemed as if he was not unduly disturbed by Pulikesi's command!

Chapter 5

The Spy from Kanchi

When the Vatapi emperor, without paying much attention to Gundodharan, flippantly ordered, 'Get an elephant to trample him,' the chief of the Vatapi spies submitted deferentially, 'Arasey, it would be good if we question him before meting out the punishment.'

'Yes, yes. I spoke absentmindedly. Bring him closer,' commanded Pulikesi. Gundodharan was brought close to Pulikesi. 'Who are you? What is your mission? State the truth!' ordered Pulikesi in a fearsome tone.

It should be noted that the Vatapi king had learnt to speak Tamil during the last eighteen months and could now understand the language. As the language spoken in Vatapi and Tamil had several common words, Pulikesi did not find it very difficult to learn Tamil.

'Aiyya! I am my mother's only son. I was heading to Thiruvengadu, which is across the Kollidam. I was going to get some medicines from the vaidhyar there,' mentioned Gundodharan.

'Why do you need medicines? What illness befell you?' asked Pulikesi.

Gundodharan pretended to tremble with fear and blurted, 'The medicines are not for me, aiyya. They are for my mother. My mother swallowed the mortar when she was pounding puffed rice!'

This answer amused some of those present. A slight smile appeared on Pulikesi's face too. 'What are you blabbering? How can your mother swallow a mortar?' chided Pulikesi.

'No, she did not swallow the mortar. She swallowed the pestle!' mumbled Gundodharan, as he continued to tremble.

'Did she swallow the mortar or the pestle? Tell me the truth!' roared Pulikesi angrily.

'No, no! The mortar swallowed my mother!' stuttered Gundodharan.

'Are you clowning around with me? Do you know what I can do to you?'

'Aiyya! Please pardon me. The sight of all of you frightens me. So my tongue is unable to articulate my thoughts.'

'Compose yourself and state what happened without any fear!'

'When my mother was pounding the puffed rice, the pestle slipped and fell on her hand. I am going to Thiruvengadu Namasivaya vaidhyar to procure medicines for my mother.'

'Is that all or is there anything else? Tell me the truth!' roared Pulikesi.

'Yes, aiyya! I promise that the pestle was injured!' blurted Gundodharan.

Suddenly, the Vatapi emperor burst out laughing. He continued laughing for some time and then asked the chief of spies, 'What do we do with this mad man?'

The chief of the Vatapi spies observed, 'Emperor, he is not a mad man, but seems to be fixated on his mission. He is tight-lipped. He ought to be interrogated in a different manner.'

The leader of the soldiers who had accompanied Gundodharan stepped forward and stated, 'Prabhu, we found this message when we searched him,' and handed over a missive.

Pulikesi took the message and, as before, handed it over to the interpreter. The interpreter read out the following message:

> 'This is the mandate to the king of the country with the fish emblem, from the king of the country with the rishabha emblem. I came to know that the monkey from the north has come to the banks of the Kollidam to meet you. Don't fall under the spell of the puli's* enticing speech. Do you remember the story of the tiger that was trapped in the marsh pretending to pray and cheating the brahmin? You must firmly believe that the puli from Vatapi cannot harm Kanchi's rishabham. If the puli languishes in the marsh, it will die of starvation. Once this happens, there is the possibility of establishing a long-lasting relationship between the rishabbham of Kanchi and the doe from Madurai. But if you help to satiate the puli's hunger, it will be dangerous for the doe from Madurai. Do keep this in mind and act as you deem fit.'

---

* Tiger, in Tamil.

Even as the interpreter read out this message, the Vatapi emperor understood the underlying meaning. His body trembled with anger. The sound of him gnashing his teeth unnerved everyone around him. When Pulikesi recollected laughing at Gundodharan's talks of mortar and pestle some time ago, he felt ashamed. This further fuelled his anger. 'You spy! How dare you clown around with Pulikesi of Vatapi? Take him away. Pluck his eyes out, behead him and feed him to the vultures!' he roared.

As he passed this cruel command, Pulikesi's reddened eyes were focused on Gundodharan. Suddenly, the anger in his eyes subsided and immense amazement was evident. This was because when the soldiers tried to drag Gundodharan away, he made some strange gestures with his head. Pulikesi, who had been attentively observing this, realized that Gundodharan had traced a swastika sign with his head. That was why Pulikesi had looked so surprised. 'Stop!' Pulikesi cried out again. 'I have to ask this spy a few more questions. You leave him alone with me. Everyone else may wait outside the tent,' he commanded.

Chapter 6

The Bikshu's Message

On hearing the emperor's command, most people walked out of the tent. When the chief of spies and certain others hesitated, Pulikesi roared angrily, 'Leave!' They too left the tent.

Pulikesi looked at Gundodharan and asked him in a calm tone, 'Who are you? Who sent you? Do you bear any confidential message?'

'Yes, mahaprabhu! The bikshu sent me. I have a message.'

'Is that so? What is the message?' asked Pulikesi, leaping up from the throne in agitation. He then fired a volley of questions at Gundodharan. 'Tell me quickly! Where is the bikshu? Is he well? Why didn't he send any message all these days? What did he tell you?'

Gundodharan's eyes suddenly filled with tears. He exclaimed in a choked voice, 'Satyasraya! My guru has been imprisoned in the Pallavan's prison in Kanchi!'

Hearing this, Pulikesi cried, 'Ah! How can I allow the bikshu to languish in jail when I'm still alive? How shameful! Has Mahendra Pallavan become so vile that he imprisons ochre-clad bikshus?' he fumed. He then asked, 'Tell me everything in detail! How was the bikshu imprisoned? When did you see him? What message did he send?'

Gundodharan replied, 'I saw him a week ago—on Friday. Mahendra Pallavan, who betrayed his religion and his guru, has imprisoned all the bikshus in the kingdom in an underground mandapam. It was there that I saw the bikshu. King of kings, let me first tell you the message the bikshu asked me to convey to you. I was worried that some danger would befall me before I could meet you. Ah! Do you know how many dangers I faced during the last seven days? I will not fear even death once I have conveyed my guru's message to you. I tried all ruses to meet you in person. When I realized that it's impossible to gain an audience with you, I intentionally got trapped by our soldiers who were coming here from Kanchi. Prabhu, the bikshu asked me to convey four important messages to you. Please heed them.' With this introduction, Gundodharan sequentially stated the bikshu's messages.

The first message was, 'Don't trust the Madurai Pandian.' Jayanta Varma Pandian had imprisoned the bikshu at Madurai. At that point of time, there were some confidential exchange of messages between Mahendra Varma Pallavan and Jayanta Varman. As the two of them could be engaged in treachery, the bikshu warned Pulikesi to exercise the utmost caution in dealing with Jayanta Varman. He advised that Pulikesi should not undertake any task relying solely on the Pandya king.

The second message was that it was the Ganga Nadu king, Durvineethan, who had exposed the bikshu to Mahendra Pallavan and ensured that the bikshu was imprisoned in

Kanchi. He had pretended to engage in a battle against the Pallavan to deceive Pulikesi and had gone into hiding with his army. If Pulikesi did not return to Vatapi, then Durvineethan's son-in-law, Vishnuvardhanan, would be the undisputed emperor of the Chalukya Empire. This was the Ganga Nadu king's secret desire. The traitor Durvineethan ought to be punished appropriately at the opportune moment.

The third important message the bikshu wanted to convey was that he had come to know that Mahendra Pallavan had made baseless allegations in message to Harshavardhana chakravarthy. Pulikesi ought to enquire into this matter and act suitably. Mahendra Pallavan could comfortably hide within the fort for a minimum of one year as he had accumulated a large quantity of food supplies. In this situation, one ought to deliberate whether it made sense to continue with the siege or make another attempt to capture the fort through force.

The fourth message was the most important message sent by the bikshu. The emperor of Utthara Bharata, Harshavardhana, was extremely passionate about sculptures and paintings. In the Pallava kingdom, there were several mandapams dedicated to these arts. Mahendra Pallavan had created exquisite sculptures at Mamallapuram for the express purpose of showing these to Harshavardhana. Should the Chalukya soldiers damage any of these sculptures, Mahendra Pallavan would use that to his advantage. The Chalukya dynasty would be subjected to Harshavardhana's wrath. So, Pulikesi ought to ensure that the Chalukya army did not harm the sculptors and sculptures of the Pallava kingdom.

After conveying these four messages, Gundodharan remarked, 'I have fulfilled the promise made to my guru. I no longer fear for my life!' and started weeping.

Pulikesi asked, 'Why are you crying?'

Gundodharan replied, 'Aiyya, apparently Mahendra Pallavar has announced that he will impale all the imprisoned bikshus on stakes the day the Vatapi army crosses the moat and enters the fort! The bikshu asked me not to tell you this. But my conscience did not permit me to do so. I am unable to control my tears when I think that crows and vultures will peck my guru, who will be impaled on a stake erected at one of the road junctions at Kanchi!'

Pulikesi was immersed in thought for some time. He then asked Gundodharan, 'How did you meet the bikshu? How did you leave the fort?'

Gundodharan responded satisfactorily. He revealed that he had joined the Pallava spy force as advised by the bikshu. He was then deputed to interrogate the imprisoned bikshus for information. Fortunately, the task of delivering the message to Jayanta Varman had been assigned to him. He stated that he had used a secret tunnel to exit the fort and that he had no intention of delivering the message to the Pandian.

Pulikesi then asked him, 'Will you be able to return and deliver a message to the bikshu?'

'Prabhu, I will return to Kanchi even if death awaits me there. Your wish is my command,' replied Gundodharan.

'Yes, you must definitely return. You must meet the bikshu in person and tell him that I myself will meet him in Kanchi in ten days. You must tell him that he should not lose heart no matter what happens and no matter what he hears. You should also tell him that I will inform him of all the details in person. Will you be able to do this?' asked Pulikesi.

Gundodharan was genuinely taken aback when Pulikesi mentioned he would meet the bikshu in person in ten days. His face and eyes displayed surprise that had not been evident earlier.

A week after this conversation transpired, the sentries at the southern gates of the Kanchi fort were as astonished as Gundodharan was. Two unarmed envoys came on horsebacks to the entrance of the fort holding flags that bore the Varaha symbol and blew the horn they were carrying thrice. Their appearance and the manner in which they blew their horns indicated that they were Pulikesi's envoys, and that they had come seeking a truce.

'Ah! What a miracle! Is it the Vatapi emperor who has sent envoys seeking a truce? Is this real or a dream?' wondered the shocked sentries of the Kanchi fort. This unbelievable news travelled at lightning speed and reached Mahendra Pallavar, who was at the ministers' council.

Chapter 7

Mahendrar's Miracles

The ministers' council had assembled at the royal court at Kanchi. The members of the ministers' council and other courtiers were alert. The chakravarthy and kumara chakravarthy were seated on their respective thrones. While Commander Kalipahayar was seated separately nearby, Commander Paranjyothi was not seen in the assembly. As he was involved in the matters of fort security, he was unable to participate in the ministers' council.

All those assembled seemed to be slightly worried. The person who seemed to be the most perturbed was the minister of food supplies, Paranthaka Udaiyar, who was standing.

'Udaiyar, when the siege began, didn't you confidently state that we had accumulated fifteen months of food stocks in our granaries? It is only seven months since the siege began. There should be food stocks to last us for at least another eight months. But now you're saying that we have food stocks for only another three months. How is that?' questioned the chakravarthy. Mahendra Pallavar's voice sounded harsh, and his face was more creased than before.

Paranthaka Udaiyar's voice betrayed fear. He stammered, 'Pallavendra, certain tasks did not happen as per my expectations. In addition, certain unexpected events also took place. Some people who had left the city returned after the Pullalur battle. You had also ordered all the sculptors in Thondaimandalam to be brought to the capital. The population increased by 5000 because of this. We had initially planned to close all schools and seminaries and send the teachers and students back home. At the last minute, you ordered us not to do so.'

'Is that all? Have five months of food supplies been consumed because of all these people?'

'I too committed a big mistake. I took into account only the men, women and children when I reported that we had fifteen months of food supplies. I did not account for the temple cows, calves and horses. As we were unable to procure grass and hay to feed the animals, we were forced to feed them with grains,' acknowledged the minister.

'O course, Paranthakar! Temple cows and chariot horses may be blamed if Mahendra Pallavan, the descendant of Thondaiman Illandirayan, surrenders to Pulikesi of Vatapi,' quipped the chakravarthy and laughed. It was impossible to make out whether his laughter was born out of anger or deprecation.

At that point, Narasimha Varmar leapt up and remarked in an angry and tearful tone, 'Appa! Why do you speak in this manner? Why should Mahendra Pallavar surrender to Pulikesi of Vatapi? Why have one lakh soldiers been confined within this fort, fed and rested for the last seven months? Father! The calculation error committed by our minister of food supplies is also for the good. Please command us at least now.

Enough that we have been hiding inside the fort for seven months. Enough of the world laughing at us! Appa, command me at least now to attack the Vatapi army and decimate them!' He then prostrated before Mahendra Pallavar, who turned away to conceal the tears that had welled up in his eyes.

When the chakravarthy turned back towards the court within a moment, he wore the same harsh and scornful expression as earlier. He lifted Mamallar, who was prostrating before him and holding his legs, and remarked, 'Mamalla, it was my mistake that I allowed you to remain at the anthapuram for a long time. Weren't you a captive amongst your three mothers? That's why you imbibed anger and agitation, qualities that are characteristic of women. Valorous men should neither lose their temper nor get so agitated. Mamalla, do I have to tell you, an expert at wrestling, all these things?' Mamallar's lips twitched as he sought to respond to what his father had just said. But he was so angry that he found himself unable to speak.

Observing his son's condition, Mahendra Pallavar observed, 'My child! You have been patient for a long time. Please be patient for some more time. You and our Pallava soldiers will get the opportunity to demonstrate your bravery. I believe that our fort will be subject to an extremely violent attack in a few days. To counter the attack, we will have to exercise all our might. This will be a great challenge to the Pallava valour. All of us must be prepared to face this!' Mahendra Pallavar then looked at the minister of food supplies and commanded, 'Paranthakar, from today, everyone in Kanchi, including the cows and horses, must follow Samana customs!'

The courtiers were shocked.

'They will follow only one Samana custom. Like Jain monks, everyone must abstain from consuming dinner.

Reduce the food supplies you have been distributing by one-third. My command includes those in the palace and temples as well. Henceforth, the residents of Kanchi will consume two meals a day. If we adopt this measure, we will have food stocks that will last us for four and a half months. Ministers! What do you say?' asked the chakravarthy.

Prime Minister Saranga Devar observed, 'Prabhu, you seem to be under the impression that the siege will not last beyond four-and-a-half months.'

'No, I don't think that the siege will last for even that much time. I asked for the food distribution to be reduced by a third as a precautionary measure. I expect Pulikesi to attack the fort within the next week . . .'

'Prabhu! There must be a reason underlying your expectation,' observed Saranga Devar.

'Yes! I wish to share the reasons with you! Courtiers! When it comes to food scarcity, Pulikesi is in a far more precarious situation than we are. The Vatapi forces have been surviving despite inadequate food for the last three months. Pulikesi left Vatapi leading an army of five lakh soldiers and fifteen thousand elephants. Now, there are only three-and-a-half lakh soldiers in the Vatapi army. Only 14,000 elephants are alive. Courtiers! If another month passes, half of those alive will die of hunger and disease. I don't know what will become of the elephants. So Pulikesi has no option but to attack the fort soon. There is also no doubt that this attack will be very violent.'

The chief minister, Ranadheera Pallavarayar, declared, 'Pallavendra! This world has not yet witnessed such a wonder. Usually, those who are subject to a siege suffer from hunger and disease. They also surrender to their attackers. I have not heard even in stories that those who laid the siege were stricken by hunger!'

'Yes, Pallavarayar! By the grace of the Peruman who reduced Tripuram to ashes, this miracle has occurred. The villagers of Thondaimandalam have refused to give our enemies a single measure of rice or a fistful of millets. They have carefully buried all the grains they possess. Even the dams of Thondaimandalam have rendered us great assistance. During the month of Thai, all the dams were breached for inexplicable reasons. On account of the floods caused by these breaches, all the plantain and coconut groves rotted. This summer, no crops were cultivated. Hence, no food was available to Pulikesi's soldiers and elephants.'

Commander Kalipahayar stood up and disclosed, 'Courtiers! It is true that the dams of Thondaimandalam joined hands with us, ruptured, and subjected our foes to hunger. But they did not break by themselves. They breached on account of the miracles performed by the Vichitra Siddhar, our king, Mahendrar.'

'I did not do anything. Our spy force headed by Shatrugnan functioned excellently. The chiefs of the kottams have also worked skilfully. Unmindful of the famine that the country may face, they broke down all the dams and canals. Courtiers, I cannot repay my debt of gratitude to the citizens of Thondaimandalam for their cooperation, even if I were to serve them in my next hundred births.' When the chakravarthy uttered these words, his voice choked with emotion.

Silence prevailed in the mandapam for some time. Then the prime minister, Saranga Devar, enquired, 'Pallavendra, it seems that Pulikesi has headed to the banks to Kollidam to meet the Pandian. The Pandian might provide the necessary food supplies to the Vatapi army, might he not?'

'Yes, minister. Pulikesi has travelled south to seek the help of the Pandian. But I do not think that he will be able to secure that assistance. Moreover, a situation that will compel Pulikesi to return to Vatapi soon has now arisen. Courtiers, I am expecting important news from the south at any moment.' So saying, Mahendra Pallavar looked towards the entrance of the mandapam. He then announced, 'Yes! That news is reaching us!'

A guard entered, bowed to the chakravarthy and whispered something into his ear. Mahendra Pallavar, who was not usually surprised by anything, seemed amazed as he listened to the guard.

'Courtiers! An amazing bit of news that neither you nor I had anticipated has come. I am unable to believe this myself. I am going to enquire and ascertain the truth. The court may now disperse and assemble again tonight. Then I will tell you everything in detail. Mamalla! You too go the palace and meet your mother.' As Mahendra Pallavar spoke, he walked to the entrance of the mandapam. He then leapt on to the horse that was waiting for him.

Chapter 8

Yoga Mandapam

A surprise awaited anyone visiting Kannabiran. His house echoed with the cries of an infant. In the dim twilight, an elderly Saivite man, sporting rudraksha beads and vibhuti, was standing inside the house carrying a six-month-old baby in his arms. This healthy, good-looking but wailing child resembled the child-God Kannan who had just consumed butter. Kannabiran and Kamali were standing in front of the elderly man and smiling.

The elderly man was trying to hand the baby back to Kamali. She was refusing to take the baby back. 'What can I do? The child is so fond of his grandfather. He is refusing to come to me,' commented Kamali.

Kannabiran felt happy observing the goings-on. The baby kicked his arms and legs around as he cried. The elderly man quipped, 'Kamali, the child is as mischievous as you are!'

Just then someone rang the bell at the palace garden, which was at the back of the house. Hearing the bell, the elderly man grew agitated. He looked around, put the baby down on the floor and ran towards the garden. Kamali, her eyes emitting sparks of anger, commented, 'Look how smart your father is. How can he bear to leave an infant on the floor and run?'

'Kamali! My father cannot be blamed. When God himself summons him, what can he do?'

'God calling him indeed! All this is fantasy. If he is so devout, why doesn't he go to the forest to meditate? What work does he have at the ornate mandapam in the palace garden? Did he get a place there to build a samadhi? Never mind, he said that the child has inherited my mischievous nature! The old man is sharp-tongued. As if his son is harmless! Look! I'm leaving. I want to meet my sister, Sivakami. As soon as the fort gates are opened, I will leave along with this mischievous child! Who will live in this prison-like palace?'

Kamali spoke without pausing as she bent to pick up the child that lay on the floor. Kannan also bent down at the same time to pick up the baby. Their heads banged against each other. 'You don't have to pick up this mischievous child!' declared Kamali.

'I will pick him up. Who are you to stop me?' retorted Kannan. While both of them were arguing, even as the child lay on the floor, the sound of horses was heard at the entrance. A few moments later, someone entered the house. Kannabiran and Kamali turned around to see who had come in and were startled.

For the visitor was none other than the chakravarthy, Mahendra Pallavar himself!

'Oh! Is there a war underway here too? It seems as though the war the nation is facing will come to an end, but the war between the two of you will never end!' When the chakravarthy said this, both of them were embarrassed and remained silent. Then Mahendra Pallavar asked, 'Kamali! Is your child doing well?' He walked up to the child and looked at his face. 'He looks exactly like Kannan. He may be christened Chinna Kannan. When Mamallan gets married and begets a child like this, the palace will be lively. It has been very long time since the sound of an infant crying was heard at the palace!' It seemed as though Mahendrar was talking to himself. He then asked, 'Kanna, where is your father?'

Kannan replied, 'Prabhu, he just left for the Vasantha mandapam.'

When Mahendrar commented, 'Ah! Has he gone there to meditate?' Kamali smiled slightly. 'Kamali is smiling! Young people like you will find concepts like meditation and samadhi amusing. When you grow old and are disenchanted with the world, you too will seek ways to attain enlightenment. Never mind, you continue with the war. I will visit the saint,' remarked Mahendrar as he walked towards the backyard. He stopped at the rear entrance for a moment, announced, 'Kamali! You will be able to meet your friend Sivakami soon!' and walked away.

When the chakravarthy disappeared, Kamali asked, 'Kanna! Why did the chakravarthy have to come suddenly and embarrass us? Kanna, did you hear him say that Sivakami will come here soon? Is the war going to end soon? Have the Chalukyas fled after losing?'

Kannabiran, not heeding those questions, was thinking about something else. Suddenly he declared, 'Kamali! I've harboured a suspicion for some time now. Today, it has been resolved!'

'Do you doubt me? What's your doubt?'

'I don't doubt you. It's my father whom I doubt. He speaks of yoga, meditation and discourses and sits in the mandapam in the garden all day. I wondered if there was a secret motive behind this. I am no longer suspicious now.'

'What suspicion? How did it get confirmed?'

'Come close to me. I will tell you. It's an extremely confidential matter. Even this infant should not hear about this. There is an underground tunnel in the yoga mandapam that leads outside the fort. I believe that the chakravarthy's spies enter and leave the city through that tunnel. Do you notice how this boy is overhearing our conversation ...!' asked Kannabiran and pinched the baby lightly. The baby gave out a sharp scream. Kamali started arguing with Kannabiran, who replied, 'He may also pinch my cheeks if he wants to.'

Kamali cooeed at the child, 'My dear!' and leaned forward to kiss him. Kannabiran placed his face in between the baby and Kamali resumed arguing with him. Commotion prevailed.

In the meantime, Mahendra chakravarthy made his way into the palace garden and reached the Vasantha mandapam. On hearing his footsteps, Ashwabalar—who was pretending to be a Shiva bhakta—peeped out of the mandapam entrance and remarked, 'Prabhu, Is that you? You have come at the right moment. Just now the bell was sounded.' So saying, he moved the central Shiva idol to reveal a poorly lit passage. Within moments, Shatrugnan's head appeared at the passage, followed by his entire body.

'Shatrugna! I was growing tired waiting for you. What was the outcome of your mission? Was it a success or failure?' demanded Mahendra Pallavar.

'Has the Pallavendrar ever failed? It was a success, swami! Everything happened as per your plan. Gundodharan was captured by the Chalukya soldiers who had escorted the envoy from Vengi. Both of them were presented to Pulikesi on the banks of the Kollidam River.'

'Did you meet Gundodharan after that? Did you receive any message from him?'

'No, I did not. I was waiting for him all this time. I've heard that Pulikesi is very short-tempered, swami! That's why I'm a little concerned about Gundodharan.'

'No harm would have befallen Gundodharan, Shatrugna.'

'How can you be so sure, prabhu?'

'Our ruse has been more successful than we expected. Listen to me, Shatrugna. Pulikesi has called for a truce! His envoys are waiting for my response at the southern entrance of the fort. I wanted to meet you before responding. That's why I rushed here.'

'Prabhu, can Pulikesi be trusted? He is known to be treacherous,' observed Shatrugnan.

'There is no room for doubt, Shatrugna! But I was hoping that Gundodharan had returned so that I could confirm a few issues with him.' Even as Mahendrar was talking, a cough was heard from the pit from which Shatrugnan had emerged. They watched, startled, as Gundodharan's head popped up from that pit the very next moment.

'Gundodhara! May you live a hundred years! We were just talking about you. How did you suddenly crop up here?' asked the chakravarthy.

Gundodharan replied, 'Prabhu, haven't you frequently asked me to follow Shatrugnan? That's an extremely difficult task. I ran through the dark tunnel trying to follow him. But I was unable to catch up with him!'

'You can clown around later! Tell me what transpired in detail,' ordered Mahendra chakravarthy.

Gundodharan related in detail his meeting with Pulikesi.

Chapter 9

Ceasefire

When the ministers' council assembled during the second jaamam of that night, everyone was tense. The city was buzzing with the news that two Chalukya soldiers had arrived at the southern gates of the fort holding aloft white flags and had delivered a missive to be handed over to Mahendra chakravarthy. Everyone was keen to know the contents of the message and Mahendra Pallavar's proposed response. Most importantly, Narasimha Varmar's face exuded fire and brimstone. His fiery eyes and deep sighs were reflective of the storm raging within him.

The chakravarthy's gait was more sprightly than usual as he walked in and sat down on his throne. Everyone's attention was on the missive he was holding. 'Courtiers, I told you this evening when the court was about to disperse that I was expecting important news. News more important and amazing than the one I was waiting for has arrived. Ministers! Commanders! Everyone listen to me! The Vatapi emperor has called for a truce. He has sent a missive in which he seeks peace and friendship!' When Mahendra Pallavar announced this and held up the message he had in his hand, the surprise and jubilation expressed by the courtiers cannot be described. Amidst this uproar, there was a lone voice of dissent. Needless to say, that voice was Mamallar's.

'Ministers! I wish to know your views. The emperor who unilaterally rules Madhya Bharata from Tungabhadra River to Narmada River is seeking our friendship. He wants to make peace with us. How should I respond to him? Shall I tell him that we will not stop the war and that we will definitely engage in a battle? Or, in accordance with the Pallava dynasty's dharma, shall we accept the hand of friendship extended by the Vatapi emperor? Courtiers! Think well before you answer. King Pulikesi of Vatapi, who leads an army of five lakh infantry and 15000 elephants, wants to end the war and enter Kanchi as our guest. He wants to stay in this city for a few days, view and enjoy the sights of this great city, and then return. May we respectfully welcome him or should we fasten the fort gates with a few more locks? Discuss amongst yourselves and state your unanimous opinion,' said the chakravarthy.

For some time, there was commotion in the assembly. The ministers enthusiastically spoke amongst themselves. Finally the prime minister, Saranga Deva Bhattar, stood up to talk and silence descended on the assembly. He stated, 'Pallavendra, everyone here has complete confidence in your statesmanship and foresight. Everyone is aware that you will do the correct thing at the right time in an appropriate manner. So we would like to know your views.'

The chakravarthy declared, 'Bhattar, isn't my opinion obvious? I do not wish to prolong the war for even a moment longer than absolutely necessary. I do not want to lose even a single life unnecessarily. All of us within this fort are comfortable to a large extent. But the Pallava citizens who reside in the villages and cities outside this fort face great difficulty. There has been no cultivation of crops during this summer in Thondaimandalam. It is possible that the citizens of Pallava Nadu will face famine within a few months. In this situation, I am unwilling to unnecessarily prolong this war. Moreover, when the brave King Pulikesi, who caused the emperor of Utthara Bharata, Harshavardhana chakravarthy, to retreat, stops the war and seeks peace of his own accord, why should we reject the offer? My opinion is that peace should be restored.'

When the chakravarthy stopped speaking, Saranga Deva Bhattar observed, 'Pallavendra, the ministers' council is in complete agreement with everything you said just now. But one issue bothers some of us. We wonder if it is wise to invite the Vatapi emperor as a guest to Kanchi. We have heard that the Vatapi king is a treacherous man who has no code of ethics, and that he is a demonic character. Can there be a hidden ruse behind his stated intention of visiting Kanchi?'

Mahendra Pallavar smiled and remarked, 'Saranga Devar, you have stated what vigilant ministers ought to say. We need to consider this possibility. But there can be no deception behind the Vatapi king's request. He has consented to send his entire infantry and elephant force two kaadam away from Kanchi. He is ready to enter Kanchi with ten to fifteen of his key ministers. Courtiers! How can we doubt someone who has sent us such a message reposing so much confidence in us? So, I want to know if you wish to continue this war or accept the truce.'

Once again the ministers consulted amongst themselves. Finally, Saranga Deva Bhattar stood up and stated, 'Pallavendra, the ministers' council desires peace. With regard to inviting the Vatapi emperor as a guest to Kanchi, the council opines that you may act in the manner you deem fit.'

Chapter 10

War of Words

When the prime minister, Saranga Devar Bhattar, conveyed the unanimous view of the ministers' council, Mahendra chakravarthy looked around at all the courtiers. He completed his visual survey without looking at Mamallar and Paranjyothi, and started talking. 'Courtiers, anticipating your opinion—'

Mamallar, unable to sit still on his throne, leapt up and asked, 'Pallavendra, may I also express my view in this great court in which monks, peace lovers, political strategists and those endowed with foresight are assembled?' Every word he uttered felt like an agniastram, an arrow emitting fire, to those assembled.

Mahendrar attempted to suppress Mamallar's agniastram with a weapon emitting water, a varunastram. 'Narasimha! Why are you raising such a question? Aren't you the kumara chakravarthy, who has the right to ascend the throne of the Pallava kingdom? Who else has more right than you to participate in the ministers' council? You may definitely state your views. But since I'm your father and those assembled in this court are mature both in age and experience, I presume you will not talk insultingly . . .'

Hearing the amusement that ensued, Mamallar threw a scorching glance at the courtiers and then turned to his father.

'Father, it is not my intention to insult you or the elders assembled here. I want to ensure that the world does not insult the Pallava dynasty or the Pallava kingdom. You have often spoken about the valorous Pallava dynasty that has ruled this country for several generations since the time of Thondaiman Illandirayan. Have members of the Pallava dynasty ever acted in this manner before? Have we ever retreated from our enemies in the battlefield? Have we ever hidden inside a fort, fearing an invasion? Now, you conclusively state that you are going to make peace with the traitor who dared to invade the Pallava kingdom. Pallavendra! I beseech you to think about how the world will interpret your actions. Won't everyone say that the Pallava chakravarthy hid inside the fort fearing the invasion of Pulikesi of Vatapi and that he finally surrendered and sought peace? No one will ever mention that it was Pulikesi who sent envoys calling for a truce. The Pandian, Cholan, Cheran and Kallapallan will pour scorn on the Pallavas. The Ganga Nadu king who fled from the Pullalur battle will raise his head again. This blemish on the Pallava dynasty will not be erased as long as the world exists.'

When Mamallar spoke in this manner, appealing to the self-respect and valour of the listeners, commotion prevailed in the court. The courtiers spoke amongst themselves, acknowledging the truth in Mamallar's words.

Mahendra chakravarthy surveyed the court with his hawk-like eyes and correctly assessed the situation. With his head held aloft, he majestically replied, 'My son! The world is not as crazy as you make it out to be. People are not fools. Even if they were so, I cannot act foolishly. I cannot engage in warfare unnecessarily. I cannot sacrifice the lives of lakhs of warriors for egoistic reasons. I cannot unnecessarily subject the citizens to untold misery. Mamalla, when I ascended the Pallava throne, wore this crown and held this sceptre for the first time, I vowed in front of the entire nation that I would safeguard the life and possessions of the citizens and that I would ensure that they faced no difficulty. I will not break that vow for selfish reasons or in fear of what the fools in this world may say!'

But there were still some arrows left in Mamallar's quiver.

'Father! You don't have to be worried about the citizens of Pallava Nadu. By God's grace, I had the opportunity to stay in a small village for three days eight months ago. At that time, I listened to the villagers' conversations. I understood that the Pallava citizens are valorous, and that honour is more important to them than their lives and possessions. Are you aware how jubilant the people in this country were when we won the Pullalur battle? They were unable to believe the notion of us hiding inside this fort with our brave army. Pallavendra, may I relate what I heard the residents of the Mandapapattu village say? "Why would Mahendra chakravarthy, who has a son like Mamallan and a commander like Paranjyothi, hide inside the fort fearing Pulikesi?" They said that you would never act in this manner. Our citizens expected the brave Pallava army to wage a war when Pulikesi surrounded the Kanchi fort. We have completely let them down. Command me at least now to fulfil their expectations. There are one lakh soldiers inside this fort itching to fight. The swords and spears made by this city's skilled blacksmiths during the last one and a half years are thirsting for blood. My dear friend Paranjyothi is keen to fight. Father, command us to lead the army. Command us to decimate the Vatapi army this very moment!'

Mahendra Pallavar was so overcome by emotion that he was unable to speak. It seemed as though his hard heart had melted, listening to his son's brave words. But the very next moment, he gritted his teeth and declared with a harsh expression on his face, 'My child, I'm happy that you spoke words that befit a true warrior. But I am unable to accept your views. You conveyed the opinion of the Pallava citizens. I am happy about that too. But the citizens are not always right. I am not going to listen to their views, which are born out of emotion and not out of forethought, and subject them and their descendants to untold misery and loss!' He turned towards the courtiers and announced, 'Courtiers, anticipating your approval, I have already communicated my acceptance to the Vatapi emperor. I have sent him a message accepting his offer of peace and communicating my pleasure in inviting him as a guest to Kanchi. I am now unable to retract my word.'

Mamallar became even more agitated than before. 'Appa! What is this? How can we welcome the sworn enemy of the Pallava dynasty to our capital? How can we extend hospitality to Pulikesi? I request you to stop at accepting Pulikesi's offer of peace. We can continue hiding in this fort till the Vatapi army leaves this kingdom if you so desire. But there is no necessity to befriend the treacherous Pulikesi. There is no necessity for the sinner who set Vyjayanthi Pattinam on fire to set foot in this holy city.'

'Impossible, Narasimha! We Pallavas do not renege on the commitments we make. I am obliged to welcome Pulikesi,' retorted Mahendrar.

When Mamallar heard this, he leapt two steps forward. The courtiers were stunned for a moment. Some of them feared that he would attack his father. No such disaster occurred. He stood with his palms folded in front of his father and requested, 'Appa, if you must welcome the Vatapi emperor, please grant me a boon. I do not wish to remain in Kanchi during Pulikesi's visit. Please permit me to leave the city when Pulikesi enters it!'

'My views on this are the same, Kumara! I had intended to send you out of this city when the Vatapi emperor visits us. There is another compelling reason for this,' disclosed the chakravarthy.

Commander Paranjyothi stepped forward and submitted, 'Prabhu, please permit me too to leave along with the kumara chakravarthy.'

Mahendrar replied, 'Ah! So be it! It is only fair that Lakshmanan follows Raman everywhere! Both of you handpick 34,000 adept soldiers from our army and be prepared. The cowardly and surreptitious Pandian who trespassed the southern border of the Pallava kingdom when the Chalukya army attacked us from the north ought to be taught a lesson. Be ready to leave soon!' The chakravarthy's words not only helped to assuage Mamallar's anger and motivate him but also shocked the ministers' council.

Chapter 11

The Welcome

Late that night, when Mahendra Pallavar met his consort at the anthapuram, Bhuvana Mahadevi voiced her concern. 'Prabhu, I heard that you and Mamallan argued at the ministers' council today. How can you and your son quarrel in public?' asked the chakravarthini.

'Devi, I don't care what the people think. But words are inadequate to describe the pride and joy I feel today. Mamallan's brave speech reflected the valour of Arjunan, Abhimanyu, Lakshmanan and Indrajit. I felt so happy. But I was unable to reverse my decision, so it was necessary for me to suppress my happiness and speak in a harsh and authoritative manner,' confessed the chakravarthy.

'What did you decide? I don't like what you're about to do either. Is it right to welcome our arch-enemy to Kanchi?' asked the Pallava chakravarthini.

'Devi, why do you speak in this manner? Doesn't the Pallava dynasty pride itself on befriending its enemies? You asked me what my intentions were. I will tell you. It is my goal to ensure the revival of Satya Yugam during my lifetime. In this holy land of Bharata, three kingdoms flourish as of today. Harshavardhanar rules the area to the north of the Narmada, Pulikesi reigns over the region between the Narmada and the Tungabhadra, and Mahendra Pallavan rules the area to the south of the Tungabhadra. If these three kings fight amongst themselves, this holy land will degenerate into a hell. The people will be stricken by famine and death. However, if these three kings are on cordial terms, Bharata will be akin to heaven. This nation will not face poverty, hunger, or famine. Education and the arts will flourish. People will be prosperous. Devi, when I was young, I used to fantasize that the Chalukya emperor would invite me to view the wonderful paintings in the Ajantha caves. I also dreamt that I would go further north and joyfully participate in the festival of arts held under the auspices of Harshavardhanar at Kanyakubja once in three years. I dreamt that I would convert Mamallapuram into a dream world of sculptures and invite Harshavardhanar and Pulikesi to view it. I don't think that my wishes will be fulfilled. But if the three of us were to become friends, why would religious strife occur in this country? Why would wars break out?'

The chakravarthini interrupted to ask, 'Prabhu, why did you, who profess to follow the religion of love and the dharma of friendship, encourage Mamallan to attack the Pandian?'

'That's a different matter altogether. Friendship is possible only amongst peers. Friendship flourishes only amongst the wise. Fools and those who don't know their place in life can be brought in line only through punishment,' replied Mahendra Pallavar.

From the following day, the city of Kanchi wore a new look. People were excited, like they were about to celebrate a major festival. They decorated the streets and the entrances of their houses. Marketplaces once again became beehives of activity. Prayers were conducted at the temples. Sculptors resumed work at the various sculpture mandapams. The sound of musical instruments being played reverberated in all directions. The sound of the Vedas being chanted was again heard at the Sanskrit seminaries. Devotional hymms were sung at the Tamil schools. There was a revival of dance performances and stage plays. The sounds of rhythm mingled with the sounds of anklets.

It is unnecessary to describe the happiness the citizens felt. Everyone seemed to be rejoicing. Men and women began adorning themselves with fine clothes and jewellery again. The fragrance of the flowers worn by the women spread in all four directions. Contrary to Mamallar's expectation, the citizens of Kanchi seemed content. Moreover, they seemed to be excited about the Chalukya emperor's forthcoming visit to Kanchi.

At noon, five days after Pulikesi's envoy came to Kanchi seeking a truce, the northern gates of the Kanchi fort were opened for the first time in eight months. Even those who lived far away from Kanchi heard the booming sound of drums and trumpets. The Vatapi emperor made his entry into the city that had no peer in education; a city he had been keen to visit since his youth. Fifty key people from his retinue accompanied him.

When he crossed the entrance and entered Kanchi, he saw Mahendra Pallava chakravarthy, who was waiting to welcome him. Their eyes met. Mahendrar's face bore a slight smile and conveyed no emotion. But Pulikesi's face reflected the fury that was simmering within him. 'Is this Mahendra Pallavan, my sworn enemy who thwarted all my plans?' thought Pulikesi.

His eyes mirrored the anger he felt. He also felt that he had seen the majestic man, who was smiling at him seemingly innocently and without a trace of hostility, before.

After the accomplishments of the two emperors were formally announced, both of them dismounted from their horses and embraced each other. Simultaneously, Pulikesi scanned Mahendra Pallavar's retinue, which was standing behind him. 'Satyasraya, whom are you searching for?' asked Mahendra Pallavar.

The Chalukya emperor remarked, 'Pallavendra, I have heard so much about your brave son, Mamallar. Who amongst those standing here is that great warrior?'

Mahendra Pallavar smiled slightly and replied, 'No, Satyasraya, Mamallan is not here. He has left Kanchi for another important task.'

Chapter 12

Three Hearts

As the Vatapi emperor was entering Kanchi through the northern entrance, the kumara chakravarthy was leaving the city through the southern gates. Thirty-four thousand Pallava soldiers, 5000 war horses, 100 elephants and the rest of the army retinue had left the city and were waiting at some distance from Kanchi to begin their campaign. The chariot wheels rattled as Kannabiran rode over the hurriedly constructed bridge across the partially demolished moat. Mamallar and Paranjyothi were seated in the chariot. After they had crossed the moat, the bridge was drawn back. Immediately the fort gates slammed shut. The sounds of the gates being shut, the locks being fastened and the chariot wheels rattling were heard in unison. At that point of time, the hearts of the three men seated in the chariot were beating fast.

Mamallar had gone to bid farewell to his mother, Bhuvana Mahadevi, prior to his departure. Tears had welled up in the eyes of that brave woman. It seemed as though she was disturbed. When Mamallar had set out to Pullalur to punish Durvineethan, Bhuvana Mahadevi had not seemed so distressed. She had then blessed her son with a smiling face and seen him off to the battlefield.

'Amma, what is this? Why are you crying? Am I a novice to the battlefield?' asked Mamallar.

The chakravarthini replied, 'My child, I am not worried about that. It's your father's actions that distress me. Your father's decision is harsher than Dasaratha's, who stopped with sending Rama to the forest. Not only is your father sending Rama to the forest, but he is also simultaneously about to welcome Ravana as a guest!'

Mamallar, hitherto serious, was quite amused by his mother's words. 'Thaye, I am not Rama. Had I been Rama, wouldn't I have to take Sita along with me to the forest? Nor is my father Dasaratha, because he is not sending me to the forest influenced by Kaikeyi's words. Pulikesi is definitely not Ravana, who is a true warrior, amma! Though he lost everything in the battlefield and stood all alone, he refused to surrender and gave up his life. The cowardly Pulikesi cannot be compared with that great warrior. After travelling a distance of hundred kaadam accompanied by his army, isn't he about to return without fighting even a single battle?' observed Mamallar.

'Kumara, no matter how much you console me, I am not at peace. I do not like your father extending the hand of friendship to the arch-enemy of the Pallava dynasty. I am unable to accept that you're leaving Kanchi at this point of time. I am concerned that the consequences of these events may be disastrous!' stated the chakravarthini of the Pallava kingdom.

His mother's words that morning impacted Mamallar deeply. He felt an inexplicable emotional fatigue. He tried hard to overcome it. He thought of the forthcoming war and how he was going to attack and punish the Pandian. He also thought of Aayanar's daughter, who was living in Mandapapattu village. If he took a short detour from his route, he could visit Sivakami and then proceed. But he himself realized that it would not be a wise thing to do. Hadn't he bid farewell to her saying that he would meet her only after defeating Pulikesi and chasing him away? He decided that he would meet Sivakami after at least defeating the Pandian. Several such thoughts rose within Mamallar like waves and tormented him.

The expression on Commander Paranjyothi's face was harsher than usual. An immense sense of responsibility weighed down his heart. That morning, the chakravarthy had secretly sent for him had instructed him as follows. 'Thambi! I am now sending Mamallan to the battlefield relying solely on you. In his current state of mind, he is bound to act aggressively without exercising caution. You must ensure that no danger befalls him. He is the sole heir to this ancient Pallava dynasty. Commander, the soldiers of Pandya Nadu are great warriors. Don't think they will be like the Ganga Nadu soldiers. You cannot easily overcome them. So, you must fight this battle exercising great caution.' He smiled mysteriously when he remarked, 'It is not enough if you protect Mamallan from the spears and arrows that are wielded in the battlefield. You must also safeguard him from the sharp eyes of the sculptor's daughter, Sivakami, who resides at Mandapapattu village. The incident that occurred when you were pursuing Durvineethan should not be repeated this time. You should complete the job at hand and return directly to Kanchi.'

When Paranjyothi took leave of the chakravarthy and was about to depart, the chakravarthy asked him to come close to him and quipped affectionately, 'Commander, what I said about Mandapapattu does not apply to Thiruvengadu. After chasing the Pandian away, do meet your mother and uncle, if you so desire!'

Every word uttered by the chakravarthy served to heighten Paranjyothi's sense of responsibility. Ah! Mahendra Pallavar was such an extraordinary person! Paranjyothi was fortunate to be the recipient of his affection and trust to this extent! But he must be worthy of such affection and trust! He must bring Mamallar back to Kanchi safely! The chakravarthy asking him to go to Thiruvengadu on his way back indicated his magnanimity. But was this the right time to visit Thiruvengadu? How would his mother and uncle feel when they realized that he was now a warrior? Umayal, by nature, was very reticent. Wouldn't she be afraid to even approach him? Paranjyothi's thoughts ran along these lines.

Kannabiran was seated at the edge of the front seat of the chariot. A scene frequently flashed in his mind's eye. He had placed his cheeks against those of his six-month-old son and had lovingly asked, 'May I leave, my dear?' That infant had smiled without any rhyme or reason and held Kannabiran's ears with his tender hands. Whenever he recollected this incident, the feeling of the child's tender hands on his ears unsettled him. He yearned to feel his son's gentle breath and wondered when he would experience that again.

He was also frequently reminded of Kamali's parting words. She, who previously used to ask, 'When are you leaving for war?' pleaded, when he was leaving for the battle in reality, 'Kanna! Why has Mahendra Pallavar gone astray? Why does he have to invite the Vatapi emperor? Why does he have to send Mamallar to wage a war against the Pandya king? My heart is in anguish, Kanna! Come what may, don't forget my sister, Sivakami! Remind Mamallar!'

Though the three men in the chariot were immersed in different thoughts, anxiety and concerns regarding what the future held in store for them united them. So, their hearts were beating on the same wavelength and at the same pace.

Chapter 13

Royal Hospitality

Kanchi wore a festive look during the Vatapi emperor's seven-day visit. Every day, the two emperors explored a different quarter of the city. Temples, educational centres, sculpture mandapams, art studios, viharams and the Jain institutions were all part of their itinerary. They also went on a procession around the city on their elephants.

It seemed as though the friendship between the two emperors was growing stronger as they spent time together. Mahendra Pallavar shared his hope with Pulikesi that this friendship would translate into greater benefits for both kingdoms in future. Mahendra Pallavar emphasized that he did not bear even an iota of hatred towards Buddhism and Jainism. He stated that he had embraced Saivism as it viewed all other religions with tolerance; an act that resulted in his being at the receiving end of the Jains' and Buddhists' unnecessary hostility. Pulikesi remarked that he too did not feel any excessive affinity or hatred towards any religion, and that he had given the Jain monks a lot of latitude in his kingdom for diplomatic reasons.

Mahendrar opined that religious gurus ought not to interfere in the affairs of the state, and that such interference would be detrimental to the gurus themselves, their faith and the country. The Vatapi emperor concurred with this view. Mahendra Pallavar referred to a religious guru whom he thought exemplified the ideal. When Pulikesi asked if he could meet the guru, Mahendrar replied, 'I myself sent him on a pilgrimage as I did not want that great soul to stay here while a war was underway. Now I don't know where he is.'

Pulikesi then asked, 'Will I not even be able to meet the greatest sculptor of the Pallava kingdom?'

Mahendra Pallavar asked in turn, 'Whom are you referring to?'

'It's the person named Aayanar,' replied Pulikesi.

'How did you come to know of him?' asked an amazed Mahendra Pallavar.

'One day I saw a sculpted house in the middle of the forest. There were no living beings in the house. But there were several life-like statues. There were several wonderful statues depicting various dance postures. When I enquired later, I came to know that a great sculptor named Aayanar lived there with his daughter, who was an accomplished danseuse. I also heard that they had headed to an unknown destination before the siege. Are you unaware of their whereabouts too?' asked the Vatapi emperor.

'I know where they are. I have also sent a person to fetch them. They may be present at the large assembly that will be congregating tomorrow,' answered the Kanchi chakravarthy. Hearing this, Pulikesi seemed excited.

Eight days after the Vatapi emperor had arrived at Kanchi, a large assembly congregated at the royal court to bid him farewell. Ministers, commanders, chiefs of mandalams, kottams and cities and influential traders of the Pallava kingdom were present. Saivite and Vaishnavite gurus, exponents of Utthara Bharata languages, Tamil scholars, multilingual poets, musicians, sculptors and painters were also seated there.

The key persons in the above-mentioned audience were introduced to the Vatapi emperor. Poets who were fluent in both Utthara Bharata languages and Tamil sang poems they had composed especially for this momentous occasion. That they did not exalt one king or belittle the other, but praised them equally, showcased their tact more than their poetic skills. Then the musicians of the Pallava kingdom demonstrated their talent. Pulikesi appreciatively examined a seven-stringed veena called Parivathini created by Mahendra Pallavar.

As time was spent in this manner, neither Mahendra Pallavar nor the Vatapi emperor seemed to be at peace; they were restless. Mahendra Pallavar's eyes frequently darted towards the entrance of the royal court. When he enthusiastically announced, 'They have arrived', the Vatapi emperor, who was close to him, asked, 'Who? Is it Aayanar and his daughter?' At that point of time, Aayanar and Sivakami were indeed entering the royal court.

Sivakami faltered as she entered. 'Ah! A bad omen!' thought Sivakami as she walked in like a doe.

Chapter 14

'Vazhi Nee Mayiley!'*

When Aayanar and Sivakami entered that enormous sabha mandapam, everyone turned towards them.

Those two thousand eyes reflected infinite amazement, joy and eagerness.

A few people in the audience had watched Sivakami's arangetram one and a half years ago. The others in that assembly had heard about that arangetram and how the news of Pulikesi's invasion had resulted in its ending abruptly. When they ruminated with wonder that the reason for the disruption, Emperor Pulikesi, was seated in the assembly, their glances darted to and fro between Sivakami and Pulikesi.

The Vatapi king, like the others, seemed dazed watching Aayanar and Sivakami enter the court. It seemed to him that one of the paintings in the deep caves of the Ajantha mountains had come to life and was walking in front of him.

_____
* 'Blessed are you, noble peacock!'

59

He had seen several beautiful women. But he had never seen one with such a graceful gait. When Sivakami walked, it was impossible to figure out if her feet were touching the ground. When an expert musician sings, not only are the individual notes clear, but there is also a flow connecting the notes. Similarly, when Sivakami walked, it was impossible to decipher if her feet were moving, or if the earth was slipping beneath her feet.

Sivakami, who was in the minds and eyes of everyone in the assembly, seemed to be oblivious of the fact that she was the centre of attention. Characteristic of women born in noble families, she felt bashful and her head was slightly lowered. She was extremely eager to know where in the assembly was the majestic person who resided in her heart. However, she suppressed her ardour and walked naturally, her gaze fixed in front.

Father and daughter approached the dais where the two emperors were seated. While Aayanar bowed, Sivakami prostrated before them and then stood up.

Mahendra Pallavar remarked, 'Aayanar, your daughter Sivakami's fame has spread far and wide and has reached the ears of the Vatapi emperor. Today, my dear friend, King Satyasraya Pulikesi, wishes to watch Sivakami dance. That's why I hurriedly summoned you here. Will Sivakami be able to perform immediately? What is your preference?'

Aayanar responded, 'Mahaprabhu, your command is my wish. Sivakami will not find a better audience and opportunity than this to demonstrate her artistic skills. Two great emperors are present at the same place, like two suns!' He then looked at Sivakami.

When Mahendra Pallavar had spoken, Sivakami had raised her head slightly and looked at the Vatapi emperor from the corner of her eye. Then her eyes broke their reserve and looked at the area around the dais. But she felt cheated. The brave and handsome countenance she was looking for was not present. 'Ah! He is not here. Why is he not seated close to the chakravarthy?' her disconcerted heart questioned. Several thoughts flashed within her like lightning and disappeared in moments. Could he be in danger? But had that been the case, Mahendra Pallavar would not have organized this celebration.

'I'm glad, Aayanar! The musicians are also ready. It is for you that this assembly has been waiting for so long!' stated Mahendra Pallavar.

When Sivakami turned around and walked towards the place designated for dancing, she looked around once again. Her eyes accidentally met Pulikesi's cruel eyes. Her heart and body trembled like a jasmine creeper caught in a strong gust of wind. This lasted only for a moment. Sivakami somehow controlled her emotions and walked towards the stage. Thoughts of an indescribable formless shadow followed her.

When Sivakami reached the stage, she brushed away thoughts of that shadow and readied herself to dance. Then it was possible for her to look around that great assembly devoid of self-consciousness. Her sight fell on the upper storey of the assembly, where the chakravarthini and the other women in the anthapuram were seated. She was reminded of the disappointment she had felt at Mamallar's absence during her arangetram, and of his subsequently informing her that he had been sitting in the upper storey with his mothers. She felt that today too he was hiding somewhere and was watching her dance. When this thought occurred to her, the disappointment, fatigue, confusion and fear she had previously felt mysteriously disappeared.

Shortly after Sivakami began dancing, the audience forgot that they were seated in a royal court, that a woman was dancing and that they were watching her. Everyone was transported from this world inhabited by humans to a new and blissful dream world.

As her performance began, Sivakami felt a sense of heightened clarity and self-awareness. She felt that it was a significant day in her life, and that her performance that day was an important incident in her life.

The two overwhelming emotions Sivakami always felt were her love for Mamallar and her passion for dancing. She too, like Aayanar, realized that it was a rare opportunity to showcase her artistic talent before an august audience.

There was another important reason behind Sivakami's determination to demonstrate the entire gamut of her artistic talent in that assembly.

Though Mahendra Pallavar might take a harsh stance in several issues, he had a soft corner for the arts. Through her performance, she wanted to earn his esteem and persuade him not to object to her marriage with Mamallar. Wasn't her dance the only weapon in her armour to make the hard-hearted emperor change his mind and make him act as per her wishes?

So, Sivakami resolved that her performance that day would be a wondrous one in the history of Bharatanatyam itself.

But all these thoughts persisted only until Sivakami began dancing. The moment she started dancing, her heart overflowed with her inherent artistic sensibility. She lost her own self and became art itself.

Sivakami no longer danced; the art of dancing possessed her and made her dance.

Sivakami's heart did not dwell on the various aspects of dancing like thalam, jathi, adavu and theermanam. The various thalams, jathis, adavus and theermanams came running at the appropriate time and rendered their services to Sivakami.

Sivakami's heart was floating in an ocean of bliss. Her body was also effortlessly floating in the boundless ocean of bliss. The audience was also immersed in this ocean of bliss. The audience returned to earth from the dream world they were residing in at the end of 'Nritham', the first part of a Bharatanatyam performance.

Thunderous applause was heard from all corners of the sabha. The two emperors also clapped appreciatively.

Prior to the performance, when Aayanar and Sivakami were walking towards the stage after being instructed by Mahendra chakravarthy, the Vatapi king had asked Mahendra Pallavar, 'Why do you have to be so deferential to them? In our country, we make artistes dance by wielding the whip!'

'Satyasraya, our country's customs are different. Here, we accord a lot of respect to the arts and artistes. They are kings and emperors in their own right. We accord titles like emperor of sculpture, "Sirpa chakravarthy", and emperor of poetry, "Kavi chakravarthy". Aayanar has been awarded the title "Sirpa chakravarthy". The people give such artistes the same respect they show to the emperors of kingdoms.'

The Vatapi king commented mockingly, 'Your country's customs are wonderful!'

Observing the Vatapi emperor joining the others in the applause at the end of Sivakami's Nritham, Mahendra Pallavar enquired, 'What do you say now? Have you changed your opinion about honouring artistes?'

Pulikesi replied, 'The dance was wonderful. I have never ever seen such a performance. However . . .' and paused. He was then immersed in deep thought.

The first song Sivakami chose to perform abhinayams for was dedicated to the primary deity of ancient Tamizhagam, Velan. Velan swears by his spear to a female devotee of his, 'I will return and claim you!' But he does not fulfil his promise, so the girl feels unhappy and cheated. Even then, she does not want to show anger against or complain about Velan. So, she lays all the blame on Velan's mount, the peacock and scolds it. Sivakami performed to the following song composed in an ancient raga named Anandha Bhairavi, set in a thalam appropriate for dancing:

> *Swear he did, on His spear. Forget that, can He?*
> *What say you, my noble peacock! Know you not, that thoughts of Him cause my heart to wither*
> *And my life to ebb.*
> *Pine as I do for my love*
> *You seem to sway in like a swan. Become wayward and swollen-headed, on carrying our Lord?*
> *Hate me? You do! Revenge is on your mind, so you sleep your way in.*
> *Shall I hail you for what you do? Oh, my golden peacock!*
> *Pity the hapless me*
> *Fallen for the matchless one. Why blame you, for*
> *Know you not by thyself nor do you listen.*
> *While elephants and horses in the world abound*
> *Chose you, His vehicle. Why?*

Chapter 15

'Namanai anjom!'*

Velan's ladylove rears a peacock. Whenever she sees that peacock, she is reminded of Murugan and her love for him intensifies. One day she commands the peacock, 'Aren't you the mount of Muruga Peruman? Go away! Go and bring him here quickly!' She doesn't stop with commanding the peacock but scares it away by pretending to beat it and chases it away. She expects the peacock to return soon with Velan mounted on its back. Despite waiting for a long time, neither the peacock nor Velan returns. She wonders for a moment whether Velan has completely forgotten her.

Immediately she recollects an old incident. During their last meeting, she had requested him to never forget her. He had sworn by his spear, 'I will never ever forget you!'

---

* 'I am unafraid of Naman'. Naman is another name for Yaman, the God of Death.

65

She immediately decides, 'He will never forget me. It is the peacock which is delaying their return.'

Sivakami formed the image of the peacock in her mind and sang the following lines as she simultaneously performed abhinayams.

Swear he did, on His spear. Forget that, can He?
What say you, my noble peacock!

The audience did not see Sivakami. They saw the presiding deity of Tamizhagam, Murugan, armed with a spear in front of them. The viewers were able to visualize Muruga Peruman looking at the girl with mercy and affection, placing his hand on the spear and swearing, 'I will never ever forget you!'

The next instant, Velan and his spear disappeared from the audience's sight and Velan's forlorn ladylove and the peacock appeared in front of the audience. They saw her pining for Velan in his absence. Sivakami then performed abhinayams to the lines:

Pine as I do for my love
You seem to sway in like a swan. Become wayward and swollen-headed, on carrying our Lord?
Hate me? You do! Revenge is on your mind, so you sleep your way in.
Shall I hail you for what you do?

The viewers saw a lone girl lovingly and eagerly looking at a seemingly endless road. When that girl mocked the peacock by mimicking its slow gait, the amused audience burst out laughing. Similarly, when the peacock became intoxicated with pride on being chosen as Murugan's mount and forgot its way back and struggled, the audience was amused. After asking the peacock, 'Have you intentionally slept on the way to seek revenge on me', she blessed the peacock with a bitter heart saying, 'Vazhi nee mayiley!' When Sivakami emoted appropriately to the above lines, the audience applauded enthusiastically.

The next moment, the ladylove changes her mind. She pets the peacock, addresses it as 'golden peacock', and pleads with it, asking, 'Don't you feel any pity for this girl? What is the use of blaming you? Cruel peacock!' When Sivakami portrayed the disturbed expression evident in the peacock's harsh eyes, the audience was dazed. Sivakami concluded the song by singing, 'There is no use in blaming you. When there are several virtuous animals like elephants and horses in this world, He who chose you as a mount ought to be blamed.' Sivakami's face simultaneously reflected the lover's sorrow, bitterness, mockery and humour as she concluded the song. The audience was mesmerized.

The abhinayams performed to the above song delighted everyone in the audience except Mahendra Pallavar. He grimaced. It seemed to him that, under the pretext of showing her love for Velan, Sivakami had demonstrated her love for Mamallar. Mahendrar understood clearly the underlying meaning of the line 'swearing by the spear'. He also understood the meaning of the look Sivakami had shot towards him when she performed to the phrase 'peerless Murugan'. 'Ah! How bold this girl is! She is trying to fulfil her desire by pleading with me! Ah! She has not yet understood Mahendra Pallavan's nature!' Thinking thus, the chakravarthy sent a message through one of the guards. That guard whispered something into Aayanar's ears. Aayanar told Sivakami, 'Amma! Please perform to one of Vageechar Peruman's verses!'

Sivakami had already understood the chakravarthy's state of mind from the scowl on his face. The message he sent confirmed this. She felt ashamed thinking that she had made a mistake in assuming she could change that stone-hearted man's mind through her art and win his support. That feeling of shame was soon transformed into anger which burnt within her. She began singing the following song:

Subject to none we are, nor scared of death we are.

Suddenly there was a transformation in the audience that had been cheerful till then. The change in the audience's emotion and expression was akin to the reaction to a sorrowful incident occurring at a house where a marriage is underway. From everyone's expression, it was evident they were wondering why the song had to be sung on this occasion.

The history behind this song is inspiring. When the Samanars of Patalipuram petitioned the Kanchi chakravarthy, foisting several charges against Marul Neekiyar, Mahendra Pallavar had summoned him to Kanchi with the intention of questioning him and ascertaining the truth. The messengers who carried the message to that great soul threatened him a little.

Thirunavukkarasar shocked the messengers by telling them, 'My God is Shiva Peruman. I refuse to obey your king's orders!'

'We will fling you in a lime pit. We will get an elephant to trample you. We will tie a stone around your neck and fling you into the sea,' threatened the messengers. Then Marul Neekiyar sang the following song:

Subject to none we are, nor scared of death we are. Hell we suffer not, trepidations we feel not.

Head up our gait, illness we suffer never, bow to none ever

Bliss living with us ever, sorrow nears us never.

White conch adorning His ears, our Shankara remains subject to Himself.

In eternal surrender and servitude at His feet offer we ourselves.

The Sivanadiyar penned the above song on a palm leaf
and instructed, 'Deliver this to your king.'

In the absence of further directions from the king, the
messengers delivered the message to him. The chakravarthy's
reaction was contrary to their expectations. Mahendra Pallavar,
after reading the verse, desired to meet the great soul who
had penned it. After an audience with Thirunavukkarasar, he
renounced Jainism and embraced Saivism.

As the courtiers were aware of these incidents, they found
the song distasteful.

But Mahendra Pallavar's state of mind was exactly the
opposite to that of the courtiers. The song gave him immense
joy. He immediately informed Pulikesi of the context in which
the song had been initially sung. It was evident that Pulikesi
was taken aback by this incident. 'Wonderful! A mendicant
composed a song that flouted your command. A woman
performs abhinayams to that song in this assembly. You are
happy watching this. I'm unable to believe this!'

'That's the greatness of art, Satyasraya! If a man were
to verbally flout my command, I would have immediately
commanded that he be beheaded. However, when that was
expressed in the form of classical Tamil poetry, I developed
the desire to meet the person who had composed such a
wonderful poem,' observed the consummate connoisseur, the
chakravarthy of Kanchi.

By then, Sivakami had completed singing the song once
and had started performing abhinayams. She was performing
abhinayams for the words 'Namanai anjom'. The audience saw
Markandeyan's story unfold in their presence.

The young girl, whose figure resembled the tender petals
of a jasmine, transformed within a moment into the fearsome
looking Yama Dharma Raja, who, wielding a rope and a mace,

took the lives of those around him! The next instant, she became a sixteen-year-old fear-stricken boy embracing the Shiva Lingam.

Yama Dharma Rajan tries to wield his rope around Markandeyan and appropriate his life. That young boy gets even more scared.

Ah! The next moment, Samhara Rudramurthy emerges from the Shiva Lingam. Sivakami's tall form appeared taller. The kind eyes of the Lord look down for a moment. His hands reassure Markandeyan. Then his eyes look ahead. The Lord's anger-filled eyes emit sparks of fire at Yaman. His knotted eyebrows seem to indicate that his third eye is about to open.

We now see traces of humility in the fearful-looking Yama Dharman. His supplicating posture indicates that he wants to ask, 'Why are you angry with me? I am only doing my duty!' The furious Samhara Rudramurthy once again appears before the audience. He lifts one leg and kicks Yaman, who falls down with a thud.

Then the audience sees the naïve Markandeyan. Ah! Now there is no trace of fear or panic on his face. It radiates the bliss of devotion and gratitude.

As soon as Sivakami started performing the abhinayams, the courtiers forgot their unpleasant thoughts. They completely forgot who had initially sung the song and the circumstances in which the song had been sung. They not only forgot the world around them but also their own selves.

When the rendition was complete and everyone had returned to earth, Mahendra Pallavar asked Pulikesi, 'How was that?'

The Vatapi king observed, 'Naganandi had written the truth', and looked intently at Mahendra Pallavar.

There was no change in Mahendrar's expression. He asked casually, 'Who is Naganandi?'

'Haven't you heard the name, Naganandi? He's a bikshu who has travelled extensively across Dakshina Bharata for a long time.'

'What had the bikshu written?'

'I had requested him to periodically write to me about his travel experiences. He complied with my request. He once wrote that the great sculptor Aayanar and expert danseuse Sivakami had no peers in Bharata Kandam.'

'It seems that Naganandi bikshu is a connoisseur of the arts. Where is he now?'

'That's not known. I thought that you may know.'

Mahendrar kept quiet.

'I heard that you imprisoned all the bikshus in the country thinking that they were spies. You may have imprisoned Naganandi bikshu too, suspecting him to be a spy.'

While the above conversation was taking place, a delighted Sivakami was surveying the applauding audience. Her eyes dwelt for a moment on Mahendrar's enthusiastic face and then on the Vatapi emperor's worried face.

When she looked at the Vatapi emperor, the mysterious mist that had been troubling her for so long cleared up. The shadow-like thought assumed a form in her mind. Ah! That face! How was it possible? Could two human beings look identical? Hadn't Mahendra chakravarthy travelled assuming several disguises? Had the Vatapi emperor also travelled across Dakshina Bharata disguised as Naganandi?

Even as Sivakami was confused by such thoughts, Mahendra Pallavar gestured to Aayanar that the performance may be concluded.

Sivakami ended the performance with a song dedicated to the God of dance and a deity worshipped across Tamizhagam, Nataraja Murthy, and abhinayams that were appropriate for that song.

The audience that had congregated in that great assembly that day unanimously opined, 'There has never ever been such a performance in the past; nor is it likely that there will be such a performance in the future!'

When Mahendra Pallavar gestured again, Aayanar and Sivakami went up and stood in front of the two emperors and bowed. Mahendra Pallavar remarked, 'Aayanar, wasn't Sivakami's arangetram that took place in the same place interrupted? The reason for the interruption, the Vatapi emperor, today watched and appreciated your daughter's performance!' He then looked at Sivakami and enquired, 'Sivakami! The Vatapi emperor is completely mesmerized by your dancing. He requested me to send you and your father to Vatapi along with him. Are you willing to go?'

An angry Sivakami lost her self-control and shot back, 'Prabhu, don't you want this poor girl to live in this country?'

These words caused shock and fear in Aayanar and those around him. But Mahendra Pallavar alone smiled. He looked at the Vatapi emperor and remarked, 'Satyasraya! Did you observe? Would artistes like to go to nations where they are whipped and asked to perform?'

Mahendrar, who failed to observe Pulikesi's face darkening and his eyes gleaming with anger, stated, 'Sivakami, I don't wish to chase you away from this country. Aayanar, I need to reward Sivakami who performed so wonderfully today. Till then, stay in this city. You can stay at Kamali's house. I will come there at leisure and talk to you.'

Chapter 16

Pulikesi's Departure

The following day, Kanchi wore a festive look again. The Vatapi emperor, Pulikesi, was scheduled to leave Kanchi.

He desired to tour around Kanchi once again before his departure. So, the two emperors mounted on their elephants and went in procession around the city. Kanchi was beautifully decorated for the occasion. The citizens adorned themselves in beautiful clothes and jewellery and stood in groups at the street corners. Some stood on the upper storeys of houses and showered flowers on the elephants that carried the two emperors.

Pulikesi did not seem to tire of repeatedly seeing Kanchi's beautiful wide roads, mansions, temples, towers, sculpture and painting galleries, dance halls, viharams and Jain temples.

Suddenly the Vatapi emperor quipped, 'I thought that Bharavi was a great poet. Only now I realize that he's a third-grade poet ...'

'How can you say that? Bharavi's *Kiratarjuniya* is such a beautiful epic . . . Haven't you read it?' asked Mahendra Pallavar.

'Ah! These poets do a good job of describing mountains, forests, rain and clouds. Their poetic skills disappear when they are asked to describe a city like this! Bharavi's description of this city does not even capture a quarter of its glory . . . Pallavendra, I will tell you something; will you accept? Both of us will enter into a barter. You take my large kingdom that stretches from the Narmada to the Tungabhadra, and give me just the city of Kanchi in exchange!' quipped the Vatapi king.

'King of kings, you may take the divine city of Kanchi! I don't want your entire kingdom in return. It would suffice if you gave me the Ajantha mountain and its caves. The city which has been constructed using stone, lime, mud and wood may fall into ruins one day. The paintings in the Ajantha caves, created with indelible dyes, will survive for a long, long time. Scion of the Chalukya dynasty, do you know something? Wasn't Sivakami, who danced yesterday, distraught when asked if she was willing to go to Vatapi? If you had only told her father, Aayanar, that you would reveal the secret of Ajantha's indelible paints, he would have immediately agreed to come with you!'

'Is that so? Is the sculptor Aayanar so interested in the Ajantha paints?' When Pulikesi raised this query, it seemed as though he was haunted by old memories.

'Oh, yes! Don't you remember that he had also sent a messenger to find out the secret of the Ajantha paints?' asked the Pallava chakravarthy. He continued talking, 'Ah! When you heard that message being read, you were so taken aback!' and then burst out laughing. Fate, a phenomenon people hold responsible for inexplicable occurrences, possessed Mahendra

Varmar's speech that instant. The Pallava king, who was a genius, a seer and a master strategist, lost control over his speech.

He, who was well aware of the following couplet penned by Thiruvalluvar, forgot it at a crucial moment.

Whatever else you guard or not, fail not to keep the tongue in leash.

Failing that, untold sorrow and ignominy may find their way to you.

He revealed all the secrets buried in his heart one by one.

The words that Mahendra Pallavar spoke had the effect of a thousand scorpions stinging Pulikesi at the same time. 'Shatrumalla,* what are you referring to? How do you know?' asked Pulikesi, and heaved a deep sigh that resembled a snake hissing.

Mahendra Pallavar laughed again and revealed, 'Yes! When I think about that incident, I feel very amused even today. You had reached the banks of the North Pennai River. First, an emissary delivered a message, which was something you had not anticipated. You were furious. At that point of time, your soldiers brought in a young boy they had imprisoned. He too had a message that was completely irrelevant; it enquired about the secret of the Ajantha paints. One ought to have seen your face then. Fortunately, you did not order that boy to be beheaded immediately but sent him to Nagarjuna mountain!'

'Vichitra Siddhar, how do you know all this? You speak as though you witnessed these incidents in person!' said Pulikesi, gritting his teeth.

'I know only because I was there in person!' confessed Mahendra chakravarthy.

---

* Decimator of foes.

Pulikesi looked intently at the king's face and remarked, 'Ah! In that case you must be the emissary, Vajrabahu!'

'It is indeed me!' concurred Mahendra Pallavar.

Pulikesi muttered to himself softly, 'One of the several mysteries that confounded me has now been unravelled. Now the other mysteries can be easily solved.'

He then asked aloud, 'What about the message that Vajrabahu brought?'

'Will the creator of the messenger find it difficult to fabricate a message?'

'Not at all! Nothing is impossible for Mahendra Pallavar of Kanchi! ... Aiyya, please tell me at least now which was the fake message, and which was the true message?'

'Satyasraya, had the original message that boy was carrying reached you, today you and I wouldn't be sitting on our elephants going in procession around Kanchi. There would have been no road to conduct a procession. There would have been no Kanchi either. Kanchi would have met the same fate as Vyjayanthi. My friend, you too must tell me the truth. Didn't you intend to raze this beautiful city to the ground then?' asked Mahendrar.

Pulikesi muttered to himself, 'I was not so keen then. I now feel like burning this city and reducing it to ashes.' He then asked aloud, 'Pallavendra, what was written in the original message?'

'Not much. It detailed the division of property. The bikshu had written to you asking you to take the Pallava kingdom and Kanchi Sundari. He asked you to give him the queen of dancing, Sivakami.'

When he heard this, Pulikesi was immersed in deep thought for some time. He then asked, 'Is it so difficult a task to capture Kanchi Sundari?'

'My friend, had you advanced to Kanchi right away, as directed in that message, it would have been an easy task. Then, not a force of elephants but a lone elephant would have been enough to break open the gates of the Kanchi fort!' replied Mahendra Pallavar.

Volcanoes erupted within Pulikesi.

He looked at Mahendrar and exclaimed, 'The author of *Arthashastram*, Kautilya, ought to be under your tutelage!'

'There is a master statesman in the southern country too. His name is Thiruvalluvar. I wish to gift you his work on political science. But you have not yet mastered Tamil,' replied the Shatrumallar.

'My friend, let bygones be bygones. Please think that they were experiences in a previous birth and forget them. During these ten days, the two of us have become intimate friends. We have understood each other. I revealed the tactics I employed to counter your invasion as I thought that I would be betraying our friendship by suppressing them. Now nothing can come in the way of our friendship; we will remain friends as long as we are alive. In my lifetime, I will not act in a manner that is inimical to the Chalukya kingdom. Isn't that the case with you too?' asked Mahendra Pallavar with genuine transparency.

'Shatrumalla, is it necessary to even ask this question?' shot back the Vatapi emperor.

After completing the procession, the two royal elephants came to a halt near the northern gates of the Kanchi fort. The time for the two emperors to part had come. The two of them dismounted from the elephants and embraced each other.

'Pallavendra, I am delighted to have visited your city as a guest. I witnessed amazing sights. But I am a little sad that I am leaving without seeing your brave son, Mamallan,' remarked Pulikesi.

'True, you neither saw Mamallan nor the brave youth who brought the message. Naganandi has rendered a great service to the Pallava kingdom. He gave us an outstanding and brave commander . . .'

Pulikesi interrupted saying, 'True; I feel cheated not seeing Commander Paranjyothi too. You did not mention where the two of them are.'

'They have gone to see the Pandya king off! Only this morning did the message reach me. It seems that they have escorted the Pandian up to the southern border of the Chola kingdom.'

'Ah, I thought as much. I heard a rumour that you and the Pandya king are about to forge matrimonial alliance!'

'Mamallar and Paranjyothi went to accord the hospitality due to an in-law!' retorted Mahendra Pallavar and laughed.

'Vichitra Siddhar, I will take leave of you. I have one question for you before I leave. Do you know who Naganandi bikshu is?' asked Pulikesi.

Mahendra Pallavar replied, 'I guessed it', and whispered something into the Vatapi emperor's ears.

'Ah! There is nothing that you're unaware of. Now that you know the truth, aren't you going to free him and send him with me?' asked Pulikesi in a commanding voice.

'There is no objection in complying with the emperor's request!' countered Mahendra Pallavar.

'Scions of the Chalukya dynasty of Vatapi do not request anything from anyone!' announced Pulikesi majestically.

'Scions of Kanchi's Pallava dynasty do not grant a boon without anyone requesting it,' declared Mahendra Varmar.

'Pallavendra, I will take leave of you,' stated Pulikesi.

'Satyasraya! Don't forget!' reminded Mahendrar.

'I will never forget,' averred the Vatapi king.

Chapter 17

Infant Kannan

The joy experienced by the childhood friends—Sivakami and Kamali—when they met after almost one and a half years, was beyond description. They hugged each other, put their heads on each other's shoulders and wept! After sobbing, they suddenly laughed. They blessed and immediately scolded each other. Both of them tried to speak at the same time and then fell silent in unison. Several important incidents had occurred in their lives during the last one and a half years. They struggled, unable to decide which incidents they ought to relate first and which ones they ought to relate later. The baby Kannan solved the problem for them.

The child, who had been sleeping in the cradle, announced the fact that he had woken up by letting out a squeal. Kamali ran to the cradle and picked up the baby. When Sivakami saw the baby, she was slightly taken aback, and she kept staring at him. Though she seemed to be shocked externally, every nerve within her throbbed. A desire that lay hidden deep within, unknown even to her, overpowered her.

When Kamali asked, 'Why are you standing like an inanimate object? What did the infant Kannan do to you? Why are you angry with him?' Sivakami snapped out of her reverie.

Sivakami stammered as she asked, 'Kamali! Who is he? Where did he come from? When did he come? Will he come to me?' and extended both her arms. The baby widened his already wide eyes as he looked at Sivakami and kicked his arms and legs, attempting to go to Sivakami.

'Are you asking if he will come to you? You have already mesmerized him! Thief, you still have some charm left even after mesmerizing Mamallar,' Kamali laughingly remarked as she handed over the baby to Sivakami.

When Kamali mentioned Mamallar, Sivakami felt joy and bashfulness. Sivakami held the child, gazed at his nose, eyes, cheeks and locks of hair and retorted, 'Sure! Didn't I use the remaining charm you had given me after mesmerizing Kannan to mesmerize Mamallar? Look at him! He's the spitting image of his father! Kamali, where is his father?'

Kamali responded, 'What kind of a question is this? His father will be where Mamallar is!'

'Oh! So annan was also at the palace today. Wouldn't he have seen me perform at the court? Why didn't you come?' asked Sivakami.

'Why are you blabbering, thangachi? How is it possible for your annan to watch you dance? Don't you know that Mamallar has embarked on a campaign to wage war against the Pandian?'

Hearing this, Sivakami was so shocked that she forgot all about the baby in her lap and stood up. The child fell on the ground and shrieked. Kamali scolded, 'You sinner! How could you drop the child? May misfortune befall you! I hope Pulikesi abducts you!' She then picked up the child, held him close to her, gently rocked him and consoled him saying, 'Don't cry, my dear!' As the infant continued crying, Kamali chided, 'Won't you be quiet? Shall I ask Pulikesi to come here and kidnap you?' In those days, if a child cried a lot, it was customary to mention Pulikesi's name to scare them into silence. That was why Kamali had also cursed Sivakami by invoking Pulikesi.

When the baby finally stopped crying, Kamali left him on the floor and looked at Sivakami. Observing that Sivakami was shocked, Kamali enquired, 'Thangachi, didn't you know that Mamallar has gone to wage war against the Pandian?'

'I didn't know, akka!' confessed Sivakami, her voice filled with emotion. She felt cheated when she recollected that she had thought Mamallar was watching her unobserved when she was performing.

Yes, Kamali must be stating the truth. Had Mamallar been at Kanchi, would he have permitted her to perform in that wild cat's presence and been a silent spectator?

Sivakami felt ashamed of dancing in Pulikesi's presence during Mamallar's absence. She felt extreme anger towards Mahendra Pallavar. Hadn't the chakravarthy, emboldened by Mamallar's absence, insulted her by asking her to perform for Pulikesi?

Amidst such confounding notions, a thought suddenly flashed in Sivakami's mind like lightning and cleared her confusion. It made her realize how treacherous Mahendra Pallavar was. She decided that the chakravarthy had summoned her to Kanchi from Mandapapattu to ensure that she and Mamallar, who had headed to Chola Nadu, did not meet.

Observing Sivakami's expressions and her eyes glistening with anger, Kamali was dumbstruck for some time. She then mustered courage and enquired, 'Thangachi, why this anger? No disaster has occurred! War is not new to Mamallar. He is going to return victorious after defeating the Pandian . . .'

Sivakami interrupted Kamali saying, 'That's enough! He has already emerged victorious by defeating Pulikesi of Vatapi. Now only the Pandian remains to be defeated. Stop talking, akka! I have neither seen nor heard of a dynasty as shameless as the Pallava dynasty!'

Kamali was shocked! Why was Sivakami talking like this? Was it the same Sivakami, who used to scold herself several times, comparing herself to a dewdrop falling in love with the sun, who was talking in this manner? Was this the same Sivakami who had been ready to give even her life in exchange for a glance from the corner of the kumara chakravarthy's eye?

Even as a dazed Kamali was thinking along these lines, there was a change in Sivakami's expression. She hugged Kamali's child and posed the following volley of questions. 'Akka, I was blabbering, please forgive me. Please tell me everything in detail. When did Mamallar leave for the battlefield? Did he leave prior to, or after the arrival of the Vatapi emperor? Who else besides annan left with him? What did annan tell you before leaving? Were they aware that the chakravarthy was going to summon me here for a dance performance? Tell me, akka! Why are you silent? Are you angry with me?'

Kamali responded by telling Sivakami everything she knew. She said that it was not fair to think that those who had left for the battlefield could have known about Sivakami's dance performance, and that she herself had found out about it only on that day.

After listening to everything, Sivakami remarked, 'Akka, don't mistake me! It's been a long time since I met you. I have a lot to share with you and I will never feel satiated no matter how long I pet this darling child of yours. But I am unable to remain here any longer. It's imperative that I leave immediately for Mandapapattu. I will tell my father right away!'

Chapter 18

Did Pulikesi Know?

The following evening, Aayanar, Sivakami, Kamali and Ashwabalar were chatting in the courtyard of Kannabiran's house. Ashwabalar was describing the procession of the two emperors around Kanchi and Pulikesi's departure through the northern gate of the fort. It must be mentioned here that, during the period of Pulikesi's visit to Kanchi, Ashwabalar had completely forgotten his meditation and had been involved in the festivities that were taking place in the city. Little Kannan was crawling around trying to attract the attention of the adults. Kamali, attempting to assist him, kept interrupting the conversation and waxing eloquent about infant Kannan's exploits. Whenever Kamali interrupted the conversation, Ashwabalar shot a condescending glance at her and continued with his narration.

When he had finished, Sivakami asked, 'Now that the Vatapi emperor has finally left for good, won't the gates of the fort be opened?'

'Everything will be known by day after tomorrow, amma. But I am not very hopeful. The happiness that was evident in that Vatapi Chalukya's face for the last ten days was missing today. His face wore a harsh expression as he took leave of the Pallavar and left the fort. Who knows what that demon is up to?'

Sivakami asked, 'What can he do?'

'He may renew his siege or try to attack and capture the fort.'

A surprised Sivakami asked, 'Will people behave in this manner after professing friendship all these days?'

'Thangachi, I am surprised that you too are raising such naïve questions. Does royalty have any qualms about doing anything? Those who are friends today will kill each other tomorrow. Those who offer their daughter's hand in marriage will wage war against their in-laws the following day!' quipped Kamali.

Aayanar asked Ashwabalar, 'What's the reason behind the Vatapi king's anger? Do you know anything?'

'It seems that the Chalukya and the Pandian are friends. They were on very cordial terms when they met on the banks of the Kollidam River. Some people say that he was angry that Mamallar had gone to wage war against the Pandian when Pulikesi was visiting Kanchi. Do you know what the other school of thought is . . .?' asked Ashwabalar and paused.

'Please tell me,' urged Aayanar.

Ashwabalar continued, 'It seems that the Vatapi king, mesmerized by Sivakami's dance performance, had asked for Sivakami to be sent along with him to Vatapi. Mahendra Pallavar's refusal to do so enraged him.'

Kamali exclaimed, 'May he go to hell! May thunder strike him!'

When a voice was suddenly heard asking, 'Ah! Who is showering their blessing in such divine language', everyone was taken aback and looked in the direction from which the voice came. That resonant voice also attracted the attention of the infant Kannan. He too sat still and looked in the direction from which the voice came. It was none other than Mahendra Pallava chakravarthy who had walked into the house through the rear entrance.

'Ashwabalar, I too heard the rumour you were mentioning. But it's not true. The Vatapi emperor did not ask me to send Sivakami along with him. Do you know what he said? You bestow so much honour on this girl. If you send her with me to Vatapi, I will wield the whip and make her dance. That foolish Pulikesi is such a connoisseur!' commented the chakravarthy. At that moment, his eyes reflected genuine anger and disgust.

Sivakami stepped forward, pointedly looked at the chakravarthy and boldly asked him, 'Prabhu, is it fair that you made me perform in the presence of such a fine connoisseur?'

'That was a mistake, my child! I ought not to have asked you to perform in Pulikesi's presence. But I never expected that the king, in whose kingdom the exquisite Ajantha paintings are located, would be completely devoid of artistic sensibility. . . . Aayanar! Did you hear this? Didn't the Chalukya emperor camp outside the Kanchi fort for so many months? He did not visit Mamallapuram even once! When I asked him about this, he told me that he did not wish to see stone statues when there were flesh and blood human beings around. Not only that. He wondered what was so wonderful about the mere pictures painted on the walls of the Ajantha caves. It is to this person you sent Naganandi's message through Paranjyothi,' Mahendra Pallavar quipped.

Aayanar's face reflected the immense surprise he felt on hearing Mahendra Pallavar's words. He hesitantly asked, 'Is it true? Had Naganandi sent a message to the Vatapi emperor? How did you . . .'

'Are you asking me how I came to know? I myself read the missive. But Naganandi is a connoisseur, unlike the foolish Pulikesi. Do you know what he had written? You advance quickly with the army, capture the Pallava kingdom and keep Kanchi Sundari for yourself. You give me Sivakami. How do you like this, Aayanar? Do you realize the magnitude of danger that was about to befall the Pallava kingdom due to your dear friend, Naganandi?' asked the chakravarthy.

But it seemed as though Aayanar had failed to register the final words uttered by the chakravarthy. He muttered softly to himself, 'Ah! Did Naganandi send the message to the Vatapi emperor? In that case, is Pulikesi maharaja aware of the secret of the Ajantha paints?'

Chapter 19

Underground Passage

When Aayanar was ruminating over the secret of the Ajantha paints, the chakravarthy asked Ashwabalar, 'Yogi, how is your meditation progressing? Ever since the Vatapi king came, you haven't had the time to concentrate on meditation!' He then signalled with his eyes to Ashwabalar, who followed him through the rear entrance of the house to the yoga mandapam located in the palace garden.

After they left, Sivakami asked, 'Not satisfied with all the arts he already knows, has the chakravarthy also started learning the art of meditation?'

Kamali winked mischievously at Sivakami and stated in a low voice, 'It has nothing to do with meditation. I will tell you later.'

After some time, when Mahendra Pallavar returned from the yoga mandapam and was walking through the house, Aayanar stopped him, bowed, and asked in a low voice, 'Pallavendra, now the task for which we came has been completed. May we return to Mandapapattu?'

Mahendrar smiled as he pointed out, 'Aayanar, I have not yet rewarded Sivakami for her wonderful performance. Please stay here for some more time. Moreover, there is no necessity for you to return to Mandapapattu. You may return to your old house in the forest.'

Aayanar remarked in a worried tone, 'Prabhu, the work I've started at every location remains incomplete. It seems to be the fate of an unfortunate person like me. If the work I started at Mandapapattu is also not completed—'

Mahendra Pallavar interrupted saying, 'Great sculptor, human life is transient. How is it possible for each one of us to complete the tasks we have begun during our lifetime? Several projects that I have begun have come to a halt mid-way. So what? Our descendants will complete them. We do not have to worry on that count. Moreover, a wedding is soon going to be solemnized at our palace. Your daughter may have to perform at the wedding!' He then continued walking, stopped at the main door of the house and stated, 'Aayanar, I do not want to force you to do anything against your wishes. If you must leave, please do so when the fort gates are opened. I will send for you should the need arise.' He then rushed out of the house.

After the chakravarthy left, Sivakami suddenly lay down on the floor and started sobbing. Kamali lifted her head, placed it on her lap and enquired, 'My dear, why are you crying? Tell me what you want to do. I will go to any length, even give up my life to fulfil your desire. It wrenches at my heart to see you cry.'

When Sivakami continued crying without responding, Kamali comforted her saying, 'You fool! I know why you're crying. Isn't it because the chakravarthy spoke about marriage? How will it take place, Sivakami? Thangachi, you don't worry! Even if the fort gates are sealed, I will somehow send you out!'

Sivakami immediately stopped sobbing, sat up and asked, 'Akka, is that true? Is it possible?'

'Nothing is impossible if I apply my mind. Who do you think I am? Mahendra chakravarthy's ruses will not work with me!'

'Akka, tell me how. How will you get us out?' asked an agitated Sivakami.

Kamali whispered into Sivakami's ear, 'Through the underground passage!'

Sivakami had already heard that there was a secret tunnel that led to a place outside Kanchi. So, she asked excitedly, 'Is there really an underground passage? Do you know for sure?'

Kamali again murmured, 'Don't speak loudly! Didn't I mention that I would tell you about mama's meditation practice? All this talk of meditation is a lie, thangachi! White lies! There is an underground passage that leads to that mandapam. I have often seen Gundodharan emerge from that tunnel. Chakravarthy also sometimes—'

'What are you saying, akka? Gundodharan?'

'Yes, thangachi! Yes! Gundodharan is the chakravarthy's spy. Shatrugnan is another spy. Both of them are wicked ruffians! . . . What are you thinking about?'

'Nothing. You continue, akka. How did you stumble upon that underground passage?'

'My father-in-law forbade me from going anywhere in the vicinity of the yoga mandapam. That's why I used to often observe that place without his knowledge. One day, when I peeped into that place, the Shiva lingam at the centre of the mandapam had been moved. There was an aperture where the lingam originally stood. Gundodharan was coming out of that hole. Who do you think was there in the mandapam then? The chakravarthy was standing there along with my mama!'

Sivakami thought for a short while and pleaded, 'Kamali akka, if you somehow send us out through that tunnel, you will be blessed. I will be your slave forever!'

'Watch your words! Are you going to be my slave?! You cunning temptress! Are you, the queen-to-be of this kingdom, going to be my slave? Don't make an impossible promise and then suffer.'

Then she offered, 'That's fine, thangachi. Be a little patient. I will figure out how to move the lingam today or tomorrow. But what is the use of your being in such a hurry? Doesn't your father have to agree?'

'He is even more impatient than me to leave Kanchi. There's a reason for that,' quipped Sivakami.

Just then, Aayanar approached them from the entrance of the house and grumbled, 'I wonder how long we have to remain trapped inside this fort . . . Sivakami! Do you know? Some time ago Naganandi had sent a message about the secret of the Ajantha paints through that boy, Paranjyothi. It seems that he had sent that message to Pulikesi maharaja. Ah! Had the chakravarthy mentioned this when the Vatapi maharaja was in Kanchi itself, I would have pleaded with the scion of the Chalukya dynasty and would have obtained the secret of the Ajantha paints!'

'How can we be sure that Pulikesi maharaja knows that secret, appa?' asked Sivakami.

'He must definitely be aware, Sivakami. I have heard that Pulikesi was hiding in the caves in the Ajantha mountains for some time during his youth,' replied Aayanar.

Kamali and Sivakami exchanged smiles. As Aayanar continued talking in this manner, their enthusiasm increased.

Chapter 20

Kabalikas' Cave

Though three days had elapsed since the Vatapi emperor's departure from Kanchi, the fort gates remained sealed. Several rumours about this were floating around the city. A few citizens alleged, 'The Vatapi army did not act as per the treaty. They have again neared the fort and surrounded it!' Others surmised that Pulikesi had sent Mahendra Pallavar a message after he left the fort and was waiting for a response. 'Mahendra Pallavar has imprisoned a bikshu who is very close to the Vatapi maharaja. Pulikesi has warned that the war would continue if the bikshu is not released,' opined some others. There was yet another rumour that Pulikesi had sent a message threatening to resume the war if Aayanar and Sivakami were not sent with him.

For the first time during Mahendra Pallavar's reign, the citizens started criticizing his deeds. Some opined, 'It was a mistake to allow Pulikesi to enter Kanchi!' 'Even if he were allowed to visit the city, why be so hospitable to him? Do

we have to demean ourselves in front of an enemy king?'
questioned others. Some others complained, 'He ought
not to have asked our goddess of art, Sivakami, to dance in
Pulikesi's presence. Pulikesi was in a stupor after seeing her
perform.'

Kamali selectively communicated the citizens' comments
to Aayanar. Of all the rumours Aayanar heard, he registered
only one piece of information. It was that the Vatapi army
had camped at some distance away from the northern gates.
Aayanar often remarked, 'Wouldn't it be good if we could leave
the fort prior to the Vatapi king's departure? I will somehow
meet him and ask him about the Ajantha paints.' Once, he
suddenly spoke as though an idea had struck him, 'There
must be an underground passage that will lead us outside the
city. We can leave if we know where it is located!'

Hearing this, Sivakami asked with her eyes sparkling,
'True, appa! If we know where the tunnel is, may we leave?'

'We can leave. I too have worked in that tunnel for some
time. But I don't know where the entrance is! How can we
locate it?' asked Aayanar in a disappointed voice.

When Sivakami replied, 'Appa, it seems that Kamali akka
knows where the tunnel is!' Aayanar hurriedly stood up.

He held Kamali's hands and requested, 'My dear child!
Is your thangachi stating the truth? If so, you must show me
where the tunnel is. I will never forget your assistance as long
as I'm alive.'

'So be it, chithappa! But I can take you there only at an
opportune moment. That place is heavily guarded,' replied
Kamali.

For three days, Ashwabalar spent most of his time at the
yoga mandapam. The sound of a bell ringing and conversations
were often heard at the mandapam. On the night of the

fourth day, Aayanar, unable to sleep, looked out through the window at the palace garden. He saw an amazing sight in the moonlight. Two people were holding a tall, well-built man by his arms and escorting him through the garden. The man in the middle was blindfolded.

When Aayanar looked closer, he realized that the person in the middle was a bikshu. That bikshu reminded Aayanar of Naganandi. *Was* he Naganandi? According to rumours heard in the city, it was for this bikshu that Pulikesi was waiting for so long. Is that why they were sending Naganandi through the underground tunnel? In that case, wouldn't Pulikesi leave as soon as Naganandi met him? Ah! Such a wonderful opportunity was slipping out of his hands!

The similarity in appearance between Pulikesi and Naganandi struck Aayanar then. Who was Naganandi adigal in reality . . . ? Aayanar, struck by several such thoughts, was unable to sleep that night.

Ashwabalar, who returned at sunrise from the yoga mandapam, looked at Aayanar and enquired, 'What is this, respected sculptor? It seems that you've not slept the whole night!'

'Yes, aiyya! Your yoga mandapam in the garden was a beehive of activity all night! What's the news?' asked Aayanar.

Ashwabalar replied, 'There was no such activity. You must have been dreaming, my friend. But one thing is true. I had an amazing experience last night at the yoga mandapam. I must immediately inform the chakravarthy about it!' Saying this, he hurriedly left the house.

Moments after he left, Kamali rushed to Aayanar and Sivakami. As they had decided earlier, they had packed their clothes in a bamboo box, so they were prepared to leave at any moment. The trio immediately headed to the mandapam in the palace garden. Kamali skillfully moved the Shiva lingam at the centre of the mandapam. A flight of stairs leading down to the tunnel was visible at the place where the lingam had originally stood. Kamali handed over the lantern she was holding to Aayanar and urged, 'Chithappa, quick!'

Aayanar took the lantern and stepped into the tunnel.

Sivakami fondly embraced Kamali. Tears glistened in both their eyes. 'Farewell, akka!' Sivakami remarked in a choked voice.

'Farewell, thangachi! When you return to Kanchi next, may you return as the consort of the Pallava kumarar!' blessed Kamali.

'Akka, till I return, please kiss the baby Kannan a thousand times every day on my behalf!' pleaded Sivakami.

Kamali laughed as she pointed out, 'He will die of suffocation!'

When Sivakami entered the tunnel, her heart was beating fast. Her chest felt tight. She felt as though she were leaving an illuminated world for an underworld filled with darkness, fear and monstrosity. Her determination helped her overcome that emotion, and she followed Aayanar.

Aayanar and Sivakami must have walked through that tunnel for almost a muhurtham. They did not converse much during that time. Aayanar often stopped, held Sivakami's hand and comforted her, saying, 'It won't be for much longer, amma. We will reach the exit soon!'

After walking for a muhurtham, the temperature dropped and the air felt cool. 'Amma, Sivakami! We have exited the fort. We are crossing the moat!' he observed.

He stopped for a moment and continued, 'My child! I remember working in this place. We had to ensure that the water from the moat did not seep down. Also, during times of danger, there is a provision to close the tunnel. Look there! If we break the stone in the place marked with a sign, the water in the moat will gush in. Then no one can either enter or leave the tunnel!'

'Thank God we'll be able to leave before some such disaster occurs, won't we?' enquired Sivakami.

After walking for another muhurtham, they observed light streaming in from above. 'Ah! The tunnel has ended!' Both of them climbed the stairs towards the place from where the light was streaming in.

The place they had reached was a small Jain temple carved out of mountain rocks. Three large statues of the Jain tirthankaras were carved there. But the horror! It seemed as though kabalikas had occupied that Samana cave. Skulls were scattered everywhere. Also, one kabalikan was sitting with his eyes closed like a fourth statue adjacent to the three statues of the tirthankaras. His body was smeared with ash and he wore a garland of skulls, presenting a horrific sight. Fortunately, he was meditating with his eyes closed tight.

Aayanar and Sivakami rushed up the stairs without giving him a second look. After walking for some time, Sivakami asked, 'Appa! What is this? A kabalikan is sitting in a Samana cave temple!'

'Amma, a Samana school used to function in this mountain. Didn't the Samanars, enraged with Mahendra Pallavar, leave the country? It looks as if the kabalikas, who were chased away from Kanchi before the siege began, occupied this cave! For them, war is a reason to celebrate! For, won't they get a lot of skulls?'

Aayanar and Sivakami were walking down the forest path conversing in this manner. They had barely walked a short distance when they heard the din of several people approaching from the opposite direction. Within a few minutes, they saw a large crowd in front of them. The ones who had come were warriors of the Vatapi army! The Varaha flag that was fluttering amidst them confirmed their identity.

Chapter 21

Flames of Fury

Vatapi warriors! From where did they come to be encountered by Aayanar and Sivakami? Needless to say, it was all due to Pulikesi. When Pulikesi took leave of Mahendra Pallavar and left through the northern gates, he was a disgruntled man. His heart was akin to a volcano filled with black smoke, molten lava and fire that was waiting to erupt.

Kanchi's multi-storeyed mansions, its prosperous citizens, the fabulous wealth at the Kanchi palace and the sights Pulikesi had seen had ignited in him an intense jealousy. Sivakami's dance performance on the final day of his visit acted like a wind that fanned the flames of his envy. The artistic pride-filled words uttered by Mahendra Pallavar during the performance instilled in Pulikesi, who had no appreciation for art, an intense hatred. What rankled Pulikesi the most was the realization that Mahendra Pallavar had been deceiving him for so long. Hadn't Mahendra Pallavar visited the Chalukya army camp all by himself on the banks

98

of the North Pennai River, delivered a fake message and returned? This had been followed by multiple acts of deceit, several ploys and illusions.

In all fairness, the city of Kanchi ought to have been under his control by now. The citizens of Kanchi, who were so proud of their wealth and knowledge of the arts, ought to have been shivering with fear in front of him and begging for their lives. Ah! He ought to have kicked Mahendra Pallavar's crown by now! Had he not waited on the banks of the North Pennai River one and a half years ago and instead headed straight to Kanchi, all this would have been possible. By now, the Varaha flag would have been hoisted not only in Kanchi but also in Uraiyur and Madurai.

What was the reason for all this not happening? It was because of Mahendra Pallavar's deceptive tactics. Pulikesi, who was feared by all the beasts in the forest, had been deceived by the tactics of a mere fox that hid itself in a hole! The more the Vatapi emperor thought about this, the more furious he became. All the veins on his forehead throbbed and stood out. All those who observed his face shuddered in anticipation of disaster.

From the moment the Vatapi emperor left Kanchi till he joined his army that was stationed one kaadam away from the city, he did not utter a single word. This dangerous silence instilled immense fear in those who accompanied him. As soon as the emperor reached his tent, a volcano erupted, spewing fire. The commanders of the Vatapi army, chiefs of the army stores and chief of the spy force were all singed by Pulikesi's fury.

When the commanders assembled at the ministers' council, Pulikesi threatened, 'I am going to get one half of you trampled by elephants and the other half mounted on stakes!'

The courtiers remained silent. Observing this, he roared, 'Why are you all quiet? Have you all been struck dumb?' He then continued to shout at them. He blamed them for all the obstacles, defeats and disappointments encountered during the invasion of the southern country.

'Brave commanders! Wise spies! Listen to me! Once upon a time, the entrance of the Kanchi fort was fitted with a single wooden gate. Had we arrived there then, the fort gate could have been demolished by just one of our elephants. Then there weren't even 10,000 soldiers to safeguard the ramparts of the fort. Our soldiers could have crossed the moat and jumped over the ramparts within a day. Had Mahendra Pallavan not come running and fallen at my feet, I would have decimated Kanchi. Mahendra Pallavan insulted me in this very Kanchi. He insulted me in the presence of a stonecutter and a gypsy girl! He said that I possessed no knowledge of the arts! Apparently I do not possess a sense of appreciation! What a proud man! How arrogant of him!' he exclaimed, ground his teeth and stamped his foot. He then commented, 'When Mahendra Pallavan was renovating the Kanchi fort, all of you were relaxing and sleeping on the banks of the North Pennai River!' and gave a terrifying laugh.

At that point of time, the chief of the Vatapi spy force mustered the courage to say, 'Prabhu, it was all on account of Naganandi's message! I had raised objections even then!'

Pulikesi looked at him with sparks of anger flying from his eyes and bellowed, 'Fool! Are you blaming Naganandi for your stupidity? Naganandi would never ever have advised us incorrectly. The message that reached us was not from Naganandi. The thief, Mahendran, intercepted Naganandi's message. Not only that. He then penned a fake message, came in disguise, and delivered it to me. Our wise spies were unable to discover this. Ah! If only Naganandi had been with us then, all this would not have happened. This Pallava fox's ruses would not have worked with him . . . What is the use of all of you being here? All our efforts have gone in vain due to the absence of the bikshu!'

When the emperor started talking about Naganandi, his heart softened, and some semblance of civility returned to his speech. Thinking that this was the right moment, the commander of the Vatapi army counselled, 'Prabhu, let bygones be bygones. Now let's think about safely reaching our army to Vatapi. As days pass, returning to Vatapi will become more difficult . . .'

In a thundering voice Pulikesi roared, 'Commander! What are you saying? Are you saying that we ought to return?' He then thundered, 'Commanders! Listen to me! Naganandi adigal is languishing in the Pallavan's prison inside the Kanchi fort. The great man who brought me up and protected me like my mother would have, a person who risked his life several times to save mine, the bikshu who instated me on the Vatapi throne, and the person who made the great emperor of Utthara Bharata, Harshavardhana, call for a truce with me is now trapped in the Pallava fox's net. You are saying that such a person ought to be left behind and we ought to return? Never! Commanders! Order our brave forces to attack the Kanchi fort. Let's capture Kanchi, reduce Mahendra Pallavan's palace to ashes, tonsure his head, tie him to the wheels of my chariot and then return to Vatapi. We will liberate Naganandi adigal, mount him on the royal elephant and take him back with us! Leave immediately!' Pulikesi then paused. For some time, pin-drop silence prevailed in the assembly.

'Why this silence? Why aren't you all saying anything? Have you all become stone statues after seeing the stone statues in Pallava Nadu?' asked the emperor.

After that, the commanders offered their opinions one by one. The chief of the elephant force pointed out that the elephants had become emaciated due to lack of food, that they had become more frenzied and that they would start injuring the Vatapi soldiers if more time lapsed.

The head of the infantry revealed that it was an impossible task to command the foot soldiers to attack the Kanchi fort as they were already fatigued and discontented. The head of stores divulged that, if a few days passed, everyone would have to die of starvation. The head of the weapons division confessed that there were not enough weapons to attack the fort, and that all the weapons they had brought along had been depleted in the previous attack.

Hearing this, Pulikesi became even more enraged. However, he did not have the courage to go against everyone's unanimous opinion and command them to attack the fort. 'Ah! I embarked on this invasion trusting all of you!' he complained in disgust. 'Never mind, all of you get lost. I will think it over tonight and inform you of my decision tomorrow!' he concluded.

Chapter 22

Pulikesi's Command

Pulikesi was immersed in thought for nearly three days. The sight of the towers and pillars of Kanchi a kaadam away enraged him even more. The thought of Naganandi adigal being imprisoned in one of Kanchi's underground prisons further intensified Pulikesi's anger. The desire to seek revenge on Mahendra Pallavan grew by the minute and assumed gargantuan proportions.

After thinking all day and night for two days, the Vatapi emperor finally made certain decisions. He summoned his commanders and ministers and communicated his diktat, which were as follows: The emperor and his key commanders accompanied by a major part of the army would return to Vatapi. Fifty-four thousand of the sturdiest soldiers in the army would be left behind. They would form small groups, plunder, and then set fire to the villages and towns that lay within a radius of four kaadam from Kanchi. These soldiers would imprison the young women in the villages and towns,

kill the young men, maim the aged and seek revenge in any
other manner they deemed fit. Importantly, all sculptures and
sculpture galleries had to be demolished. One arm and one leg
of the sculptors had to be amputated. After passing such cruel
commands and appointing the appropriate persons to execute
them, the Vatapi emperor, accompanied by a large part of his
army, embarked on his return journey.

Seeing the Varaha flag, Sivakami realized that they had
run into the Vatapi soldiers. Her body trembled while her
heart palpitated. Though there were only a hundred soldiers,
Sivakami felt as though 16,000 soldiers were standing in front
of her. But Aayanar did not feel an iota of fear. His smile
indicated that he was filled with enthusiasm. He asked the
soldier who was at the front, 'Aiyya, aren't you a Chalukya
soldier? Where is your king?' From the expression on the
soldier's face, Aayanar realized that he did not know Tamil.
So, he repeated his question in Prakrit. As the soldier did not
understand Prakrit either, he turned around and looked for
the leader of the group, who was following behind.

By then, the leader, who was on horseback, had reached
the front of the group. He looked intently at Aayanar and
Sivakami and exclaimed, 'Oh!' in surprise.

This was because he had been part of the retinue that had
accompanied Pulikesi to Kanchi and had watched Sivakami's
dance performance at the Pallava chakravarthy's court. So, he
was happily surprised when he recognized them. He rode his
horse up to them, stared at them, and then asked Aayanar,
'What was your question?'

Aayanar enthusiastically enquired, 'Aiyya, where is your
emperor? I want to meet him.' Commander Sashankan's
eyebrows knotted. He asked with an amused smile, 'Why do

you want to meet the Vatapi emperor? What do you hope to accomplish by meeting him?'

'I can share the details of the task only with the emperor. It's a secret matter,' replied Aayanar. Hearing the warrior laugh mockingly, Aayanar thought they might not lead him to the Vatapi emperor if he did not disclose the task at hand. So, he stated, 'But it's not my intention to hide the details from you. I came here thinking that your emperor may know the secret of Ajantha's indelible paints. I wanted to know how the indelible paints are prepared. Will you please lead me to the emperor?'

Listening to this, Commander Sashankan laughed even louder than before. He looked at the soldiers standing next to him and ordered, 'Why are you standing still? Blindfold them.'

Aayanar asked in a shocked voice, 'Why do you want to blindfold us?'

Commander Sashankan responded, 'Do you need to really know? Then listen to me. The Vatapi emperor has commanded us to imprison all the young women in the Pallava kingdom. Not only that, but he has also ordered us to amputate one arm and one leg of all the sculptors. This order applies to average sculptors. You are a great sculptor who is a guru to all other sculptors. So, I am going to cut off both your arms and legs. I asked them to blindfold you so that this girl does not have to see you being amputated!'

A shrill voice that resembled the final call of a cuckoo injured by an arrow was heard. Sivakami fell and lay on the ground like a corpse.

When Sivakami regained consciousness, she still felt dizzy. She observed that her feet were moving and that two men were holding each of her arms firmly. Gradually, she regained her memory and recollected the incidents that had occurred. When she realized that her father was not by her side, she experienced an agony that she had not experienced thus far in her life. Supported by warriors on both sides, she walked a few steps ahead in a dazed condition. She then observed a figure emerging from the dense forest. The moment she saw the figure, she realized that it was Naganandi adigal. Immediately she extricated herself from the soldiers' hold like one possessed and leapt towards Naganandi adigal. She fell at his feet and pleaded, 'Swami! I seek refuge in you! Please save me!'

Chapter 23

Plea for Refuge

'Sivakami! Is that really you? Or are my eyes deceiving me?' asked Naganandi adigal, feigning disbelief.

'Adigal, it is me, the orphaned Sivakami. Please save this daughter of an impoverished sculptor, swami!'

'Don't talk like that, amma! You're neither an orphan, nor are you poor! You are the fortunate one with whom the kumara chakravarthy of the Pallava kingdom is in love. Aren't you going to become the daughter-in-law of Chakravarthy Mahendra Pallavar?'

'Swami, this is not the time to seek revenge on me! I beseech you to rescue me,' Sivakami pleaded.

'I am an ochre-clad mendicant! How can I save you?'

'You can, swami! You can! If you wish to, you definitely can save me!'

'How did you get trapped by them? Why did you leave the fort? How did you come out of the fort?'

'Please don't ask me all that now, swami! It was stupid of me to have come out. I am the cause of my father's death . . . I don't mind going to hell. Please save my father . . .'

'Where is your father, amma? What danger befell him?' asked the bikshu.

'Aiyya, ask these people where my father is! Some time ago, I heard terrible things being said. There, that man sitting on the horse passed an order. Ask him where Aayanar is! Ask him quickly!'

As Sivakami was talking, Commander Sashankan had been observing them, and he now rode towards them. He mockingly greeted Naganandi saying, 'Buddham saranam gacchami!' and bowed to him. Commander Sashankan was one of those who were envious of Naganandi bikshu's influence over the Vatapi emperor.

Naganandi reciprocated in a harsh voice, 'Buddham saranam gacchami!'

'Ah! Naganandi bikshu! How did you suddenly spring up here? In which hole was the snake hiding all these days? Why is it raising its hood now?' asked Commander Sashankan.

The sound of a cobra hissing, that caused everyone to shudder, was heard there at that point of time. One man screamed, 'Snake, snake!' Everyone fled from there. A cobra slithered past the legs of the horse on which Commander Sashankan was seated.

'Commander! Beware! A cobra doesn't usually bite. But when it does bite, its venom can be extremely harmful!' quipped the bikshu.

Sashankan ground his teeth and retorted, 'Bikshu! Thanks for revealing this amazing truth. I have a lot of tasks to attend to. I don't have the time to talk to you. Excuse me . . .' He then rode a few steps away and told the soldiers, 'You! Catch this girl and bind her with a rope!'

Hearing this, the soldiers approached Sivakami.

'Commander! It is indeed your fortune to imprison a reputed artiste of the southern country. I will inform the emperor of this incident at the earliest . . .'

'Oh! It seems that the bikshu is also travelling to Vatapi . . .'

'Yes, Sashankar! But I do not have to travel up to Vatapi to inform him of this incident. I saw the chakravarthy some time ago in another part of this forest . . .'

'Lie! Lie! By now the Vatapi emperor must have reached the banks of the North Pennai River.'

Naganandi warned in a resonant voice, 'Truth and deceit will soon become known, commander! But do remember one thing. If a cat eyes a doe that a tiger proposes to prey on, the consequences will be disastrous!' All Sashankan did was grunt in response. Then Naganandi told Sivakami, 'Amma, listen to me attentively. If you act in the manner I tell you, no harm will befall you. Go along with them without resisting. As you have learnt dancing, your legs must be strong enough to walk long distances. You don't hesitate to walk, do you?'

Sivakami, who till then had stood immobilized like a stone statue listening to the conversation between Sashankan and Naganandi, seemed to regain consciousness. 'Swami, I am not at all concerned about myself. Your friend Aayanar is in great danger because of this vile man. Aiyyo! Please save him!' she pleaded.

Immediately Naganandi bikshu asked, 'Commander, where is this girl's father?'

Sashankan let out a terrifying laugh and replied, 'Ah! Do you want to know that? I will tell you. The emperor has commanded us to amputate one arm and one leg of all the sculptors in the Pallava kingdom. Her father is a great sculptor, isn't he? I have ordered for both his arms and legs to be amputated as a mark of respect! I have asked my men to take him to the rock there, cut off his arms and legs, and push him down. I have asked my men to take him to the peak of the rock so that those on the ramparts of the Kanchi fort will be able to see his limbs being amputated.'

Sivakami, who was looking at Sashankan intently as he was talking, turned to Naganandi with indescribable fear and sorrow-filled eyes and cried, 'Adigal!'

Naganandi responded saying, 'Amma, trust me. I will save your father. You go along with them in peace!'

Sashankan warned, 'Bikshu, are you aware of the punishment that awaits the person who prevents the Vatapi emperor's command from being executed? You must keep that in mind!' He then instructed Sivakami, 'This bikshu has given you good advice. Heed his words and come with us without resisting!'

Chapter 24

Atrocity

Aayanar's mind had lost its capacity to think. He was unable to believe what he had seen and heard. He was even unable to decide if it was all real or a dream! It was natural for kings who ruled nations to wage war. Generally the command issued would be, 'Don't harm women, children, calves and artists.' If the kings were aggressive and cruel, they wouldn't be conscientious enough to pass such a command.

But was it possible that an emperor ruling a large kingdom had commanded his soldiers to amputate the limbs of sculptors? How was it possible that such a demon continued to rule a kingdom? Would the denizens of that country tolerate such behaviour? Was it possible that Emperor Pulikesi had passed such a command? Could this king, whose kingdom housed amazing, world-renowned, life-like indelible paintings, have passed such a cruel command? Was the cruel-looking commander, who claimed that the emperor had passed such an order, stating the truth? Had his ears heard accurately what the commander had said?

Did Sivakami actually faint after hearing his cruel words? When he had rushed to prevent her from falling on the ground, did the Vatapi soldiers actually grasp him with their iron-like hands and restrain him? Had he in reality heard the words, 'Take him to the top of the rock and amputate his arms and legs there so that those on the ramparts of the fort can observe the sight'? Or had these incidents occurred in a terrible nightmare? Was it true that he was climbing that rock and that his fatigued legs were trembling? Or was this merely a hallucination?

All this was a hallucination! Or a dream! This could never be true. But were the ramparts of the Kanchi fort visible at a distance also a figment of his imagination? No, never! It was true that he could see the Kanchi fort. It was also a fact that the soldiers had made him climb the rock and had made him stand on the top of the rock. These demons holding his hands and raising their swords to amputate his arms were also real. Ah! Sivakami! My dear daughter! The sinner that I am, I have put you in such a precarious situation! I have sacrificed you for my obsession with the Ajantha paints. Aiyyo! My dear daughter!

When one of the soldiers lifted his sword, Aayanar closed his eyes tightly. But the raised sword did not cut off his arm the next moment, as he had expected. An authoritative voice commanded, 'Stop!'

When Aayanar opened his eyes . . . 'Ah! What is this? Isn't he Emperor Pulikesi? How did he reach here?'

The soldiers, shocked at the sight of the emperor, abruptly loosened their grip on Aayanar. Aayanar's leg slipped into a nearby ditch, and he rolled down the slope of the rock that extended to the ground below. Within moments, he lost consciousness.

When Aayanar regained consciousness, it seemed as though a major scuffle had occurred in the vicinity. The sound of several men screaming and stones colliding was heard. The same authoritative voice that he had heard earlier again commanded, 'Stop!'

Aayanar opened his eyes and observed the scene. He realized that he was lying in his own house in the middle of the forest. When he looked around, he saw the Vatapi emperor standing majestically and heard him order, 'Leave this place!' The entire group of violent Vatapi soldiers walked towards the entrance.

The statues and beautiful dance postures he had taken such immense effort to sculpt lay broken. When he saw this, he felt devastated. He tried getting up to inspect the damaged statues but felt a sharp stab of pain in his right leg. He was unable to get up. It was only then that Aayanar realized that he had fractured his right leg. At that point of time, Aayanar's sister came running to him from the rear portion of the house. She was trembling and her eyes were filled with tears. The poor lady had been shocked when she witnessed the Vatapi soldiers committing atrocities.

After all the soldiers had left the house, the Vatapi emperor walked calmly to where Aayanar was lying down.

Aayanar shrieked, 'Prabhu! How can your soldiers engage in such atrocities?'

Chapter 25

Masquerader

Emperor Pulikesi came and sat next to Aayanar, who lay on the floor, unable to get up because of his injured right leg. He remarked, 'Great sculptor, forgive me. I came rushing here only to protect your wonderful sculptures. I tied you to the horse and brought you here, without even waiting for you to regain consciousness. Despite that, some of your statues were damaged. Please forgive me. But be happy that at least a few statues are undamaged!'

Aayanar looked at the emperor's face eagerly. A doubt lingered in his mind. What a miracle! The Vatapi emperor spoke fluent Tamil. Was it the cruel King Pulikesi who was sitting next to him and comforting him? Would such a good-natured king have commanded his soldiers to amputate the limbs of sculptors? Would he have commanded his soldiers to destroy statues and sculptures? Had the commander whose face resembled that of a wildcat stated the truth? Or was the emperor not speaking the truth?

Aayanar suddenly thought of Sivakami! Aiyyo! What had happened to her? He forgot everything else. 'Prabhu! Your soldiers captured my daughter Sivakami and took her away. Aiyyo! Please save her. How could I have forgotten about Sivakami and talked about sculptures?' shrieked Aayanar.

Pulikesi reassured, 'Aayanar, by God's grace no harm will befall your daughter. She will reach Vatapi safely!'

'Aiyyo! What are you saying? Is Sivakami going to Vatapi? Then why should I remain here? Take me there too!'

'I initially thought so too. But you've now injured your leg. If you move even slightly in this situation, your life will be in danger.'

'Prabhu, if you are concerned about my life, please send my daughter back!'

'That's an impossible task . . .'

'Ah! Aren't you an emperor too? Is it only possible for you to command your soldiers to amputate the limbs of sculptors, to mutilate statues and to imprison young girls?' screamed Aayanar furiously.

Pulikesi pointed to Sivakami's athai, who was sitting close to Aayanar, trembling in fear, and instructed in a patient tone, 'Aayanar, I have to tell you something important. Please ask your sister to go inside!'

'Prabhu, you tell me! My sister is hard of hearing. She cannot even hear the sound of thunder!'

'Even then, please ask her to go in!' repeated Pulikesi.

When Aayanar gestured to his sister, she went inside, more confused than before.

Pulikesi asked, 'Aayanar, please understand what I have to say and then respond. Your daughter is now on her way to Vatapi. If I rush back, I may be able to trace her. After finding her, I may even be able to send her back. But you

need to consider one more issue. A huge force has headed to
Mamallapuram to damage the wonderful sculptures there. If
I go there, I will be able to stop that force. Shall I proceed to
stop the force headed towards Mamallapuram or trace your
daughter?'

The doubt that lingered in Aayanar's mind became
stronger. Was it truly Emperor Pulikesi who was speaking
such fluent Tamil? Aayanar looked intently at him and
hesitated while asking, 'Aiyya! You ... you ... !'

Emperor Pulikesi immediately removed the crown from
his head and put it down.

Aayanar blurted out, 'Ah! Is that you Naganandi adigal?'

'Yes, Aayanar! It is me, the impoverished bikshu!'

'Swami! Why have you assumed this disguise?'

'I donned this role to help my friends. I was also able to
render timely assistance.'

'Ah! It is amazing that both of you look identical. You
are naturally endowed with this resemblance! Swami, who are
you? Probably ... !'

'No, Aayanar! Emperor Pulikesi of Vatapi and Naganandi
bikshu are not the same person. Due to some amazing
miracle of evolution, God has endowed us with an identical
appearance. I was able to use this resemblance to save the
great sculptor of Bharata Kandam.'

'Ah! Swami! What is the use of saving my life? My
daughter ... my daughter, Sivakami!'

'Aayanar, you tell me what I'm supposed to do today. Shall
I go in search of your daughter or shall I go to Mamallapuram?'

Aayanar pleaded in a distressed tone, 'Swami, God will
protect my daughter. You go to Mamallapuram! Please leave
immediately!'

The disguised bikshu kept turning around and looking at Aayanar as he left the sculpted house.

Sivakami's athai, who had been inside the house till then, hesitantly stepped out and sat next to Aayanar. She enquired, 'Thambi, what affliction ails you?'

Aayanar did not respond to her. Suddenly athai became agitated and asked, 'Where's my child? Where is Sivakami?'

Aayanar sat up erect and asked in a tone that echoed across the sculpted mandapam, 'Akka, where is Sivakami? Where is my daughter Sivakami?' After asking this question, he lowered his head and wept inconsolably. Hearing Aayanar's voice, Rathi and Suga Rishi came running to him from the backyard. Seeing Aayanar weep, those animals stood still like statues.

Chapter 26

Humbling of Pride

At Kanchi, Mahendra Pallavar was seated in the palace chamber where the ministers' council discussed confidential matters. General Kalipahayar, Prime Minister Saranga Devar, Chief Minister Ranadheerar, the chief of spies, Shatrugnan and Gundodharan were standing in front of him. Mahendra Pallavar's face was glowing with happiness. He asked, 'Gundodhara, did you see it in person? Have the Chalukya forces actually retreated from Mamallapuram? Are you sure that the sculptures were not destroyed?'

'Yes, Pallavendra! How can I express my surprise on observing this? Two thousand Chalukya demons, armed with crowbars and other iron weapons, came running towards Mamallapuram. I was distraught that they were going to damage the lifelike sculptures created painstakingly by thousands of sculptors. I was thinking how pained you would be when you saw that horrific sight. The very next moment, Emperor Pulikesi appeared from nowhere atop a rock.

He majestically gestured with his hands. That was it! The Chalukyas who came running and shrieking like demons stood immobilized. They did not expect to see the Vatapi emperor at Mamallapuram then. Neither did they expect him to rescind his previous command and ask them to return without damaging the sculptures. Prabhu, I too was shocked and stood frozen like a statue for some time. I regained consciousness only after everyone had left that place. I immediately came running here!' reported Gudodharan.

Saranga Devar exclaimed, 'Prabhu, your magical prowess seems limitless! How did you cause the Chalukya emperor to rush to Mamallapuram and rescind his own command?'

Mahendrar remarked, 'How can I change that fool's heart, which is devoid of artistic sensibility? Even Brahma cannot do that!'

The chief minister, Ranadheera Pallavarayar, asked, 'Then how did this miracle occur, Pallavendra? How did you save Mamallapuram?'

'Isn't there a proverb that even a miniscule splinter may be of help? My hunch that the bikshu might be useful turned out right!'

'Prabhu! You speak in riddles; we're unable to understand anything!'

'Hadn't I kept Naganandi bikshu in prison? I had incarcerated him anticipating such a situation. Pulikesi had asked for Naganandi bikshu's release just before his departure from Kanchi. For a moment, I felt like acquiescing. I thought of sending Naganandi along with Pulikesi. Fortunately, I did not do so and detained him here. That's the reason for Mamallapuram surviving now!'

Shatrugnan confessed, 'I now understand the import of your command. I did not understand anything when you ordered, "Keep the entrance to the underground tunnel open and sit beside it. Don't be surprised by the people who exit through the underground tunnel! You should continue to be in meditation!" I was stunned when Naganandi was released. That moment I felt like catching the fake bikshu by his neck and strangling him. It was due to your unequivocal command that I kept quiet.'

Commander Kalipahayar asked, 'The rest of us are still unable to understand! Are you saying that Naganandi bikshu fetched Pulikesi and saved Mamallapuram?'

When Mahendra Varmar revealed, 'Naganandi did not fetch Pulikesi; Naganandi became Pulikesi,' the listeners gasped in surprise. 'What is the use of all of you being endowed with eyes? You don't use them. Didn't you observe that Naganandi's face and Pulikesi's face were identical? I even wondered whether Naganandi was actually Pulikesi. It was only later that I realized they were different people. I thought that Naganandi would be useful during times like these and had imprisoned him as a precautionary measure. When Pulikesi visited Kanchi, I asked our goldsmiths to replicate his crown and ornaments. I handed over the ornaments to Naganandi yesterday and asked him to head straight to Mamallapuram.'

'Were you able to convince Naganandi so easily, prabhu?'

'Even bikshus and spies fear for their lives and may be tempted by freedom,' quipped Mahendrar.

'But how could you trust that treacherous masquerader and release him?'

'Ah! Naganandi is not a human in the first place. He is a demon in human form. That sinner wields poisoned knives! Nevertheless, he is a connoisseur! I was aware of his love for the arts. I was sure that he would protect Mamallapuram from harm. That's why I sent him. I wouldn't have cared what became of him had he also saved Aayanar's house of sculptures!'

Listening to all this news, the chief minister and others stood speechless in shock. The sound of a woman howling outside shattered that silence. A sentry rushed in, bowed and then stated, 'Prabhu, please forgive me. Kannabiran's wife, Kamali, is insisting on seeing you now. When we stopped her, she created a commotion!'

The chakravarthy looked concerned. He commanded, 'Allow her in!'

Kamali came in running with her hair undone, fell at the chakravarthy's feet and implored, 'Pallavendra! Please forgive the sinner that I am; I have committed treachery.'

That morning, Kamali's father-in-law, Ashwabalar, had asked her, 'Where are Aayanar and his daughter, Sivakami?'

Kamali had cleverly replied, 'Time weighed heavily on their hands in this house. They were unable to tolerate the baby's pranks. They have gone to visit the temples in Kanchi. Aren't they crazy about sculptures and statues?'

'Thank God! Didn't they say that they wanted to leave the fort? Do you know what would have become of them had they left the fort? It seems that the cruel Pulikesi's men are setting fire to the villages. They are amputating the limbs of sculptors. They are taking young unmarried girls as hostages . . .'

When Kamali heard this, she had shrieked, 'Aiyyo!' Even as she was weeping, she related what had transpired to Ashwabalar.

He had scolded her to his heart's content and then instructed, 'Go! Run to the chakravarthy and tell him what has happened!'

Hence Kamali had hastened to meet the chakravarthy.

By the time Kamali had completed relating the incidents even as she sobbed and stammered, the chakravarthy's facial expression had undergone a complete transformation. The proud smile on his face was replaced by indescribable sorrow. He asked Shatrugnan, 'Is she stating the truth, Shatrugna? Are you aware of this?'

Shatrugnan replied in a quivering voice, 'Yes, prabhu! Shortly after Naganandi left, a man and a woman left through the tunnel. They looked like Aayanar and Sivakami. As you had commanded me not to be surprised by the people who left, I kept quiet.'

Mahendrar looked at the chief minister and the others present and admitted, 'Some time ago, wasn't I so proud of my astuteness? God has humbled my pride. I cannot face Mamallan after losing Sivakami. Commander! Mobilize the forces immediately! They must be ready to exit the fort through the northern gates within the next muhurtham.'

Chapter 27

Victorious Warrior

Joyous commotion prevailed in the Chola village of Thiruvengadu. The villagers were ecstatic when they heard the news that the kumara chakravarthy of the Pallava kingdom, Narasimha Varmar, was visiting the village that day, accompanied by his dear friend, the brave Commander Paranjyothi.

The villagers had heard about the fierce battle fought between the Pallava and Pandya forces on the banks of the Kollidam two days ago. They also knew that Jayanta Varma Pandian had fled from the battlefield following his ignominious defeat. Those who had witnessed the battle in person had related how the Kollidam was transformed into a river of blood. Everyone was aware that the Pandya army was larger than the Pallava army, and that it was due to the valiant deeds of Mamallar and Paranjyothi that the Pandya army had lost, disintegrated and taken flight.

It was not surprising, therefore, that the villagers were heady with delight when they heard of the arrival of these gallant warriors.

Fortune had already smiled on the villagers once. Ten days ago, Thirunavukkarasar Peruman had visited the Saivite monastery in that village. That holy soul had not only mowed the grass that grew in the temple praharam but, had also in the evenings sung along with his disciples the nectar-like pasurams he had composed.

The villagers, who were already immersed in the bliss of devotion and appreciation of Tamil, became even more exultant when they came to know of the impending visit of the kumara chakravarthy and his brave commander. A rumour also spread that Mamallar and Paranjyothi were visiting the village for an audience with Thirunavukkarasar.

But those in Namasivaya vaidhyar's household alone knew the actual purpose of their visit. Paranjyothi's beloved mother was living in Namasivaya vaidhyar's house. This being the case, did Commander Paranjyothi and his friend need another reason to visit Thiruvengadu?

Namasivaya vaidhyar's residence buzzed with joy and activity far exceeding that in any other house in Thiruvengadu.

That day, the usually composed Namasivaya vaidhyar paced to and fro between the entrance of the house and its interiors at least a hundred times. His wife adorned their daughter Umayal with clothes and ornaments with the meticulousness she had not demonstrated till then. Umayal's younger brother and sister were bent upon teasing her. However, Umayal's heart was akin to a turbulent sea amidst a raging storm.

Paranjyothi's mother was awaiting her only son's arrival, teary-eyed.

It must be mentioned that, between Mamallar and Paranjyothi, both of whom were a yojanai away from Thiruvengadu, it was Mamallar who was more enthusiastic. Not only did Paranjyothi appear more fatigued, but his horse also frequently lagged behind. Mamallar teased him and tried to hurry him up. He teased, 'What is this, commander? Why is your horse retreating in this manner? Doesn't the horse understand your urgency? Shall we exchange horses?' He further pulled Paranjyothi's leg, remarking, 'Why is your face so radiant? Are you going to meet your lover? Or are you headed to the battlefield? Don't worry! I will put in a word so that your family does not reprimand you too much.'

Paranjyothi tolerated this banter for some time. Finally, unable to bear the mockery any longer, he exclaimed, 'Aiyya! You are unable to comprehend my situation and hence, speak in a manner that adds insult to injury. I truly have no desire to come here. You forced me to agree and I now regret it. You will be blessed if you allow me to return at least now. You meet my mother on my behalf and inform her that I am well. Please inform her that I am ashamed to meet her as I have not kept my word!'

Mamallar was taken aback on hearing Paranjyothi's emotional outburst. 'Commander! What promise did you make to your mother? Why were you unable to fulfil it?' he asked in a worried tone.

'Prabhu, do you remember the reason why I had left my native village and my house? My uncle, Namasivaya vaidhyar, was reluctant to get his educated daughter Umayal married to an illiterate person like me. I left my house with the intention of heading to Kanchi, which offers boundless education, enrolling at Navukkarasar Peruman's monastery, and attaining proficiency in education and the arts. But what happened? I am returning home as illiterate as I was when I left. I did not even get an opportunity to see Thirunavukkarasar Peruman . . .'

Narasimha Varmar laughed heartily at Paranjyothi's words.

'Pallava kumara! Your laughter scorches my heart! When the chakravarthy sent me back from the northern battlefront, he asked you to educate me! But neither did you teach me anything, nor did you permit me to even touch manuscripts. You frittered away the little leisure time we had by speaking about Aayanar's daughter! Ah! I have never seen people who are as self-centred as the royalty!' When Paranjyothi said this in a sorrowful tone, the kumara chakravarthy laughed even more loudly.

When Mamallar and Paranjyothi reached the outskirts of Thiruvengadu, a tumultuous reception was awaiting them. Mamallar was reminded of the reception at Mandapapattu, where Aayanar and Sivakami had been accorded special attention and he had followed them incognito.

Ah! Several incidents had transpired after that! By now, Kannabiran must have reached Mandapapattu and informed them about the battle on the banks of the Kollidam, in which the Pandian had fled after losing. Sivakami must have been so happy! She must be expecting his arrival with her head held high! This time, would she and the other villagers come to welcome him? As Mamallar was immersed in such daydreams, he heard loud cheering that reached the skies.

'Long live the kumara chakravarthy Narasimha Pallavendrar!'

'Long live the brave Mamallar who vanquished the Ganga king and the Madurai Pandian in battle!'

'Long live the bravest of the brave, Commander Paranjyothi!'

Mamallar's fantasies came to an end. The cheering made him aware that they had reached Thiruvengadu.

Chapter 28

Rustic Maiden

When the welcome ceremony was over, Mamallar and Paranjyothi entered Namasivaya vaidhyar's residence. The family members stood stunned, not knowing what to do when the kumara chakravarthy of the Pallava kingdom entered their humble dwelling. As Paranjyothi was dressed in the robes of a commander, they felt shy to look him in the eye and converse with him. Paranjyothi was even more tongue-tied.

Mamallar sat on a single seat that was placed in the hall of that house, without anyone asking him to do so, and looked around. He understood the situation. Guessing that the elderly woman with tear-filled eyes was Paranjyothi's mother, he observed, 'I was eager to meet the fortunate mother who begot our brave commander. Today, I have the good fortune of meeting you!' He then looked at Paranjyothi and chided, 'Commander! What is this? Please prostrate before your mother. Won't people comment that you have forgotten even your etiquette after leaving for Thondaimandalam?'

Paranjyothi immediately stepped forward and prostrated before his mother, who was eager to embrace him. But she hesitated to do so in the kumara chakravarthy's presence, and also because her son was dressed like a warrior. Paranjyothi, after prostrating before Namasivaya vaidhyar, sat next to Mamallar and looked at the roof of the house.

Namasivaya vaidhyar told Mamallar, 'It is our good fortune to host you in our humble dwelling!'

Mamallar told him, 'Oh! So you are Namasivaya vaidhyar. I want to caution you. It seems that your daughter has frightened my friend a lot. Isn't the girl standing by the door your daughter? She appears extremely docile. But she has scared the great warrior who is the finest commander in the Pallava army, the person who caused Vatapi's elephant force to disintegrate and made the kings of Ganga Nadu and Pandya Nadu flee. Please ask your daughter not to act in this manner henceforth. Do you know how much I had to struggle to bring Paranjyothi here? I held his hand and dragged him here forcefully. Amma! Why don't you ask your son if he was reluctant to come here or not?'

Paranjyothi's mother shot a look filled with pride and affection at Paranjyothi and asked, 'My child! Is Mamalla prabhu stating the truth? Were you unwilling to visit us?'

'Yes, amma. The Pallava kumarar states nothing but the truth. But please ask him why I was hesitant to come here!'

Without waiting for Paranjyothi's mother to ask him, Mamallar continued, 'It seems that your dear son had promised you that he would go to Kanchi, educate himself and return as a scholar. He was unable to keep his word. He is now as illiterate as he was when he left. So, he feels ashamed to even look you in the eye. How do you like this story?'

After listening to Mamallar, Paranjyothi's mother sat by her son and asked, as she caressed his face, 'My child! Does it matter whether you are educated or not? I am happy that by Lord Shiva's grace you have returned home safely. Did I ever get angry with you when you thrashed and chased away the teachers who came to teach you?'

Mamallar laughed and teased, 'What? What? Did your son hit his teachers and chase them away? Thank God, I escaped! This meek boy pestered me to teach him. Had I trusted him and started teaching him, wouldn't he have hit and chased me away too? Thank God, I escaped!' So saying, Narasimha Varmar laughed again.

Paranjyothi looked at him piteously and mentioned, 'Prabhu! Do you think that this is a laughing matter? It is not so. As every parent cherishes their child, my mother does not mind my returning uneducated. But ask my mama if he will get his daughter married to this uneducated fool!'

Namasivaya vaidhyar, desirous of participating in the playful banter, quipped, 'Why ask me? Why don't you ask the bride herself? If she is agreeable, so am I!'

The sound of a door opening was heard then, and everyone turned in that direction. Umayal had opened the door and was stepping into the inner chamber. 'What will my poor child do if everyone teams up and teases her?' Umayal's mother murmured.

Then Namasivaya vaidhyar informed the kumara chakravarthy, 'We often heard accounts of Paranjyothi's valorous deeds. He has made Chola Nadu proud. We were all yearning to see him. It is our good fortune that he could come here so soon. It is on account of our penances in our previous births that you too have accompanied him. You, who are the Puvikkarasar, the ruler of the earth, have come here at the same time as Navukkarasar.

An opportunity like this does not arise often. We will conduct the wedding on an auspicious day right away. You may take Umayal along with you!' Namasivaya vaidhyar then paused.

Then Mamallar remarked, 'Did you hear that, commander? It's obvious that the vaidhyar is determined to educate you and make a scholar out of you. As no other ploy worked, he has decided to get his daughter to educate you. Ah! Finally, you are going to get a teacher whom you will not be able to hit and chase away.' Hearing this, everyone present, including the women, burst out laughing. The kumara chakravarthy then informed Namasivaya vaidhyar, 'Aiyya, that's not possible. The brave commander of the Pallava kingdom ought to get married in the capital in the presence of the chakravarthy. This is my father's command. We will send escorts as soon as we reach Kanchi. All of you should come there. I would like to mention one more thing. If your daughter is keen to marry a well-educated scholar, there's a way out. Our dynasty's guru, Rudrachariar, resides in Kanchi; he is only ninety years old. His beard is at least a cubit long. There is no art that he is unaware of and no literary work that he has not read. I can get your scholarly daughter married to him!'

There was uproarious laughter.

He then stood up saying, 'Commander, come, let's go! We'll return after an audience with Thirunavukkarasar.'

When Mamallar and Paranjyothi returned after visiting Navukkarasar at the monastery where he was staying, Paranjyothi's mother held her son's hand and led him to an inner chamber saying, 'Come here, thambi! I have to tell you something.' Umayal lay on the floor there, weeping. She pointed out Umayal to him and remarked, 'See how your taunting banter has tormented this girl! How can you behave in this manner?'

Paranjyothi's heart melted. He remonstrated, 'Aiyyo, why this blame? I did not mock her!'

'After all that you said, you insist that you did nothing! Do you know what this child said? After you went to the city of Kanchi, you joined the royal service and have also befriended the chakravarthy. So you are unwilling to marry this rustic girl. That's why you're speaking in this manner!'

'Aiyyo! That's not at all the case, amma!'

'If it's not so, you console this girl yourself. No matter how much I tried, she did not heed me!' So saying, Paranjyothi's mother left the room.

Paranjyothi, who took his mother's command very seriously, tried to console Umayal. But Umayal showed no signs of being comforted. It seemed as though she was desirous of Paranjyothi consoling her for a long time. She appeared to regain her composure for a moment; the very next instant she would start sobbing. Despite Umayal being a rustic girl, she knew how to fulfil her heart's desire. She created a situation that necessitated Paranjyothi remaining in the room and consoling her for a long time.

No matter how long a play lasts, it will ultimately have to come to an end. Similarly, when it was time for this (fake) sorrowful play to end, Umayal extracted a promise from Paranjyothi. She asked him to promise her that he would indeed marry her. After giving his word, Paranjyothi explained, 'But, Uma, I need to tell you one thing. Our wedding will not be solemnized as early as your father desires. You may have to wait for a long time. It is only when my friend Mamallar's wedding is solemnized that our wedding also will take place. I will not assume a householder's role before he does.'

'If necessary, I will wait for several yugams for you!' promised Uma.

Chapter 29

The Wind Too Stood Still!

The following dawn, Mamallar and Paranjyothi took leave of Namasivaya vaidhyar and his family. The brave Pallava army that had routed and chased the Pandya army had crossed the Kollidam River and was in a state of readiness. Crossing the Kollidam was easy as the water level was fortunately low. On crossing the Kollidam, Mamallar and Paranjyothi commanded the Pallava cavalry to follow them, asked the infantry to advance at a leisurely pace, and rode ahead. They reached the banks of the South Pennai River at sunset. Mamallar was downcast during the journey that day. His face reflected the anguish he felt.

His concerns were not unfounded. The previous evening, when Mamallar had sought an audience with Thirunavukkarasar, the great soul had affectionately blessed him. The ascetic praised him for defeating the Pandian. He also expressed his delight at the Vatapi emperor calling for a truce and seeking peace. He acquiesced to Mamallar's wishes and promised to return to Kanchi soon. Then Navukkarasar recollected the incident that had occurred when he last met Mamallar at his monastery in Kanchi. 'Pallava kumara, are Aayanar and his daughter, Sivakami, well? I can still recall the abhinayams that girl performed for the verse "Munnam avanadhu naamam kettal". Overcome by emotion, didn't she finally faint? Are father and daughter safe?'

As the saint was enquiring in this manner, Mamallar was haunted by old memories. He hesitantly admitted, 'I last saw them before the siege of Kanchi. They were on the banks of the Varaha River in a village named Mandapapattu. I am thinking of visiting them on my way back.'

Hearing this, Navukkarasar remarked, 'Is that so? Mandapapattu is a very scenic village. If you meet them, please tell them that I enquired about them. I wonder why my heart goes out to Sivakami every time I think of her. Pallava kumara, I even told Aayanar then. When I saw Sivakami that day, I was concerned that no harm should befall her. Ekambaranathar should be merciful to her.'

These words had a severe impact on Mamallar and dampened his spirits. His heart repeatedly chanted, 'No harm should befall Sivakami', like a mantra. An intense desire to see Sivakami that very instant arose within him and filled every nerve of his body. He rode so fast that the cavalry that followed him lagged behind by a great distance. But even that pace seemed inadequate to him. Paranjyothi had to caution him several times asking, 'Prabhu! Do you intend killing the horse?', and restrain him.

Mamallar fervently wished that Kannabiran, whom he had sent to Mandapapattu two days ago, would meet him on the way and convey some news about Sivakami. His wish was fulfilled after he had travelled for some distance after crossing the South Pennai River. Kannabiran was approaching him from the opposite direction, driving his chariot swiftly. For a moment, Mamallar eagerly surveyed the chariot, hoping to see someone inside it. The next moment he consoled himself thinking that it was not fair to expect anyone to be seated in the chariot.

The news that Kannabiran bore initially disappointed Mamallar. Subsequently, that very news somewhat reassured him and gave him peace of mind.

Mamallar learnt that Mahendra Pallavar had fetched Aayanar and Sivakami to Kanchi two weeks ago. It was true that he could no longer meet Sivakami on his return journey, but so what? Wouldn't they be safe in Kanchi?

Mamallar was extremely gratified that Mahendra Pallavar had remembered Aayanar and Sivakami as soon as the war came to an end and had accorded the utmost priority in fetching them to Kanchi. He started building several castles in the air. Why had Mahendra Pallavar hastened to summon them to Kanchi? Why had Mahendra Pallavar commanded him not to pursue the Pandya army but to return to Kanchi? Probably Mahendra Pallavar understood his desire and had decided to solemnize his wedding in the near future.

Mamallar spent that night on the banks of the Varaha River indulging in several such fantasies and discussing them with Paranjyothi. By then, the cavalry that had lagged behind caught up with them.

At dawn the following day, all of them headed towards Kanchi. As they had decided to reach Kanchi that very night, excitement levels were high.

When they had travelled one kaadam from the banks of the Varaha River, the sight of two horsemen approaching the retinue further increased the excitement. The two horsemen must be emissaries from Kanchi. What message did they bear?

When the two horsemen neared the retinue, they dismounted and bowed to the prince. One of them removed a missive from its protective case made of cow's horn and submitted it to Mamallar saying, 'Prabhu, a message from the chakravarthy.'

The second horseman handed over another message to Paranjyothi.

Both of them immediately started reading their respective messages. The horses on which they were mounted stood still.

The messengers who brought the missives remained standing.

The sixteen thousand horsemen who had raised a storm of dust, also stood still.

For some time, even the wind stood still. The branches of the trees and the leaves did not move.

Mamallar became suspicious as soon as he read a few lines from Mahendra Pallavar's message. He shuffled through the leaves of the missive and checked if the confidential insignia was in order. He also observed the messengers closely. There was no doubt that the message was indeed written by his father.

Mamallar's body trembled, and his eyebrows knotted; beads of sweat appeared on his face and the tears that welled up in his eyes clouded his vision and he somehow managed to read the message. The contents of the missive were as follows:

'This message is from the humbled and distressed father, Mahendra Varman, to his son, the brave Narasimhan.

'My child! All my Chanakya-like tactics have finally proved futile. I have been cheated. I experience untold sorrow for not paying heed to your straightforward counsel. Son! That sinner, Pulikesi, has cheated me.

After having enjoyed my hospitality at the Kanchi palace for two weeks and professing friendship, he has betrayed me. It seems that the hot-headed demon has ordered his forces to set fire to the villages and towns of Thondaimandalam, deface the statues and torture the citizens. Aiyyo! Kumara! How can I tell you this? I am afraid that we have lost the priceless artistic treasure of the Pallava kingdom.

Narasimha, please forgive me! I am now leaving to atone my sins. I am going to rescue our citizens from the atrocities perpetrated by the vicious Chalukya warriors. I am leaving with the army stationed inside the fort. Commander Kalipahayar is coming along with me.

'Kumara, Kanchi Sundari will be orphaned, devoid of any security. You and your friend, Paranjyothi, must safeguard her. I doubt if I will ever return to Kanchi fort. There is no certainty that I will be alive to meet you again. There is no greater glory I can attain now than embracing death valorously on the battlefield.

'Son, please forgive and forget the treachery I have committed! Please forget me once and for all! But please do not forget that the Pallava lineage that has remained unbroken for the last six hundred years relies solely on you for its continuance!'

Commander Paranjyothi had finished reading the message sent to him long before Mamallar had completed reading the above message. Unlike the message to Mamallar, the missive to Paranjyothi was brief.

'Dear Paranjyothi!

'You have often asked me if I had committed any mistakes in my life. I have haughtily responded in the negative. I have now committed the biggest blunder of my life. I tried utilizing diplomacy to make a friend of an enemy. The result was contrary to my expectation. I am now proceeding to the battlefield to redress that blunder.

'I feel sad that you are now not by my side. Nevertheless, it is essential that you remain with Narasimhan at this point of time.

'Don't forget what I have told you several times. The Pallava dynasty should not come to an end without a successor. I am handing over Narasimhan to you.'

After reading his message twice or thrice, Mamallar attempted to speak to Paranjyothi. But he was unable to find the words. So he handed over his message to his friend.

Paranjyothi quickly read the missive and stated, 'Aiyya, I will go ahead, along with the cavalry. You stay here till the infantry reaches this place and then come to Kanchi.'

'Indeed, commander! Only my body is still here; my soul is with my father. Now there is no question of breaking the journey. Let the infantry come at its pace. We will proceed with the cavalry,' retorted Mamallar.

Within a short time, that region trembled under the impact of thousands of horses galloping at break-neck speed. The entire region was enveloped by clouds of dust.

Chapter 30

'Whither Sivakami?'

Aayanar had been distraught ever since he had returned to his old house. His right leg, which was fractured when he fell down the mountain, was a source of extreme pain and untold misery. His heart was weighed down with indescribable sorrow on account of Sivakami's disappearance.

When Aayanar and Sivakami had rushed from Mandapapattu to Kanchi in the palanquin sent by the chakravarthy, they had asked Aayanar's sister to follow them at a leisurely pace in a bullock cart. That lady had taken with her important household objects, Rathi and Suga Rishi, and reached the forest house before Aayanar. Her reaching early helped Aayanar survive.

Aayanar's sister conscientiously nursed and tended to Aayanar. But the one question she often posed had the effect of rubbing salt into Aayanar's wounds and hurt him deeply. That question was, 'Where is Sivakami?' Aayanar, in an attempt to stop her from asking the question which caused him immense sorrow, was evasive in his replies. As Sivakami's athai was unable to comprehend any of Aayanar's responses, she continued enquiring about her niece's absence.

As if this was not enough, Rathi and Suga Rishi often came and stood close to Aayanar with their heads raised and asked the same question silently. Aayanar would chide them harshly and chase them away. These days, Suga Brahma Rishi hardly raised his voice. Whenever he did, he seemed to be enquiring, 'Where is Sivakami?'

It seemed as though the surrounding forest was in great turmoil. From time to time, one could hear people crying and screaming as they ran. War cries could be heard from near and far. At night, one could see fire and dense smoke. At times there was unusual calm among the birds of the forest. At other times, thousands of birds shrieked in unison.

One day, there were indications of a major combat occurring somewhere very close by. The din of trumpets, soldiers raising slogans of victory, the movement of humans and horses, and the clashing of weapons were heard incessantly. In the evening, a few soldiers who had sustained severe injuries entered Aayanar's house and pleaded for water. When Aayanar realized that they were Pallava soldiers, he welcomed them from where he was lying down, asked them to sit down and then asked his sister to bring water for them. Then he asked them where and how they had been injured. Those soldiers exclaimed, 'Don't you know anything?'

Aayanar pointed to his fractured leg. Observing his injured leg and the damaged statues that lay around, the soldiers asked, 'Aiyyo! Did the Chalukya demons enter this house too and perpetrate such atrocities?' Then one of the soldiers related in detail what had happened from the time Pulikesi had left Kanchi to the fearsome battle that had been fought in Manimangalam that day. The summary of it is as follows: As soon as Pulikesi left the Kanchi fort, he divided his army into smaller forces and commanded them to set the villages of Pallava Nadu ablaze, to torture the citizens, to destroy the statues and to amputate the limbs of sculptors. When the chakravarthy came to know of this, he had left the fort accompanied by a small army. That morning, the Pallava soldiers and Pulikesi's soldiers had fought near a village named Manimangalam. Pulikesi's army had outnumbered the Kanchi soldiers both in strength and weapons. But as Mahendra chakravarthy himself had headed the army, the Kanchi soldiers fought valorously. Both the emperors had met in the middle of the battlefield, argued with each other, and subsequently attacked each other.

When the Pallava army had been on the verge of losing, the din of a large cavalry approaching the battlefield had been heard. Seeing the rishabha flag, the soldiers had exclaimed, 'Mamallar has arrived!' Soon Mamallar's cavalry had struck the Chalukya army like thunder and attacked them. The Chalukya soldiers had started fleeing. The demon Pulikesi had fled too. But as he was fleeing, he had aimed a small dagger at Mahendrar. Mahendrar had lost consciousness and fallen on the ground. After the Vatapi soldiers had fled from the battlefield, Mamallar and Paranjyothi reached the spot where Mahendra Pallavar lay unconscious. After making arrangements for Mahendrar's treatment and safe passage back to Kanchi, they had pursued the fleeing Vatapi soldiers.

After relating the above incidents, the injured Pallava soldiers headed towards Kanchi. Aayanar was distraught when he heard that Mahendra Pallavar had sustained a fatal injury. But the news that Mamallar and Paranjyothi had gone in pursuit of the Chalukya soldiers comforted him a little. He felt a glimmer of hope that they would release Sivakami from captivity and bring her back.

A week had passed after the Manimangalam battle. Aayanar eagerly anticipated good news every day. He became alert whenever a noise was heard at the entrance of the house. He sat up eagerly, expecting someone to walk in bearing good news. And one day, two horses did actually come galloping towards the house. The horses came to a halt outside the house.

Aayanar was anxious to know the identity of the visitors. He stared eagerly at the entrance; his heart was beating wildly. His expectation was not in vain. Yes! Mamallar and Paranjyothi walked in. Happiness blossomed on Aayanar's face as soon as he saw them. But the quizzical expression on Mamallar's face agonized Aayanar. So, he decided to pre-empt Mamallar by asking him the very question that Mamallar was about to ask him. He called out in a sorrowful tone that echoed across the sculpted mandapam and the forest outside, 'Prabhu! Where is my Sivakami?'

Chapter 31

Pulikesi on the Run

What had prompted Mamallar and Paranjyothi to reach Aayanar's forest residence?

When Mahendra Pallavar's small force was on the verge of being decimated in the Manimangalam battle, Mamallar and Paranjyothi—accompanied by the cavalry—had arrived there. Soon after, the outcome of the battle had undergone a complete change. The Chalukya warriors had started retreating. As Mamallar was thinking of pursuing and annihilating them, news of Mahendra Pallavar lying fatally injured in one corner of the battlefield had reached him. When Mamallar and Paranjyothi rushed to that spot, they came to know that Mahendra Pallavar had been taken to the royal guest house in Manimangalam village and was being treated there. The two friends had immediately hastened to the royal guest house. After undergoing treatment for some time, Mahendrar had opened his eyes. Happiness had been visible on his face when he saw his son. The next moment his face had worn a sorrowful expression.

'My son! I have betrayed you! Will you forgive me?' he had murmured.

'Appa, please don't worry. Didn't we reach here at the right moment? The Chalukyas dispersed and fled . . .' Even as Mamallar was talking, Mahendrar had lost consciousness.

Mamallar and Paranjyothi had made arrangements for Mahendra chakravarthy's safe passage to Kanchi and then assessed the situation on the battlefield. They had realized that the majority of the soldiers who had accompanied Mahendra Pallavar from Kanchi had died fighting bravely on the Manimangalam battlefield. Commander Kalipahayar had also lost his life on the battlefield. Mamallar and Paranjyothi had pondered over what they ought to do next. News had reached them that small forces of Chalukya soldiers were entering the villages around Kanchi and were torturing the citizens. So they had decided that it was their foremost duty to obliterate such cruel demons and save the villagers. They had also decided to pursue Pulikesi's massive army once the infantry reached Kanchi.

For three days they had ridden across the region to the east, south and west of Kanchi, decimated the Chalukya forces, and ensured that they were no longer in the country. As the infantry had reached Kanchi by then, they had proceeded northwards. A fierce battle had been fought in a village named Sooramaram, three kaadam from Kanchi. It was Sashankan who had led the Chalukya army in this battle. Sashankan and a majority of the Chalukya soldiers had lost their lives in this battle. The Chalukya soldiers who survived had fled. The Pallava army had pursued them up to the banks of the Vellaru.

Mamallar and Paranjyothi had found out that Pulikesi had left Commander Sashankan behind and had crossed the Vellaru. Mamallar had wanted to cross the Vellaru and pursue Pulikesi. Paranjyothi, who had assumed charge of the Pallava army after Kalipahayar's demise, disagreed.

'Prabhu, do you remember the condition in which we left the chakravarthy? Is it right for us to leave him behind in this state and travel a long distance? Kalipahayar also lost his life on the battlefield. What will become of the Pallava kingdom if something were to happen to the chakravarthy during our absence? What will happen to the suffering villagers who have been plundered and tortured by the Chalukyas? Who will protect them and distribute food and clothes? How can you be so sure that the Madurai Pandian will not re-enter the Pallava kingdom and invade us? Prabhu, consider all these issues and decide,' Paranjyothi had counselled.

Mamallar's resolve had weakened the moment Paranjyothi referred to Mahendrar's health. For some time, he had remained immersed in thought, his head lowered. He had then acknowledged, 'Commander, what you say is true. Not only that. If we were to advance with our army now, we do not have adequate food stocks. The Chalukya demons must have already looted the villages on their way back. If we were to follow them, how will the villagers procure food for us? We too will end up torturing them. We will return to Kanchi and ascertain the state of my father's health. We will return after making the necessary arrangements.'

On their way back to Kanchi, they observed the atrocities perpetrated by the Chalukya soldiers. The Chalukyas had set fire to houses, huts, haystacks and crops ready for harvesting. Ash covered the entire region. It seemed as though Pallava Nadu had become a large and horrific graveyard. In some villages, houses were still burning. People were crying out in agony every now and then. On seeing Mamallar and

Paranjyothi, the subjects had wailed loudly and started complaining. They had related the brutal acts committed by the Chalukya soldiers. When they recounted instances of the sculptors' limbs being amputated and young women being kidnapped, Mamallar had been heartbroken. He had been so overwhelmed that he could not say a word. He could not even share his feelings with Paranjyothi.

When he heard of the fate that had befallen sculptors, the thought that Aayanar and Sivakami were inside the Kanchi fort had comforted him somewhat. Nevertheless, when Mamallar had heard about sculptures being disfigured, he wondered about the safety of the wonderful statues at Mamallapuram and felt tormented. Mamallar and Paranjyothi had hurried to Mamallapuram to ascertain in person what had happened to the sculptures there. When they saw that not much damage had been inflicted on the statues, they had returned to Kanchi. Aayanar's house was en route to Kanchi from Mamallapuram. In addition, it was the shorter route to Kanchi. So, Mamallar decided to visit that house and ensure that the divine sculptures depicting dance postures were undamaged.

When they reached the entrance of Aayanar's house, they had been unnerved by the open front door. The appearance of the façade had caused them anguish. With an uncanny feeling of impending calamity, they had stepped into the house.

When both of them saw the broken and mutilated statues, they had felt as though their own limbs had been broken. Aayanar, who had been lying down, heard their footsteps and sat up. Mamallar was surprised to see Aayanar, whom he thought was safe within the Kanchi fort. His horror-stricken face and rage-filled eyes sent a chill down their spines. When the sculptor Aayanar asked, 'Where is my Sivakami', Mamallar had felt as though the sky had fallen on his head.

Chapter 32

Blood Oozed Out

Paranjyothi held on to Mamallar lest he fall down. Both of them stood speechless, staring at Aayanar. Aayanar repeated his question in an emotionally charged tone, 'Pallava kumara, where is Sivakami? Where is the apple of my eye? Where is my dear child? Where is Mahendra Pallavar's adopted daughter? Where is Bharata Kandam's peerless queen of dancing?'

Mamallar's heart was turbulent, like an ocean in a raging storm. Nevertheless, due to his anxiety to know what had become of Sivakami, he composed himself and asked in a voice devoid of emotion, 'Aiyya! Please compose yourself. Shouldn't I be the one asking you where Sivakami is? What happened to Sivakami? Please tell me.'

Aayanar's fury subsided; his emotions assumed another form. He exclaimed with tear-filled eyes, 'Yes, prabhu! Yes! It is you who ought to question me. You gave this sinner the responsibility of looking after Sivakami. It is I who lost my dear daughter. Aiyyo! My daughter! It is my misfortune that

I am the cause of your misery.' He then wept with his head lowered.

Every word that Aayanar uttered tore at Narasimha Varmar's heart. He concluded that Sivakami was dead. Amidst the anguish and fury he felt, there arose a desire to know how Sivakami had died. The thought that the Chalukyas had caused her death occurred to him like a flash of lightning and tore his body and soul apart. He roared in a harsh tone, 'Aayanar! Please respond and then cry. How did Sivakami die? When did she die?'

Aayanar who was lying down shrieked, 'Ah! Is my dear child dead?' and attempted to get up. His legs were unsteady; he gave out a terrible cry as he fell down.

When Aayanar asked if Sivakami was dead, Mamallar realized that she was alive. When Aayanar failed in his attempt to stand up, the kumara chakravarthy noticed that the sculptor had injured his leg. Mamallar's heart mellowed at the sight of Aayanar's plight. He exclaimed, 'Aiyyo, what happened to you?' and sat down next to Aayanar.

'When I fell from the mountain, I injured my leg. I don't care about that. You said that Sivakami is dead! Is that true?' questioned Aayanar.

'Aiyyo! I don't know what has befallen Sivakami. I came here straight from the battlefield. I thought that you and Sivakami were safe in Kanchi. How did you come here? When were you separated from Sivakami? Is she still alive?' asked Mamallar in an extremely calm tone.

In direct contrast, Aayanar shrieked, 'Aiyyo! It would have been good if Sivakami were dead!'

'What happened to Sivakami?'

'How can I tell you what transpired? It was all because of this sinner. Prabhu! The Chalukyas have imprisoned Sivakami and taken her away!'

At that, Mamallar exclaimed in horror. It was clear that
he had immediately understood the gravity of the situation.

'Yes, prabhu! They have imprisoned her and taken her
away. When I heard that you had pursued the Chalukyas,
I was hoping that you would free Sivakami and bring her
back. You have let me down! But it's not your fault. All this
happened because of this sinner. I was obsessed with paintings
and sculptures. I have now lost my live painting; my sculpture
endowed with life! . . . Aiyyo! I have become the Yaman for
my daughter!'

Mamallar did not register a word of Aayanar's lament.
For some time, he sat motionless, as though he was in a
trance. Then he cleared his voice and enquired in a low tone,
'Respected sculptor, how did all this happen? Why did you
leave Kanchi? How was Sivakami imprisoned? How did you
hurt your leg? Please explain everything to me in detail!'

Aayanar told him all that had happened. He stammered
and sobbed as he narrated everything. Mamallar, while
listening to Aayanar, pulled out his sword from its sheath
and held it in his hand. His left hand kept running down the
sword's sharp edge. A few cuts appeared on his fingers as they
stroked the edge of the sword. The blood that oozed out of
those cuts dripped onto the floor, forming a puddle.

Chapter 33

Darkness Enveloped

It was noon when Mamallar left Aayanar's forest residence and headed towards Kanchi. It was the month of Purattasi; the sun was glowing brightly in the clear blue sky. But Mamalla Narasimhar's world was enveloped in darkness. The foreboding gloom was without any silver lining. But occasionally, he experienced blinding lightning in the sky of his mind. It was like a flash of brightness caused by the clash of weapons in the battlefield.

Mamallar concluded that he had permanently lost Sivakami. He was unable to imagine Sivakami being alive after being captured by the Chalukyas. He imagined that she would have given up her life within a short time of the Chalukyas capturing her. Would she continue to live like other ordinary women after being captured by the enemy? It would be impossible for Sivakami to place her life above her honour.

That divine glow of light had permanently disappeared from his life and this earth. Neither this world nor he deserved such a beautiful, artistic and virtuous soul! Their fathers had together put an end to Sivakami's life. They had also stymied his life. Despite this, Mamallar was not able to remain angry with them for long.

Aayanar was in a state of shock after being separated from his daughter. Further, he was immobile as his leg was fractured. How could one be angry with Aayanar? Also, what was the point in being furious with Mahendra Pallavar who, after being grievously injured on the battlefield, was fighting with Yaman?

Mamallar was unable to bear the thought of living in a world in which Sivakami was no longer present. Nevertheless, he knew he would have to endure everything for some more time. The reason was that he had to take his revenge on the cruel and treacherous demons in human form, the Vatapi Chalukyas!

His revenge must be such as the world had never witnessed nor heard of so far! He must perpetrate atrocities that were ten times as grievous as the ones committed by the Chalukyas in Thondaimandalam. Rivers of blood must flow in Chalukya Nadu. The reflection of the flames rising from the cities set on fire must be seen in the overflowing rivers of blood! The noise of people wailing in that demonic country must be heard for generations!

Though he was enthused slightly by the idea of revenge, it did not last long, for the thought of Sivakami not being alive followed immediately. His enthusiasm then was replaced by fatigue. His nerves slackened, pulse abated and the reins of his horse slipped from his hands. Mamallar tried to revel in old memories to overcome his tiredness.

When Mamallar thought about the relationship that had blossomed between him and Sivakami during the last three to four years, he felt a choking sensation. He was so overwhelmed that he could not even shed tears. Ah! People speak of fondness, affection and love! None of these words were capable of describing the relationship between him and Sivakami.

Maybe the world would use terms like 'fondness', 'affection' and 'love' to describe the relationship between Commander Paranjyothi and the maiden in Thiruvengadu. But there was a vast difference between Paranjyothi's experience and his. Mamallar knew that Paranjyothi did not even think of Umayal for several days at a stretch. But the thought of Sivakami was integral to his, Mamallar's, existence. Even if all the water in a well were drained, wouldn't water sprout from the spring beneath? Similarly, images of Sivakami incessantly emerged one after the other from Mamallar's heart.

Sivakami smiling, Sivakami laughing, Sivakami with her eyebrows knotted, a sad Sivakami, Sivakami staring with fright, a blissful Sivakami with her eyes half-closed and Sivakami engaging him in a mock fight—several such Sivakamis appeared in Mamallar's mind.

Whatever be his activity, like conversing with his parents, listening with utmost attention to matters of the state, swiftly riding a horse, appreciating music and dance performances in the royal court, or fighting with adversaries, the thought of Sivakami always remained with him.

If this was the case during the day, it is needless to mention his condition at night. While residing at the Kanchi palace, Mamallar used to look forward to the time after dinner when he could retire to his chamber all by himself. He could then wholeheartedly think about Sivakami. Wasn't the very thought of her rolling her black eyes in mock anger while looking at him intoxicating?

When sleep overcame him after dwelling on Sivakami in this manner for a long time, he dreamt of Sivakami. He dreamt of her numerous times. They encountered several instances of happiness, sorrow, dangers and disappointments in those dreams.

When Sivakami faced danger in his dreams, he was able to rescue her sometimes. There were instances when he woke up before the dream ended. He would then fret about her safety all night and visit Sivakami the following day to ensure that she was safe. Mamallar recollected those incidents. All those fearful dreams had come true now! When she was really in danger, he was unable to save her.

That helpless maiden must have had a premonition that such grave danger would befall her. That's why she had asked him often, 'You won't forget me, will you?' and 'Will you forsake me?'

Mamallar used to casually ask in return, 'Why these meaningless queries?' In reality, they were such meaningful questions!

'Sivakami! My dear! I will never forget you! I will not forget you no matter how many births I take! I will first seek revenge on the sinners who separated us! Then I will come in search of you. I will follow you to Yama Loka and ask Dharma Raja, "Where is my Sivakami?" I will go to Svarga Loka and ask Devendran, "Where is my Sivakami? Rambha, Urvashi, Menaka and Tilottama reside in your world. But I have only one Sivakami! Give her to me!"

'Sivakami! I will not forsake you if you're not in Svarga Loka! I will search for you in Brahma Loka, Vaikuntam and Kailasam and find you. Even the Mumurthi cannot separate us! I am coming, Sivakami! I am coming! I will soon come to the place where you are!'

Chapter 34

Who Was That Woman?

The city of Kanchi witnessed the kind of calm it had hitherto not seen. It was akin to the quiet after a storm. The city-dwellers were also in a similar state of mind.

News about the atrocities perpetrated by the Vatapi forces in Thondai Nadu before they retreated, and the battles fought at Manimangalam and Sooramaram, had trickled into Kanchi. As the citizens had heard that Mahendra Pallava chakravarthy was practically on his deathbed after sustaining injuries at the Manimangalam battle, and that the palace physicians were exercising great efforts to save him, they were anticipating the sorrowful news of his death.

The people of Kanchi had heard from a few soldiers who returned from the Manimangalam battle that Aayanar had fractured his leg and that the Chalukyas had captured Sivakami and taken her away. These incidents heightened their sorrow and also resulted in their respect for Mahendra Pallavar waning.

For these reasons, an unnatural calm had descended on the great city of Kanchi, which had lost its charm, bustle and grandeur. If this was the atmosphere in the city, it is needless to describe the situation in the palace. From the day Bhuvana Mahadevi had set foot in Kanchi after her marriage to Mahendra Pallavar, not even for a single day had the Kanchi palace worn the haunted look devoid of gaiety and radiance as it did now.

Even when Kanchi had been under siege, the sounds of musical instruments, trumpets, conches and temple bells had been heard periodically. The tinkling sound of anklets worn by the ladies-in-waiting at the palace could be heard incessantly. The melodious sounds of Vedas being chanted and Tamil songs being sung were also occasionally heard. The sounds of horses entering and leaving the palace were heard continuously in the front courtyard.

Now a deep silence—a fear-instilling silence—pervaded the previously lively palace.

When Mahendra Pallavar was brought back from the Manimangalam battlefield, the royal physicians strove day and night to save him. He was unconscious for several days. The chakravarthy continued to remain unconscious even after Mamallar returned from the Sooramaram battle. Then, gradually, he was able to open his eyes and recognize those around him.

The physicians advised that the chakravarthy would recover and that he should be looked after diligently for some more time. As Mahendrar became emotional and tried to speak every time he saw Mamallar, they felt that it would be good if the kumara chakravarthy did not visit his father often.

Mamallar became even more sad and restless because of this. He could confide in no one in the palace. Commander

Paranjyothi, accompanied by the army, had left the fort and was engaged in relief efforts in the villages the Chalukya forces had plundered.

Bhuvana Mahadevi was perpetually in tears. She kept recollecting her warning that inviting Pulikesi to Kanchi would have disastrous consequences. She also felt that it had been a big mistake not to have got Mamallar married to the Pandya princess. This remark was intolerable to Mamallar.

As days passed, Mamallar felt that his heart would explode if he did not speak about Sivakami to someone. But whom could he speak to? Only Aayanar was there. Aayanar was the only one who could empathetically listen when he spoke about Sivakami. Also, Mamallar was keen to know how Aayanar's health was. Wasn't Aayanar like a father to him? Wasn't it wrong to ignore him? Thinking thus, Mamallar rode all by himself to Aayanar's forest residence.

As he was riding down the forest path, he remembered the lotus pond. It was the place where he and Sivakami had spent several joyful days. It was where they had exchanged several affectionate words and had been blissful. He wanted to see that lotus pond. So, he took a detour and slowly rode towards the pond.

After he had ridden down the forest path for a while, he saw a woman walking from the opposite direction. She was taken aback on seeing Mamallar and stepped aside. Mamallar, characteristic of a person born in a cultured dynasty, rode past her without giving her a second look. But after riding for some time, he felt that the woman's face had been familiar. Mamallar thought, 'Who is she? Where have I seen her before?' as he reached the lotus pond.

Chapter 35

Murky Pond

Ah! Was this the same lotus pond on the banks of which Sivakami and Mamallar had met so joyfully on numerous occasions? Yes, this was the very pond where the lovers had often met. But its appearance had undergone a complete transformation. The lotus pond now reflected the state of Mamallar's mind. The pond, which used to be filled with crystal-clear water, was now mostly filled with slush. The flowers, buds and leaves that had covered the pond like a green canopy captivating onlookers were missing. A few lotus leaves that had been trampled under the feet of elephants lay scattered. Along with the dried leaves lay a few wilted and lifeless lotus shoots.

The low-lying branches of the trees on the banks of the lotus pond had been broken and the trees appeared tonsured! Ah! That wooden plank! Even that was broken and a part of it lay on the ground, smashed to smithereens. The other part stood in its original place with broken edges. A shattered

Mamallar sat on the broken wooden plank. Old memories, competing with each other, flooded his mind.

He had come here looking for Sivakami several times during spring, when the trees in the forests had been covered with tender shoots and flowers, and the birds used to chirp merrily. He and Sivakami would sit quietly on the wooden plank, unaware of time slipping away as their eyes, hands and hearts did all the talking. When the moon rose in the horizon amidst the green trees, how many times had Mamallar compared Sivakami's face to the full moon. For several days, when they had stood at the edge of the lotus pond filled with crystal-clear water, he had blissfully alternated between looking at Sivakami's face and the reflection of her face in the water! These memories initially made Mamallar happy. But when it occurred to him time and again that he would never encounter such joyful experiences again, his heart grew heavy. Mamallar finally felt that he could not bear to recall such memories anymore; he stood up abruptly. He rushed towards his horse, leapt on it and rode towards Aayanar's house.

The peace he had felt when he was leaving Kanchi had vanished. Anger and rage filled his heart now. He felt enraged at his foes, the Chalukyas, who had abducted Sivakami. He was also furious with Aayanar, who had foolishly lost her. He felt an indescribable suspicion and anger towards the bikshu. Ah! He had never held that masquerader in high esteem. Wouldn't the bikshu have saved Sivakami, had he so desired? Why hadn't he saved her? Why hadn't he sent any message to Aayanar? What had become of the bikshu? How had he mysteriously disappeared?

The night when Sivakami's arangetram had abruptly ended, Mamallar recollected the chakravarthy pointing out the bikshu, who had been near the royal viharam, and cautioning him. Immediately, Mamallar's anger was directed towards his father. Wasn't the Pallava kingdom in its current state due to Mahendra Pallavar's ruses, treachery and disguises? It was because of Mahendra Pallavar that he had lost Sivakami! Suddenly a strange thought occurred to him. Was it on account of one of Mahendra Pallavar's ploys that Sivakami had been imprisoned? If that were not the case, why did Mahendra Pallavar have to send him to the battlefield and to fetch Sivakami from Mandapapattu? Why did he have to arrange for a tunnel to be built in the palace garden, and make it known to Kannabiran's wife? Probably, that woman Kamali was also the chakravarthy's accomplice in this ruse! Everyone had joined hands and betrayed him! Ah! This deceitful world was filled with perfidy and ill-will!

Mamallar reached the entrance of Aayanar's house in this state of mind. He wanted to ask Aayanar about certain mysterious and incomprehensible aspects of Sivakami's imprisonment. He stopped the horse some distance away from the house and composed himself. Then he walked up to Aayanar's house calmly. He was surprised when he heard the sound of conversation coming from within the house. Who was Aayanar speaking to? When Mamallar recognized the man sitting with Aayanar near the sculpture mandapam, he was taken aback. That man was the chief of spies, Shatrugnan!

It was not Shatrugnan's presence in Aayanar's house that surprised Mamallar. When he saw Shatrugnan's face, he immediately recollected another face. It was that of the woman he had seen on the forest path some time ago. The two faces were amazingly similar. Was she Shatrugnan's younger or elder sister? Or was it Shatrugnan himself . . .? The doubt was resolved in a moment. Narasimha Pallavar observed a saree and a few pieces of women's jewellery lying next to Shatrugnan.

Chapter 36

Shatrugnan's Story

Neither Aayanar nor Shatrugnan noticed Mamallar standing at the doorstep—they were so engrossed in their conversation.

When Mamallar entered the mandapam, both of them looked up in unison. Shatrugnan immediately stood up and exclaimed, 'Prabhu!' Shock rendered Shatrugnan speechless.

Aayanar, who had been reclining, enthusiastically pulled himself to a sitting position and exclaimed, 'Prabhu! Please come in! Welcome! I was just thinking about you! Shatrugnan has brought good news. My child Sivakami is alive and safe!'

Hearing this, Mamallar felt faint. He walked up to Aayanar, looked at Shatrugnan and asked, 'Shatrugna! Is this true?'

'Yes Prabhu! It's true!' Shatrugnan replied with his arms folded. 'Pallava kumara, when I met you on the forest path some time ago, I passed by you without talking to you. Please forgive me. When I saw you all of a sudden, I felt embarrassed to talk to you!' he explained humbly.

'Was that woman you? It was a good disguise!' observed Mamallar.

'Yes, even I was taken aback some time ago. The disguise of a woman suits him so well. The chakravarthy chooses the right person for every task,' commented Aayanar.

Mamallar murmured softly, 'Only you find the chakravarthy's wisdom praiseworthy!' He then asked Shatrugnan, 'Why did you assume the guise of a woman?'

'It was only because Shatrugnan donned that disguise that he was able to trace Sivakami. Please sit down; Shatrugnan will explain everything in detail. I too will listen to what he has to say for a second time.'

Mamallar sat down. Shatrugnan followed suit and started narrating his story:

'The chakravarthy was shocked beyond words when he found out that Aayanar and Sivakami had left Kanchi through the underground tunnel. He immediately decided to leave the fort and commanded the forces to get ready. He then called me aside and commanded, "Shatrugna! You have rendered stellar service to the Pallava kingdom thus far. But your service now is more important than all that you've done in the past. Had Mamallan been present here, I myself would have performed that task. I am now headed to the battlefield to uphold the honour of the Pallava dynasty. I am entrusting you with the task of tracing Sivakami and bringing her back. If you're unable to rescue Sivakami and bring her back, you must at least ensure her safety." I asked, "Prabhu, if the Chalukya forces have captured Sivakami ammai, what can I do single-handedly?" "I have indeed entrusted you with a difficult task. Shatrugna! You have donned several disguises thus far. But there is one disguise which will suit you the most; it's the guise of a woman!" I immediately understood the chakravarthy's intention. I donned the disguise you saw me in some time ago, left Kanchi, and reached this house.

'When I arrived here, an unconscious Aayanar was brought to this house. He was not accompanied by Sivakami devi. So, I realized that she must have been imprisoned and left this place. Wherever I heard the voices of Chalukya soldiers, I hid myself and observed them. Finally, to the northwest of Kanchi, I stumbled upon a large Chalukya force that was marching northwards. The sounds of women complaining and wailing could be heard from amongst the mob. When I neared the force and looked closely, I realized that those weeping were our women who had been taken prisoners. There was also a palanquin amidst the women. I came to know that Sivakami devi was seated in that palanquin.

'Soon, I ran towards that force with my hair untied and crying loudly. I pretended that someone was chasing me. I repeatedly looked back while running. The Chalukyas mocked me saying, "Have you come? Come!". They took me along and left me with the other captive women. For some time, I too wept like the other women. Then, I slowly neared the palanquin and confirmed that it was indeed Sivakami ammai who was seated in it. I guessed the reason for their taking Sivakami ammai along so respectfully. The commander of that force, Sashankan, wanted to carefully hand over the greatest artistic treasure of Pallava Nadu to the Vatapi emperor and ask for a reward for successfully stealing that treasure! This thought comforted me. I was confident that no harm would befall Sivakami ammai immediately. However, she was surrounded by the demonic Chalukya forces. It was an impossible task to extricate her and bring her back. I was unable to think of a way to free her.

'All of us were headed northwards. We soon reached the banks of the Vellaru, which is also known as Ponnmugaliaru.

Commander Sashankan seemed very confused. I was able
to ascertain the reason for this from the Chalukya soldiers'
conversation. The reason was the message brought by
emissaries about the major battle being fought between the
Vatapi emperor and Mahendra Pallavar at Manimangalam.
I also surmised why this message had confused Commander
Sashankan so much. Sashankan had thought that the Vatapi
emperor, accompanied by a large part of the army, would
have reached the banks of the North Pennai River by then.
Wouldn't Sashankan be surprised then if he received the
news that Pulikesi had stayed back and fought a battle at
Manimangalam, which is close to Mamallapuram? Sashankan
was struggling to decide whether or not the Vatapi emperor
would be angry with him for advancing ahead of him. The
day after we reached the banks of Ponnmugaliaru, Sashankan,
along with his forces, stayed back on the southern banks of
the river. The imprisoned women, escorted by a few Chalukya
soldiers, were made to cross the river.

'As soon as we reached the opposite bank, I decided, "This
is a good opportunity. I will take Sivakami ammai along and
hide in the nearby hills. As there are only a few soldiers, we
can escape without their knowledge in the night." That night,
when everyone was about to sleep, I arranged to be close to
Sivakami ammai. When all the other women had gone to sleep,
I introduced myself in Prakrit. Sivakami ammai was initially
extremely taken aback. Then she enquired about Aayanar and
you. But I was then unaware of your whereabouts. I did not
know that you had returned from your campaign in the south.
So I only told her that Aayanar had been saved and that he
was still alive. Then, gradually, I informed her about my plan.
Prabhu! I cannot describe my disappointment . . .'

Chapter 37

Pulikesi and Sivakami

When Shatrugnan paused for a moment during his narrative, Mamallar felt that he would stop breathing. He was extremely impatient to know what had happened. His imagination ran riot, conceiving a myriad of possibilities. He thought that Shatrugnan and Sivakami had probably fled that place. But they might have met with a perilous situation on the way back. His heart ached to save her from that dangerous situation and bring her back.

He angrily asked, 'Shatrugna, why are you prolonging the story? Where did you leave Sivakami before coming here? Tell me quickly . . .'

'Prabhu! Sivakami ammai must have crossed the North Pennai River by now! I left her in the area between the Ponnmugaliaru and North Pennai River, the sinner that I am!' lamented Shatrugnan sadly.

Sparks of anger flew from Mamallar's eyes. It seemed that he was angrier with Shatrugnan than with Pulikesi.

'What is this? Did you leave Sivakami behind with Pulikesi and come here all by yourself? Shatrugna! Don't be frivolous. Tell me what transpired quickly!' he roared.

Then Aayanar, with an enthusiasm that Mamallar found difficult to comprehend, suggested, 'Prabhu! Let Shatrugnan continue with his narrative. I beseech you to listen patiently!'

Shatrugnan continued with his narrative:

'I expected Sivakami ammai to happily consent to my plan and agree to escape with me. But I was extremely disappointed. Sivakami ammai, who had been courageous till then, started weeping after listening to my plan. She covered her face with her hands and sobbed. I was unable to understand what was on her mind. I attempted to console her. Then she stared at me wide-eyed and remarked, "I trusted his word and am now in this condition." She then observed, "No! No! This danger has befallen me because I did not listen to him. How can I face him?" She then spoke irrelevantly. Her behaviour shocked me. I was worried that she was hallucinating.

'Then Sivakami ammai narrated the atrocities she had witnessed the Chalukya forces perpetrating in our villages. It was only then that my doubts regarding her clarity of thought disappeared. I patiently listened to what she had to say for some time. Then I assured her, "Amma, Mahendra Pallavar and Mamallar will avenge all this!" You ought to have seen Sivakami ammai's fury and ferocity then. When she cried out, "Yes, Shatrugna! Yes! They must seek revenge", I was concerned that the guards would become suspicious. Fortunately, as the women were mumbling and blabbering in their sleep, the guards did not hear Sivakami ammai shouting.

'Then, slowly, I calmed her down. I repeated my plan to escape. She stared at me and observed, "Aiyya! There are a thousand women like me. Some of them have been separated from their husbands. Some of them have left behind their new-borns. How can I alone escape, allowing the Chalukya demons to abduct all the other women? I am neither married nor have I given birth to a child. How does it matter what becomes of me? You leave me here. You will be blessed if you can rescue even one mother of an infant from here." Even my heart softened. Nevertheless, I strengthened my resolve and urged her, "Amma, Mahendra chakravarthy has commanded me to bring you back safely. I am the chakravarthy's servant. I am duty-bound to obey his command." I knew that these words would not make her change her mind. Nevertheless, I repeated, "Amma, it's true that you're neither married nor do you have a child. But don't you have a father? Won't the separation from his only daughter cause him distress? Don't you have to think about that?"

'Tears glistened in Sivakami ammai's eyes then. She asked in a choked voice, "Yes, I have betrayed my father. Aiyya, he has escaped, hasn't he?" I replied, "Amma! If you want him to recover, you must leave with me immediately!" Sivakami ammai again covered her face with her hands and sobbed. She soon removed her hands from her face and requested, "Aiyya, please give me a day's time to think. My body and soul are overcome by fatigue. Even if I wanted to leave now, I would not be able to take a step forward. I will tell you for sure tomorrow." I too thought it would be best to give her a day's time and agreed, "So be it, amma! Nothing will be lost in a day. You decide by tomorrow."

'I thought that I would be able to change her mind by the night of the following day and bring her back with me. But an incident that I had not anticipated occurred the following evening. The Chalukya emperor, Pulikesi, joined us on the banks of the Ponnmugaliaru. He was accompanied by a small

army! I guessed that he had left Commander Sashankan
behind to lead the rest of the army. That night itself everyone
started travelling northwards. Words cannot describe my
disappointment and sorrow. When I found an opportunity
to meet Sivakami ammai alone on the way, I asked, "Amma!
What have you done?" Sivakami replied, "What did I do? If it
is so ordained, what can I do?"

'After travelling for two days, we halted at the foot of the
Thiruvenkata mountain. During the two days of the journey,
Pulikesi did not meet us. On the third day, we were resting
in the shadow of a rock. We heard the sound of horse hooves
nearby. Soon, Pulikesi and a few horsemen came riding and
stood at the bend of that rock. I expected the emperor to
dismount from his horse and approach us. But he did not do
so. After the emperor surveyed the area for some time, he was
about to mount the horse. It was then that the most unexpected
incident occurred. Sivakami swiftly detached herself from the
women, leapt forward and ran. She then stood in the way of
Pulikesi and cried out, "Emperor! I implore you!"

'Hearing Sivakami's cry, even the hard-hearted Pulikesi
must have softened. Immediately, Pulikesi came close to
Sivakami and asked, "Lady! What do you seek?" Ah! There
are no words to describe the enraged words Sivakami ammai
spoke then! I don't know where she derived such courage,
astuteness and eloquence from. Sivakami ammai looked
majestically at Pulikesi and spoke. I will relate what Sivakami
ammai said in a choked voice to the extent I remember.

'"Aiyya! Sovereigns like you who rule the world wage wars
to demonstrate your valour and to earn fame. You befriend those
whom you had regarded as your foes at one time. One day you
are the guest of another sovereign in his palace. The following
day the two of you wage a battle on the battlefield. Why should

we poor women be tortured amidst your conflicts? How did we harm you? I beseech you to be merciful and send us all back. Some of the imprisoned women here have left behind wailing new-borns. Many of them are married. If you don't free them and send all of them back, they will go mad before they reach your capital city, Vatapi. When you return to your capital after a victorious campaign, would you like to enter the city with a thousand dazed women? How do you stand to benefit by this? Please allow these women to return home. They will bless you wholeheartedly!" That blockhead devoid of artistic sensibility retorted, "Lady! You ought to demonstrate your proficiency in abhinayams in a dance performance. What is the use of demonstrating your expertise here?"'

When Shatrugnan related this, Mamallar heaved a deep sigh and quipped, 'Ah! Didn't Aayanar's daughter fall at the feet of that mean man and seek a boon? She deserved this!'

Shatrugnan continued with his narrative: 'Yes, prabhu. It seemed as though Sivakami ammai too thought along those lines. After listening to Pulikesi's response, she lowered her head. She continued staring at the ground for some time. Then that sinner remarked, "Lady! I will not be cheated by your abhinayams. But there is an element of fairness in what you say. So, I condescend to consent to your request. However, I have a condition. You spoke very forcefully on behalf of these women. You must prove that your sympathy for these women is not a pretence. Didn't you mention that they have been separated from their husbands and children? But you are neither married nor do you have children. You tell me whether you consent to come to Vatapi with me! If you consent, then I will free these women and send them back this very instant." When I heard those words, I felt like killing that sinner.'

Mamallar angrily interrupted asking, 'Did Sivakami agree to that condition?'

'Yes, prabhu! Sivakami did not hesitate even for a moment. She immediately replied, "I agree, Emperor! I agree to your condition!" At that moment, Sivakami ammai's posture and expression were divine. It seemed as though the Sita who faced Ravanan, the Panchali who stood in Duryodhana's court, the Savitri who debated with Yaman and the Kannagi who argued with the Pandian had come together in the form of Aayanar's divine daughter . . .'

'Shatrugna! Enough of your ecstatic description! What happened next?' demanded Mamallar.

'Shortly thereafter, the emperor released all of us. He commanded a few soldiers to escort us up to Ponnmugaliaru. All the women who had been teary-eyed and anxious till then became exultant. They heartily blessed Sivakami. But I was thunderstruck. I fell at her feet and beseeched her, "Amma! I will not leave you and go. Ask another boon of the emperor and retain me with you." Sivakami stubbornly insisted, "It is of paramount importance that you leave. You should go and meet my father." She refused to pay heed to my advice. Finally, I decided to leave as I had no other alternative. I feared that if I stayed there any longer, my disguise would come off, that I would not be of help to Sivakami, and that I would not be able to bring her message here. So I asked, "If you so desire, I will go. What should I tell your father?" Sivakami ammai replied, "Ask him not to worry about me. Tell him that I will be safe in Vatapi. By the time I return from Vatapi, I would have learnt about the secret of the Ajantha paints . . ."'

As soon as Shatrugnan said this, Aayanar rejoiced saying, 'Did you hear that, Pallava kumara? Sivakami is safe. Not only that, she has also said she will return after learning about the secret of the Ajantha paints. It was unnecessary to have sent Paranjyothi for this purpose. It's my dear daughter who is going to fulfil my desire! Not only that! We now have to change our opinion about the Vatapi emperor. Didn't we think that he was incapable of appreciating art and devoid of artistic sensibility? If that were so, would he have sent back the thousand women and taken only Sivakami along? Prabhu! Once I recover, I myself will go to Vatapi . . .'

As Aayanar spoke, Mamallar felt as though someone had pierced his ears with an iron rod. Hearing that Sivakami had consented to go to Vatapi, he felt as though a thousand scorpions had stung him at the same time. That instant, his pure love for Sivakami became a little tainted. He was unable to bear the thought that Sivakami had volunteered to go to Vatapi with Pulikesi. Aayanar's words had the effect of piercing his already wounded heart with a sharp spear. Mamallar desired solitude then. He wanted to return to the lotus pond. He stood up abruptly and questioned, 'Shatrugna, do you have anything else to narrate? Did Sivakami send any other message?'

Shatrugnan hesitantly looked at Aayanar. When he observed that Aayanar was immersed in deep thought, he reported softly, 'Pallava Kumara, Sivakami ammai sent a message for you too. She asked you to remember the vow you had made by swearing on a spear. She stated that she was waiting in Vatapi for you to fetch her like Sita Devi, who waited in Lanka.'

Just a few moments earlier, this world had seemed like a barren arid desert to Mamallar. Now he felt that a lush green oasis existed in that desert.

Chapter 38

The Road to Vatapi

Pulikesi's army was marching towards Vatapi. The size of the army returning was merely half that of the force that had left Vatapi. Nevertheless, it was still large. There were approximately three lakh soldiers and 7000 war elephants. The army left a trail of death and destruction on its way back. Villages and cities were plundered. Those who tried to safeguard their homes and possessions were mercilessly killed or mutilated. Houses, huts and haystacks were set ablaze. Dam embankments were demolished.

The Chalukya soldiers committed such atrocities both on account of hunger and a desire to seek revenge. They also goaded their elephants to assist them. The elephants, being hungry and demented, destroyed all the fertile lands on the way. They trampled the farms where crops were cultivated. They grabbed the roofs of houses and flung them away. They tore haystacks apart. On account of all these incidents, the Vatapi army's return route was easily identifiable. It resembled an area hit by a fierce cyclone. The sound of people crying and complaining was heard long after the Vatapi army had passed through. Eagles and vultures circled the region. Foxes howled in broad daylight.

Sivakami was also travelling to Vatapi along with the Chalukya army. But Sivakami did not feel as though the palanquin-bearers were carrying her to Vatapi. She felt that it was her inexorable fate that was leading her somewhere. The fear and worry regarding what might befall her when the Chalukyas had captured her had now disappeared.

Sivakami had gained a courage that was completely unexpected of a helpless girl in her situation. She not only felt emboldened but had also developed an awareness of her strength of character! She had developed this confidence ever since she had successfully appealed to Pulikesi to liberate the imprisoned women. An emperor who ruled a kingdom that was considerably larger than the Pallavas' had acceded to her request! Not only that, but Sivakami had also gathered from his expression that he was willing to fulfil her wishes.

At the same time, Sivakami was witnessing another mystery (or thought she was witnessing one). She was puzzled on seeing Pulikesi at the Kanchi court the other day. She now understood what it was. The bikshu Naganandi's and Pulikesi's faces were identical. Ah! She had solved the mystery! The emperor Pulikesi and the bikshu were one and the same person! As she was aware that Mahendra chakravarthy used to travel across the country in disguise, she assumed that it was natural for Pulikesi too to do so. She was reminded of the interest the bikshu had shown in her dancing. She thought that Pulikesi had probably invaded Kanchi for her sake.

Sivakami was both shocked and amazed that she wielded so much influence. Pulikesi, who was known to be violent and cruel, was willing to accede to her requests! This thought occurred to Sivakami often and made her more arrogant. This thought also reassured her about her safety. She was emboldened by the belief that nothing would happen in contradiction to her wishes, and that no harm would befall her.

Did Sivakami think of Mamallar during those days? Good question! Thoughts of Mamallar formed the basis of all her emotional experiences. But occasionally, those thoughts assumed strange forms. Affection became anger, anger became sorrow, which instilled in her hatred and a desire to seek revenge. Mamallar, who was born to rule the Pallava kingdom, had been unable to prevent the imprisonment of the women of Pallava Nadu. This humble sculptor's daughter had been able to free them! 'How will he feel when Shatrugnan conveys this news to him? Will he be pleased? Or will he be angry? His opinions on this matter are of no consequence to those present here. Didn't he treat me lightly thinking that I am a mere sculptor's daughter? Wasn't he a silent witness to all the insults his father heaped on me? If he was truly in love with me, would he have accorded greater importance to the kingdom? Wouldn't he have courageously expressed his desire to Mahendra Pallavar and married me? Would this disaster have occurred had he done so?

'Good; I will teach him a lesson. Now a great emperor who rules a kingdom thrice as large as the Pallava kingdom is willing to accord the utmost importance to a casual request of mine! Mamallar should come and observe this! Mamallar should come in person and understand that I'm willing to give up such a prestigious position and return with him! But what if he never turns up?' The instant this thought occurred to Sivakami, she felt that all the blood in her had evaporated and that her body had become a cage made of skin. The next instant, she regained her courage. 'Can he refrain from coming?

He will never ever act in that manner. He is not of such base character; nor is his love so shallow. He will definitely come to fulfil the promise he made while swearing on the spear.'

Sivakami strengthened her resolve and thought about what she would do if Mamallar did not come. 'If he does not come, what does that indicate? It means that his love for me is not genuine. It means that he was just pretending to be in love with me. In that case, all that happened is for the good! Why should I regret being separated from someone who does not love me? I possess the wonderful art of dancing, which my father imparted to me. There lies the expansive kingdom of Vatapi and that of Harshavardhanar beyond. Why should I destroy myself pining for someone who doesn't love me?'

Even as Sivakami was thinking along these lines, she was pining for that love-less man. 'No! Why am I unnecessarily imagining things? If he does not come to take me, is there any purpose in my life? Why should I live? Dancing and artistic pursuits are all useless! I should not deceive myself unnecessarily! It's only because of him that I continue to be alive despite being imprisoned by the Chalukyas. I am going to Vatapi despite witnessing all the atrocities on the way because of him. I believe that he will seek revenge on these criminal Chalukyas and take me back. It is his love that is keeping me alive. I am going to Vatapi to uphold his honour. What if he forgets me? Good, it won't take me long to commit suicide!'

When Sivakami danced, her expressions used to change at lightning speed in accordance with the emotions expressed in the song. Sometimes it was impossible for the audience to follow her swift movements. Now, Sivakami was experiencing a myriad of emotions that rose and ebbed at lightning speed.

Emperor Pulikesi did not approach Sivakami till the womenfolk of the Pallava kingdom, who had been freed, had reached the banks of the North Pennai River. Sivakami felt that the underlying reason was Pulikesi's concern that she would come to know about his donning the guise of a bikshu. She decided that she ought not to reveal that she had already unravelled this secret.

A large part of the Vatapi army had camped on the opposite bank of the North Pennai River. The small force that was accompanying Pulikesi had, meanwhile, joined the larger contingent. That night, Sivakami had an astounding dream. However, she was unable to decide for a long time whether it had been a dream or an actual occurrence. That incident, irrespective of whether it had been a dream or was real, aroused several new doubts and anxieties within her.

Sivakami's palanquin was set down at a short distance away from the Vatapi army camp. The area in which the army had camped was scenic and tranquil. The full moon was showering its milky white light across the sky and on the earth. A gentle breeze was blowing across the area. Sivakami, who was exhausted after a long journey, lay down under a tree. Her eyes closed of their own accord. Soon she fell under Nitra Devi's spell and slipped into deep sleep. Her slumber was disturbed by the sound of conversation. Her eyelids had lost their ability to open, but her eagerness to know who was conversing intensified. Her eyelids opened slightly upon her exercising great effort. She saw an unexpected sight in the moonlight.

Emperor Pulikesi and the bikshu were standing next to each other. Their height, build, facial structure, nose, eyes and eyebrows were identical. Only their clothes were different. One wore the crown and ornaments befitting an emperor. The other sported a tonsured head and ochre robes. Observing this, Sivakami muttered to herself, 'Ah! What's this! Aren't Pulikesi and the bikshu the same person? But here they appear to be two different people! So this is not reality, I'm dreaming. I'm fantasizing in my dream!' Her eyelids closed again.

Though her eyes were closed, her ears were open. She heard the following conversation: 'Anna! Weren't you referring to this girl?'

'It's indeed her.'

'Is she Sivakami?'

'Yes; she's Sivakami!'

'In the message you wrote to me, you had asked me to retain Kanchi Sundari and hand over Sivakami to you. Was this the Sivakami you were talking about?'

'Yes, thambi. Yes.'

'I'm unable to understand why you're so mesmerized by her beauty. I have seen several women who are more beautiful than her in Vatapi itself.'

'If you watch her dance, you will think differently!'

'I saw her dance too, at Mahendra Pallavan's court! There was nothing spectacular about her performance.'

'You cannot understand. You need to have an eye for the arts. Weren't you the one who said there was nothing outstanding about the Ajantha paintings?'

'Never mind! It suffices that you're the one in our lineage who possesses an artistic sensibility. Our campaign to the south has been a dismal failure. I am, however, satisfied that your desire has been fulfilled.'

'Thambi, you must safeguard her with utmost caution. You should ensure that she does not suffer any discomfort till I return.'

'Why are you worried, anna?'

'I am not worried about her. I am concerned for the art that resides in her. I am worried that the divine art should not be affected in any manner.'

'You are indeed worried about the arts! If you are interested, I will share with you what I told Mahendra Pallavan!'

'What did you tell Mahendra Pallavan, thambi?'

'These lowly folks don't deserve so much respect! I told him that we whip the artistes and make them dance in our country.'

'Look, how can I entrust her to you? I will not go to Vengi.'

'No, anna. No! Don't take my words seriously! I said so playfully. Have I ever acted in a manner that contradicts your wishes? I will make the necessary arrangements to keep her happy. You may go without worry!'

With this, the conversation seemed to have come to an end. Sivakami slipped into an unconscious state again.

The following dawn, when Sivakami woke up, she gradually recollected the conversation. She was confused about whether it had been real or a dream. After thinking for a long time, she decided that it must have been a dream. It was not possible for two people to be endowed with an identical appearance. Even if it were so, it was not possible that one person was a bikshu and the other, an emperor. Both of them conversing in that manner in her presence was an impossibility. Their conversation was conjured up by her dazed mind. Hadn't she often wondered about the artistic appreciation that surprisingly lurked somewhere within the cruel Pulikesi? This must be the reason for her dreaming about two identical individuals conversing in that manner. Despite Sivakami concluding that Pulikesi and the bikshu were the same person, the dream still confused and worried her immensely.

Chapter 39

Brothers

It's not surprising that Sivakami thought that Pulikesi and the bikshu were the same person. Pulikesi himself had been stunned by the similarity. This happened some time ago, when the exhausted emperor was seated in his tent all by himself. None of the goals he had set for himself when he left Vatapi had been achieved. They had all come to naught, due to Mahendra Pallavan's ruses.

There was no news about the man who could defeat Mahendra Pallavan by countering his ploys. Pulikesi's spirits were sagging on account of this. His sole consolation was that he had arranged to teach Mahendra Pallavan a lesson through his commander, Sashankan. Ah! Wouldn't that fox Mahendra Pallavan realize that it was a great folly to deceive Pulikesi, when he came out of his hole?

The emperor was waiting on the northern banks of the North Pennai River for Commander Sashankan to join him. He was wondering why Sashankan was taking so long to return after executing his command. It was then that he heard that an army was advancing towards them from the south. Thinking that it was Sashankan who was coming, Pulikesi eagerly waited to hear what the commander had to say. When he heard a lone horse coming to a halt outside the tent, he was about to upbraid Sashankan for being so late. But it was not Sashankan who entered the tent. A tall person wearing a crown, bracelet and other ornaments befitting an emperor entered the tent. Words cannot describe Pulikesi's confusion and amazement when he saw that person. 'What is this? Have I gone mad? Or am I fantasizing? How can I, sitting here on the throne inside the tent, enter the tent from outside?' he wondered.

Observing Pulikesi's baffled look, the person who entered the tent smiled. 'Thambi! Why are you so scared? Am I a ghost or a monster? Are you unable to recognize me?' Enquiring thus, the person removed his crown. The bikshu's tonsured head was visible.

Pulikesi immediately stood up and asked enthusiastically, 'Anna! Is that you?' He was about to embrace the bikshu but then stood rooted to the spot. 'Ah! Why have you assumed this disguise? Your vow . . .?' he asked. Traces of envy and anger were then evident in Pulikesi's eyes.

'Thambi! Don't be hasty. Wasn't this disguise useful in saving your life once? Now it came in handy to save my life. I have no second thoughts regarding my vow. Didn't I promise you that I will not assume this role within your kingdom? Have we reached your kingdom yet?'

When Naganandi asked thus, Pulikesi angrily retorted, 'Yes. But why is this region not a part of our kingdom? Why hasn't the Varaha flag been hoisted in the Pallava kingdom? Why is the gigantic Vatapi army retreating after being defeated by Mahendra Pallavan's miniscule army? It's all because of you!'

'Thambi! Don't even utter the word "defeat"! Who was defeated? Neither the Vatapi army nor you were defeated. I was also not the cause of that defeat. Let's discuss this at leisure. First, fetch me two pieces of ochre robes. If I continue donning this disguise, there will be unnecessary confusion. When I was entering, the sentries were gaping at me!'

'Yes; there's a reason for their gaping, isn't it? They must have been shocked, wondering when and how the emperor who was seated inside the tent had left it. Even I was confused for some time,' Pulikesi observed. He then commanded the sentries posted outside, 'Fetch two pieces of ochre robes from the spies' quarters immediately!'

The moment the ochre robes were brought, Naganandi changed his attire. The two brothers sat next to each other on the same throne. 'Thambi, tell me in detail what transpired since you left Vatapi!' asked Naganandi.

Pulikesi related everything. The bikshu attentively listened and then acknowledged, 'Ah! Mahendra Pallavan is even more astute than I thought. He has been misleading us for a long time!'

'Anna! I thought there was no one in this world to surpass you in statecraft.'

'Initially, I made one mistake. It had far-reaching and disastrous consequences!'

'Adigal, what was that mistake?'

'My heart softened when I saw that youth, Paranjyothi.'

'You entrusted the message to that stealthy boy!'

'You were the reason for that, thambi!'

'Me, how is that?'

'I had visited Pandya Nadu, made the necessary arrangements and was returning to Kanchi. A tired young boy was sleeping on the banks of the lake. I was reminded of the first time I saw you in that very state. So, I developed a fondness for that boy and trusted him too. It was evident from his physiognomy that he would attain great heights. So, I was tempted to bring him into our fold. I sent a message for you through him. Had that message reached you and you had advanced, we could have captured the Kanchi fort in three days. Mahendra Pallavan would have lain at your feet.'

'Instead, the message penned by Mahendra Pallavan reached me. On account of that, I wasted eight months on the banks of the North Pennai River. Mahendra Pallavan, heading a small cavalry, was pretending to attack us without engaging in actual warfare. After that, I advanced to Kanchi and laid siege to the fort. It was futile. Anna, this is my first defeat after ascending the Vatapi throne . . .'

'Appane! Don't utter those words! What do you term as defeat? Who was defeated? Haven't you learnt the first lesson in statecraft yet? The lesson is that one ought to never acknowledge defeat. If you yourself acknowledge your defeat, your subjects will also say the same thing. Your foes will echo your words. The news of Emperor Pulikesi's defeat will spread across the country. The false message that Mahendra Pallavan wrote may come true. Harshavardhana's army may cross the Narmada and enter your kingdom. Never ever utter the word "defeat", thambi!'

'If I don't mention it, will my defeat be transformed into victory, anna?'

'Why are you again brooding over defeat? How can you term your campaign a defeat? Think about it! You started your campaign to the south accompanied by an ocean-like army.

You razed Vyjayanthi to the ground. You overcame the Pallava army on the banks of the North Pennai River. You laid siege to the Kanchi fort and progressed further south up to the banks of the Kollidam. You set Durvineethan, who was imprisoned by the Pallavan, free. Three key monarchs of Tamizhagam, the Cholan, Cheran and Pandian, acknowledged your supremacy and paid tribute to you on the banks of the Kaveri.' 'Anna! The Cholan did not come!'

'Kallapallan came instead of the Cholan. Who is going to enquire about the details, thambi? When you returned to the Kanchi fort, Mahendra Pallavan surrendered to you. Just like Mahavishnu, who placed his leg on Mahabali's head, you too placed your leg on Mahendra Pallavan's head and deigned to let him remain alive. You collected tributes from him and left Kanchi . . .'

'I haven't brought any tributes, anna!'

'So what if you haven't brought any tribute. I have!'

'What's that?'

'I will show you tonight. When news of your campaign, as I just related it, spreads across Utthara Bharata, won't people say that you've returned after a victorious campaign? Or will they say you retreated after being defeated?'

'Anna, words are inadequate to describe your astuteness! You can transform even defeat into victory. After listening to you, even I think that I was victorious. But how will this news of my victory spread across Utthara Bharata?'

'Ah! What is the purpose of the existence of Buddha sangams and samana seminaries? We must immediately dispatch someone to Nagarjuna mountain.'

'Anna! It would be good if you go there in person. You also have a task to complete at Vengi.'

'What task?'

'Vishnuvardhanan is grievously injured. Apparently, chaos prevails in the kingdom of Vengi, which he successfully conquered last year.'

'But what will my visit to Vengi achieve?'

'You must go there and counsel him. There is nothing that you cannot achieve, anna! You will transform defeat into victory.'

'I cannot go to Vengi now.'

'Why?'

'There's a reason.'

'Tell me.'

'I will tell you tonight, thambi, when the sun sets, and darkness envelops this region; I will tell you when the full moon rises. Why are we confined in this tent? Come, let's step outside!'

'Yes, yes! The beauty of nature ought to be appreciated!' remarked Emperor Pulikesi caustically as he stood up.

'What is the use of your being blessed with several fortunes? You are not blessed with the fortune of experiencing beauty,' quipped Naganandi as he stood up. The two brothers stepped out of the tent arm-in-arm, like two intimate friends of the same age.

Chapter 40

Foothills of Ajantha

'So what if the sun disappears? Will darkness envelop the world? Here I am,' announced the full moon as it rose in the east. The golden-hued moon that appeared between two tall palm trees resembled the glowing face of a young girl looking out of a framed window. To the bikshu, the full moon resembled Sivakami's face. Naganandi and Pulikesi were sitting on a rock. 'Anna, what are you thinking about?' asked Pulikesi.

'Thambi, when I entered the tent, wasn't I dressed like you? Do you remember my assuming this disguise once before?'

'How can I forget that anna? I can never forget it.'

'Since that incident occurred twenty-five years ago, I thought you may have forgotten about it.'

'It does not matter whether twenty-five years or twenty-five yugams pass. I will remember that incident not just in this birth but in all subsequent births, anna!'

'Do you remember when we first met, thambi?'

'Of course. I had escaped from our chithappa, Mangalesan's heavily guarded prison. I was hiding from that tyrant's soldiers and was wandering aimlessly in the forests. After running for a long time, my legs had slackened, and I felt exhausted. I understood how difficult it was to withstand hunger and thirst. Finally, one day, overcome by fatigue, I fainted. When I regained consciousness, I realized that I was lying on your lap and that you were squeezing the juice of some green herbs into my mouth. What would have happened to me if you hadn't reached there by God's grace? Anna, what prompted you to exercise so much effort to save me that day?'

'I had been living with the bikshus in the caves in the Ajantha mountain for as long as I could remember. I was learning to paint and to sculpt. Nevertheless, I was often restless. The desire to see the world and mingle with young men of my age arose within me. Occasionally, unknown to the elder bikshus, I used to walk along the riverbank and leave the mountainous territory. But forests lay beyond the mountain and there was no human activity. It was when I was pining for company that I saw you lying unconscious in the forests at the foothills of Ajantha. I showered on you all the affection I had bottled up for the last twenty years. I felt as much love for you as young men in cities and villages would feel for their lovers. I nursed you back to consciousness by squeezing the juice of green herbs into your mouth.'

'Anna, when I saw you for the first time, I reciprocated your affection with the same intensity. I was very fond of our brother, Vishnuvardhanan. But the affection I felt for you far exceeded what I had felt for Vishnuvardhanan ...'

'I did not return to the Ajantha caves the day I found you. I did not return the following two to three days either. The two of us were inseparable and were wandering around the forest arm-in-arm like newlyweds strolling in a garden. You related what had transpired in your life to me in detail. The two of us discussed ways to overthrow Mangalesan and regain control of the Vatapi kingdom.'

'Then Mangalesan's men came there searching for me.'

'When you heard the sound of men approaching in the distance, you were scared. You hugged me pleading, "Anna! Please do not hand me over to them!" I thought for a moment and then came to a decision. I asked, "Thambi, will you obey me?" and you gave me your word. Then we swapped our clothes. I also showed you the way to the Buddha sangramam located in the Ajantha caves. I told you how one ought to behave there. I asked you to hide amidst the dense branches of a tree that stood at a distance.'

'I had barely hidden myself amongst the branches of the tree when Mangalesan's men, who resembled Yaman's emissaries, reached there. Their chief commanded, "Catch him and tie him up!" My heart bled. "I've escaped from grave danger," I thought. I felt immensely grateful to you.'

'Thambi, I had observed the similarity in our appearance even before. When we reached the banks after bathing in the river and waterfalls, I observed the similarity in our reflections on the river surface. It was this knowledge that enabled me to save you then.'

When Emperor Pulikesi admitted in a choked voice, 'Anna! You asked me if I remembered those incidents. How can I forget that you dared to risk your life for the sake of a stranger like me?' tears filled his eyes. Even the full moon wondered 'Ah! What is this? Is it really the cruel and merciless Pulikesi who is shedding tears?' In the moonlight the emperor's tears glistened like pearls from the deep seas.

Chapter 41

At the Ajantha Cave

The bikshu, seemingly oblivious of the emotional and tearful Pulikesi, gazed at the full moon and recollected: 'Those barbarians thought that I was you, imprisoned me and took me away. After crossing the forest, they asked me to mount a horse. Seeing me struggle to mount a horse, they became suspicious. Initially, they thought that I was feigning ignorance. When they realized that I really did not know how to mount a horse, their leader asked me disparaging questions. They were taken aback when they heard my responses. You used to wear earrings, and so your ears were pierced. When they saw that my ears were not pierced, they knew for sure that I was not you. The anger they felt at not having been able to imprison you prompted them to torture me. The scars on account of the blows they inflicted are still visible on my body!'

Saying this, the bikshu felt his face.

'Aiyyo! Anna, seeing those scars I was unable to sleep for several nights. But why are you reminding me of all that now?' cried Pulikesi.

'Thambi, I did not say it to remind you. I meant to remind myself. When I recollect those incidents today, I don't feel sad. I only feel happy. That's the fruit of helping others. When we experience hardship in order to help others, the pain is short-lived. Soon the impact of the hardship disappears. Then only the happiness lingers all our lives. But thambi, if my relating those old stories causes you sorrow, I will not proceed further,' remarked Naganandi and paused.

'Anna, what are you saying? I too feel happy when I recollect those days!'

'In that case, I'll continue to reminisce. I tolerated the torture inflicted by those barbarians for some time. When I was no longer able to withstand their cruelty, I announced that I belonged to the Buddha sangramam at Ajantha. Immediately, they were frightened. They asked me how I had got the clothes I was wearing. I told them that I had found them on the banks of the river, and that I had felt like wearing them. They brought me back to that very spot on the riverbank. They searched the surrounding forest area. Concluding that some wild animal must have preyed on you, they left me behind and returned. I started walking towards Ajantha, wondering whether you had found your way back.'

The Vatapi emperor interrupted him saying, 'I walked along the riverbank as instructed by you. Despite travelling a long distance along the serpentine river, there was no sign of human habitation. Frequently the mountain slopes formed a wall ahead of me and it seemed that there was no way beyond that point. The landscape did not change as I walked ahead. I wondered if I had misunderstood your directions and whether I was walking in the wrong direction. Another terrifying thought struck me. I thought that you may have deceived me and that you might attempt to rule the kingdom by making peace with chithappa, Mangalesan. I finally reached the Ajantha caves, which had exquisite paintings on the walls. As instructed by you, I spoke to no one and spent time pretending to be the sculptor's disciple. You reached there after a week. After listening to your story and observing the wounds on your face, I cried aloud, repenting the injustice I had meted out to you . . .'

'Thambi! You were not at peace even after weeping over what I had gone through. The head bikshu of the sangramam saw both of us together one day. He saw us when we were swimming in a secluded spot in the river. He enquired about you; I stated the truth. I was scared that he would punish me for flouting the rules at Ajantha by bringing you there. But the guru was neither angry with me nor did he punish me. That evening, he summoned us to the main viharam when no one was around and chronicled our past. Hearing it, you became even more agitated. Thambi, your envy of me was akin to a fire that was progressively becoming an inferno.'

'Yes, anna! That's true; but, at the same time, I was ashamed of my baser instincts.'

'It's not your fault, thambi. There was not an iota of fault on your part. I thought so even then. The head bikshu told us that we were twins, and that I was the elder sibling. Our father had kept me hidden ever since I was born and had handed me over to the bikshus when I was five years old. He had asked the bikshus to disclose my identity and hand over the reins of the kingdom to me only if some danger were to befall you. The bikshu guru narrated all this, expressing his wonder at fate that had beckoned me to rescue you. He profusely lauded my virtuous character. He said that you were born within half a nazhigai of my birth, and since the horoscope indicated that you were destined to rule the kingdom, our father had selected you to ascend the throne. When I came to know about this, my love for you increased manifold. But, at the same time, your mind was poisoned. From that moment, you started hating me. That did not surprise me; nor was I angry with you. I understood that it was natural for you to suspect me as, by convention, I had the right to ascend the Vatapi throne. I decided to set your suspicions at rest. I prostrated at the bikshu guru's feet and requested him to allow me to join the bikshu mandalam. Though the guru initially objected, he finally agreed. I tonsured my head, donned ochre robes, and was ordained as a bikshu in your presence. I vowed to forego worldly pleasures forever. The flame that was ablaze in your heart was extinguished. You felt love and gratitude for me like before.'

'Anna, since then I have considered you, my God. I acted in accordance with your wishes. I never flouted your words.'

'You did not suffer any setback because of this. Thambi, I left you behind at Ajantha and went away. I travelled across the country for three years. I convinced the government officials and army chiefs to join hands with you. I also incited the citizens against Mangalesan. At the opportune time, I fetched you from Ajantha. You advanced to Vatapi leading a massive army. Mangalesan was killed in the battle. You ascended the Chalukya throne on which our famous grandfather, Satyasraya Pulikesi, had once sat and ruled over the kingdom.'

'Anna, I ascended the Vatapi throne with your assistance. You forsook the throne that was by right yours. You renounced all worldly pleasures and became a bikshu to set my fears at rest. It was due to your herculean efforts that I was able to kill Mangalesan and ascend the throne. Ever since then, for the last twenty years, you have been a mother, father, minister and military strategist to me. It's because of you that the Varaha flag is fluttering in the area spanning the Naramada and North Pennai Rivers. I acknowledge all this and am grateful to you. But why are you reminding me now of these old stories? How should I demonstrate my gratitude to you?' asked Pulikesi, and eagerly looked at Naganandi's face in the moonlight.

Pulikesi observed a gentleness that had not been perceptible previously on the bikshu's face, which had hardened on account of harsh penances. 'Yes, thambi, there is one thing you can do in return for all the services I have rendered to you,' replied the bikshu.

'In that case, tell me what it is immediately. I will repay at least a fraction of the debt of gratitude I have owed you for the last twenty-five years.'

'Thambi, didn't I send you a message even before you left Vatapi? Do you remember what I had written?'

'You had written about several things; what are you referring to?'

'I had asked you to retain Kanchi Sundari and give me Sivakami Sundari!'

'Why are you bringing that up now?'

'I am asking you now for what I asked you then.'

'Anna! What is this? We were unable to capture Kanchi Sundari.'

'Kanchi Sundari is out of your reach. Despite that, I am asking you to hand over Sivakami to me.'

'How is that possible? I was truly reminded of your message when I watched that girl dance in Mahendra Pallavan's court. I asked the Pallavan to send her with me. Do you know what he said? He believed that she would not come with me as I had no artistic sensibility! Now are you asking me to invade Kanchi again?'

'That's not necessary, thambi. You do not have to invade Kanchi again. You were unable to assume control of Kanchi Sundari. But as I found Sivakami Sundari, I brought her along with me.'

'What? What? Is it true?'

'Thambi, I disguised myself as you just for her sake. I saved her father's life. It was for Sivakami's sake that I assumed charge of the army and engaged in a battle with Mahendra Pallavan at Manimangalam. It was for her that I stopped fighting mid-way and retreated.'

'Anna! Tell me everything in detail!' demanded Pulikesi.

Naganandi related all that had transpired since he had arrived at Dakshina Bharata three years ago.

Pulikesi, after listening to everything, asked disbelievingly, 'Anna! Are you telling me that you are truly in love with that dancer?'

'Yes, thambi! I swear.'

'But what will happen to the vow you took in the presence of the guru at Ajantha? Are you going to join the ranks of the fake bikshus across the country who don ochre robes and womanize, anna?'

'Thambi, I expected this question. I am prepared to respond but not in a few words. I have to explain in detail; will you listen to me?'

'I will definitely listen; but I will not compel you to tell me. You may confide in me if you so desire!' remarked the Vatapi emperor. In truth, Pulikesi was keen to know what Naganandi had to say. At the same time, the seeds of jealousy had been sown in his heart. All these days there had been no place for anyone but him in the bikshu's heart. He had been the sole recipient of the bikshu's affection. The bikshu had neither paid attention nor worried about anything but his well-being. After all these years, a woman, a dancer, had found a place in the bikshu's heart! 'Yes! The bikshu is more devoted to that girl than to me these days! She must be a consummate temptress!' thought Pulikesi enviously.

Chapter 42

The Bikshu's Love

Naganandi bikshu, who was unaware of envy raising its head in Pulikesi's heart like a snake raising its hood, began to share his most intimate thoughts. 'Thambi, from childhood—for as long as I can remember—I grew up in the Ajantha caves. Bikshus and their disciples used to reside in the Ajantha sangramam. I did not see a living woman till I was twenty years old. My eyes had not beheld mortal women in flesh and blood. But I had seen soulful women with wide eyes that were capable of penetrating one's heart and perceiving one's innermost thoughts. I had seen women endowed with divine beauty not found in mortal women. I had seen maidens adorned with divine ornaments, which enhanced their beauty. I had observed women who added to the splendour of the flowers they wore in their hair. I had seen tranquil women, those who were mercy personified and also enticing women whose appearance resembled Mohini's. I had seen them all on the walls of the Ajantha viharam, painted by expert bikshu artists. In my eyes, all those wonderful forms were living men and women. When I approached them, they welcomed me, extended courtesies to me and enquired about my well-being. I used to converse with them without inhibition; I used to enquire about their well-being and also about the outside world. They responded to me through the language of silence.

'Amongst the paintings I used to see and converse with every day, I was attracted to the painting of one maiden. A blue silk fabric was draped around her waist and the upper cloth she wore was of the hue of tender mango shoots. These fabrics enhanced the beauty of her golden-hued body. The red of her smiling lips competed with the red water lilies adorning her black tresses. When the black pupils encased in her eyes, which were shaped like lotus petals, looked straight into my heart, I experienced a kind of sorrow and joy that I had not experienced till then. No matter in which nook or corner of the viharam I stood, it seemed as though that Padmalochini was gazing at me. It must have been the creation of an artist, who was an incarnation of Brahma himself. Though the painting was over three hundred years old, the colours had not faded, and it seemed as though it had been painted only yesterday.

'There was another remarkable feature about the portrait of that maiden. The posture in which she stood, with her waist curved and arms and legs bent, indicated that she was engaged in a strange task. But I was unable to comprehend what she was doing. Despite thinking about her posture for a long time, I was unable to figure out what she was doing. I finally asked a bikshu who was residing in the chaithyam, who revealed that the maiden was performing Bharatanatyam. I then wanted to find out what Bharatanatyam was. Realizing that there was a treatise titled Bharata Shastram, I procured it and read it. I became well-versed with several aspects of the art of Bharatanatyam.

'Following this, I could imagine the maiden in the portrait performing Bharatanatyam. She appeared in several Bharatanatyam costumes. Several mudras, hasthas and abhinayams flashed in my imagination. That imaginary maiden resided in my heart all day and night. That was when I felt the urge to step into the outside world and observe the men and women living in cities and the countryside. I was tempted to think that such a maiden existed in reality somewhere. This craving egged me on to walk along the Ajantha River into the forests at the foothills of the mountain and wander there. That was when I saw you one day, thambi. Your unconscious body still had life in it. After that, a change occurred within me. The maiden whom I had observed in the portrait and had tended in my imagination gradually faded away. You replaced her in my heart. When I realized that you were my own brother, a blood relation, there was no longer a place for that maiden in my heart.

'Thambi, soon thereafter you and I left the Ajantha caves. You ascended the Vatapi throne. You and I waged several wars, employed numerous political and military tactics, and won. We were responsible for the Chalukya kingdom expanding and spanning the area from the Tungabhadra to the Narmada. The emperor of Utthara Bharata, Harshavardhana, grew wary of the Varaha flag.

'During those days, it was not difficult for me to uphold the penances I was supposed to perform as a bikshu. I saw countless women in Vatapi and in the cities and villages I travelled through. When compared to the portraits of the maiden painted in the Ajantha cave, these women seemed to be lacking in beauty and grace. I was incapable of looking at these mere mortal women after appreciating the beauty of the maiden in the painting. I was amused by men who lusted for mortal women. Thambi, when you married six women one after the other, I sympathized with your pitiable condition!'

Pulikesi, who had been listening silently thus far, interrupted. 'Yes, anna! When I recollect that, I too am shocked, wondering why I engaged in such crazy activities! But what can we do? We become wise only with experience. You realized very early that it is unwise to lust after women!'

When Emperor Pulikesi uttered these words, a tinge of sarcasm was evident in his tone. But the bikshu, despite being endowed with a razor-sharp intellect, failed to notice it. He continued speaking: 'No, thambi, no! I am not worthy of your praise. All of you realized the truth after experiencing life. But I, after abstaining from worldly pleasures for several years and losing my youth, fell in love with a woman. However, my love is unlike the love professed by other men. Before I describe my love, I must tell you how I fell in love.

'After Emperor Harshavardhana of Utthara Bharata had concluded a treaty with us and promised that his troops would not cross the Narmada river and reach its southern banks henceforth, I headed to Dakshina Bharata to make arrangements for our proposed invasion. As there were several Buddhist and Jain monasteries in Dakshina Bharata, my task was rendered easy. I was able to find bikshus who were willing to work for us even at the Kanchi royal viharam. Subsequently, I sent you a message asking you to come to Dakshina Bharata with your army. After sending this message I was about to leave for Madurai when the singular most important incident of my life occurred.

'Thambi, though I was wholeheartedly immersed in the task of expanding the Chalukya kingdom, my attention was drawn now and then to painting and sculptures. I saw some exquisite sculptures at Kanchi. I heard that some wonderful sculpture work was being carried out at the harbour city recently christened "Mamallapuram". I headed there to view those sculptures before proceeding to Madurai. The sculptures at Mamallapuram were truly remarkable. I heard that Aayanar, a senior sculptor under whose supervision these works were being carried out, lived in a house that he had built in the middle of a forest. I went looking for his house, as I wanted to meet him.

'I witnessed several wonders in that great sculptor's residence. Importantly, I was attracted to the sculptures portraying dance postures that Aayanar was then sculpting. Those sculptures reminded me of the portrait of the dancer I had seen in the Ajantha caves. When I was admiring those sculptures, a miracle occurred. A female form came walking towards us from the backyard of the house. The figure had both body and soul. But there was not an iota of difference between the portrait I had seen on the wall of the Ajantha cave and this female form. Her face that resembled the full moon, her golden-hued body, the colour of her clothes, wide eyes that were capable of penetrating one's heart and her hairdo were identical to those in the portrait. For some time, I wondered whether she was real, or if I was hallucinating. That maiden's red lips parted slightly, and she asked, "Appa, who is this swamigal?" It was only then that I realized that she was real. The sculptor Aayanar informed me, "She is my daughter, Sivakami; I am sculpting statues of her in various dance postures." Shortly thereafter, Sivakami started dancing.

'Thambi, from that moment onwards, the entire world seemed new to me. I realized that there were more important facets to life than war, statecraft and the burden of ruling a kingdom. I was attracted to Sivakami in the same manner that I had been to the portrait of the dancer before I met you at the foothills of Ajantha. I thought of Sivakami day and night in the same manner as I had thought of that dancer. Not only that, my soul and every nerve of my being were attracted to her.

'Yes, thambi! I fell in love with Sivakami; I was enthralled by her; I felt attracted to her. The intensity of my love for her is such that all the words for love in all the languages in this world are inadequate to describe the depth of my emotion. Words like "love", "enchantment" and "attraction" have been used by crores of people crores of times ever since this world came into being. But these words do not hold the same meaning for them as they do for me. My love does not have a physical aspect.

'I was not attracted towards Sivakami's appearance. I have seen paintings and sculptures that are far more beautiful than her. I did not fall in love with her golden-hued body. The golden glow of the full moon shining tonight is more luminous than her body. The beauty of Sivakami's eyes did not captivate me. The soulful eyes of Sivakami's fawn, Rathi, are more beautiful than her eyes.

'I did not fall in love with Sivakami's tender body. There are numerous flowers in this world that are more tender. Yes, thambi. There is not an iota of physical attraction in my love for Sivakami. The vow of celibacy I undertook for your sake twenty-five years ago has not been affected in any manner by Sivakami . . .'

As Naganandi spoke in this manner, his face exuded an uncommon joy. Pulikesi thought to himself, 'This seems to be a strange madness. Has he become insane on account of languishing in Mahendran's prison for a long time?'

The bikshu, who guessed the train of Pulikesi's thoughts by observing his expression, averred, 'No thambi, no! I have not become insane. I have never possessed the clarity of thought that I do now. In truth, it's not Sivakami with whom I'm in love; I am captivated by the god of art who resides within her. When an unselfconscious Sivakami blissfully dances in the cosmos, I too lose my consciousness. The joy I experience watching her dance far exceeds the joy I experience while performing all other tasks. Thambi, I have antagonized Mahendra Pallavan on several issues; I have hated him. But Mahendran and I concur on one issue. One day, Mahendra Pallavan told Aayanar that Sivakami was not destined to wed a mere mortal, and that her wonderful art was worthy of being offered to God. I heard him when I was hiding behind the Buddha statue; I wholeheartedly agreed with his view. Thambi, trust me; my love for Sivakami will not compromise in any way the vows I undertook when I became a bikshu!' concluded Naganandi adigal.

Chapter 43

Pulikesi's Promise

Emperor Pulikesi smiled and observed, 'Adigal, you may not have reneged on the vows you undertook when you became a bikshu. But our invasion of Dakshina Bharata has been adversely affected by that dancer!'

The shocked bikshu asked in an angry tone, 'How is that? What is the connection between the invasion and Sivakami?'

'Adigal! Is your ability to engage in subterfuge in any way inferior to Mahendran's? We may have faced defeat in the battlefield before. But have our political strategies ever failed? Had you not been captivated by Sivakami and the god of art who possesses her, could Mahendra Pallavan have imprisoned you? Please introspect and state the truth!'

When Pulikesi spoke thus, the angry expression on the bikshu's face was replaced by a shy stubbornness. He lowered his head and requested, as he stared at the ground, 'Emperor, please forgive this bikshu who lost his mind! I am no longer worthy of being of service to the kingdom. Please forgive and free me considering the service I've rendered all these years!'

'Anna! Why are you joking?'

'No, thambi, I am not joking; I am stating the truth. Please relieve me. I shall leave.'

'Where do you intend to go?'

'I will go to some uninhabited place. I will discover another mountainous territory like Ajantha and disappear deep inside the inaccessible mountains. There, I will spend the rest of my life watching Sivakami dance . . .'

'Anna, if you take Sivakami away with you, will she consent to dance?'

'You don't understand the character of artistes, thambi! The authority of an emperor who rules a vast kingdom cannot make Sivakami dance. But she will accede to the request of an impoverished bikshu who does not even have a roof over his head.'

'Oh!'

'Yes, thambi! That's why I did not ask her to dance when I had disguised myself as you.'

'Anna! This craziness does not befit you. I will send Sivakami back to Kanchi. If that's not possible, we will get her married to one of our commanders.'

The bikshu's eyes emitted angry sparks. He warned, 'Thambi! The man who approaches Sivakami with the intention of marrying her will have to be prepared to be despatched to the world of Yaman.'

'Anna, has Mamallan gone to Yama Loka?' asked Pulikesi mockingly.

'No. That fool will face a punishment that is harsher than death in this world itself. Listen, thambi. I had resolved to kill Mamallan with my own hands. Two or three opportunities presented themselves. But I changed my mind at the last minute.'

'Ah! Had you killed Mamallan, the Varaha flag would have been fluttering in the Pallava kingdom by now. Mahendra Pallavan and the Madurai Pandian would have lain at our feet.'

'That may have happened. But that would not have been the appropriate punishment for Mamallan, who wanted to make Sivakami an object of his pleasure.'

'How has he been punished now?'

'He will be tortured all his life, thinking about the Chalukyas abducting his dear lover. This thought will gnaw at his heart day and night. There can be no greater punishment for him.'

'Good, anna! What do you have to say now?'

'I want to dissociate myself entirely from the affairs of the state. I have toiled for you and the kingdom for twenty-five years. I want to live for myself for a few years. Thambi, please give me leave. I will go in search of an uninhabited place.'

'Anna! You may dissociate yourself from the affairs of the state by all means. But you don't have to go in search of forests and mountains. You may reside at Vatapi itself in a beautiful mansion. Build a dance hall in that mansion. Sivakami may dance blissfully there, and you can appreciate her dancing.'

'Thambi, do you really mean that? Will you make these arrangements for me?'

'I will definitely make the necessary arrangements—but on one condition.'

'Condition? Are you imposing a condition on me, thambi?'

'Yes. It is a condition I beseech you to accept. It's a task which no one but you can execute. Please be of assistance to me for one last time. Then I will ask nothing of you.'

'What is it?'

'It was the matter I mentioned some time ago. News of Vishnuvardhanan lying grievously injured in Vengi has reached me. You must go immediately to Vengi and nurse him back to health. Isn't Vishnu a brother, like me, to you?'

'He is indeed my brother, but he dislikes the very sight of me! He has not yet forgiven me for having separated Bharavi from him and chasing Bharavi away . . .'

'Anna, why did you separate the poet Bharavi from Vishnu? The consequences were disastrous!'

'It was for Vishnu's good. He was whiling away his time by incessantly reading and writing poetry . . .'

Pulikesi smiled and thought to himself, 'Of my two brothers, one is obsessed with poetry while the other is obsessed with art. It is essential that I save the bikshu in the same manner that he saved Vishnu years ago.'

He then quipped, 'Yes, anna, you did it for his good. I had asked Bharavi to leave the country, as you desired. But what was the outcome? Bharavi went to Ganga Nadu. Then he lured Vishnu with his descriptions of Durvineethan's daughter and got them married. He went next to Kanchi. He sent messages describing Kanchi, because of which I was allured by Kanchi Sundari.'

'Why are you relating those old tales now?'

'I will refrain from doing so if you dislike it. But please help me one last time, anna! We have returned without capturing Kanchi. There can be no greater ignominy to our dynasty than Vishnuvardhanan too returning vanquished from Vengi. Please help me this once. Take half our army along with you.'

The bikshu thought for some time and then stated, 'So be it, thambi, but you must give me your word!'

'You want me to take care of Sivakami, don't you? I promise I will. Won't I do this for all the assistance you have rendered to me all these years? I will house her in a beautiful palace in Vatapi, ensure her well-being till you return, and then hand her over to you.' 'Thambi, Sivakami is the goddess of art. He who approaches her with lust will meet his end.'

'I will not forget that. But the more you speak of the art of dancing, the more I am drawn towards it. May I ask Sivakami to dance for me?'

'She will not dance.'

'If she were to willingly dance . . .?'

'I have no objection.'

'I am glad.'

'Thambi, our grandfather was conferred the title "Satyasraya". You too bear the same title. Your behaviour should befit your title at least once.'

'I promise that I will take the utmost care of Sivakami and hand her over to you.'

The long conversation between Emperor Pulikesi and the bikshu ended in this manner. It was during the second jaamam of that night that the two of them walked up to Sivakami, who lay half asleep. And in the moonlight they could see her clearly.

Chapter 44

Midnight Journey

For a month after the Manimangalam battle, Mahendrar lay bed-ridden in an unconscious state. It came to be known that the knife that struck him in the battlefield had been dipped in venom. Though the palace physicians tried their utmost to nurse him back to health, their efforts were not fruitful. Namasivaya vaidhyar reached Kanchi in these circumstances. Commander Paranjyothi had despatched emissaries to fetch him from Thiruvengadu. Namasivaya vaidhyar's treatment soon bore fruit. Mahendrar's thinking grew clearer.

The moment Mahendra Pallavar was more lucid, he enquired about Aayanar and Sivakami. He was devastated when he learnt that Aayanar had fractured his leg, and that the Chalukyas had imprisoned Sivakami and taken her away. It seemed as if he would suffer a relapse. When Mamallar visited his father, Mahendrar asked him the same question Aayanar had asked some time earlier. He enquired, 'Narasimha, where is Sivakami?'

An extremely sorrowful Narasimhar replied, 'Appa, why do you worry about that now? You should first recover!'

'Narasimha, it is obvious that the love you had professed for Sivakami was superficial. I will leave right away; I will find Sivakami and bring her back!' declared Mahendra Pallavar as he tried to get up.

Mamallar, who was both embarrassed and agitated, retorted, 'Appa! I'm waiting for you to recover. I was wondering what you would say. When you yourself speak thus . . . '

'What else can I say, Narasimha? Aayanar's and Sivakami's skills are well known from the Himalayas to Lanka. Is there a greater ignominy to the Pallava dynasty than the Vatapi demon abducting a renowned dancer like Sivakami? I would rather lose my life in the battlefield than live under the shadow of such a slur.'

'Appa, don't speak in this manner. The commander and I have made arrangements to take leave of you as soon as you recover . . . '

'What arrangements have you made so far?'

'We have mobilized an army.'

'How foolish! If you go with an army, you will neither be able to fetch Sivakami nor will you return yourselves.'

A surprised Mamallar asked, 'What else can be done, appa? What do you suggest?'

Mahendrar advised, 'Bring Paranjyothi and Shatrugnan here. I will tell you what I have in mind.'

When Mamallar, Paranjyothi and Shatrugnan met the chakravarthy that evening, he suggested that Paranjyothi and Shatrugnan should travel to Vatapi in disguise and bring Sivakami back. Mamallar initially objected to bringing Sivakami back in this stealthy manner. Mahendrar said that there was nothing wrong in doing so, as she had been taken away in a similar fashion. Mahendra chakravarthy also stated that travelling to Vatapi incognito would help them in invading that kingdom in future.

When Mamallar realized that Mahendra Pallavar's intent was to invade Vatapi, he felt elated and stopped objecting. After the discussions were over, he prostrated before his father and pleaded, 'Appa, I will go along with the commander. Kindly give me leave!'

Mahendrar initially objected. Finally, Mahendrar made Mamallar promise that he would not act rashly, and that he would act in accordance with Commander Paranjyothi's counsel in all matters, and then gave him leave to go.

Two days later, at midnight, six men mounted on horses were in the muttram of the Kanchi palace, prepared to embark on a journey. The six men, who sported fake beards and moustaches as part of their disguise, were Mamallar, Paranjyothi, Shatrugnan, Gundodharan, Kannabiran, and Ashwabalar. They frequently looked up at one of the upper storeys of the palace. In a short while, Mahendra chakravarthy and Bhuvana Mahadevi could be seen in the front area of the upper storey. When Mahendra Pallavar gave leave saying, 'You may leave; return victoriously', Mamallar and Paranjyothi bowed and then patted their horses. When the horses exited through the outer gates of the palace and reached the road, Mahendra Pallavar told Bhuvana Mahadevi, 'Devi, this is the punishment for being born in a royal dynasty!'

Chapter 45

Mahendrar's Secret

That night, neither Mahendra Pallavar nor his chief consort, Bhuvana Mahadevi, slept. They sat in the upper storey of the palace, which was lit up by the crystal-clear light of the stars and spoke about the past and the future.

'Devi, I never expected to face such humiliation during the last days of my life. My dreams have been shattered! The political dictum which states that even a person's most intimate friends will desert him during times of misfortune is so true! Look at the stars twinkling in the sky! They once seemed to laud me saying, "Mahendra, is there anyone else on earth who is wiser than you! No one can match you in philanthropy, virtues, valour, and love of arts." Now those very stars wink at me, laugh mockingly and ask, "Mahendra, will this humiliation suffice? Haven't your cunning and strategizing come to naught when fate intervenes?"'

As the chakravarthini was aware that Mahendrar's body and soul were grievously injured, she did not wish to hurt him further. However, she involuntarily uttered the following words. 'Prabhu, how can we blame fate for the activities we undertake of our own volition?'

Mahendrar smiled sadly and observed, 'No matter how shrewdly we humans act, fate does intervene and defeats our purpose. Fate appeared in the form of Sivakami to prevent me from achieving my goals.'

'Ah! Why do you blame that poor girl? What could she do?' asked the Pallava queen sympathetically.

'It is only to be expected that, as a woman, you will understand her situation and support her. But it is on account of Aayanar's daughter that all my intentions have been thwarted. I have been trying to separate Sivakami from Mamallan. I adopted several ruses and ploys to achieve this. They were futile; it was fate that finally emerged victorious.'

'Didn't fate fulfil your objective? You tried hard to separate that girl and Mamallan. Fate came to your assistance and carried her away to Vatapi. That being the case, why are you attempting to trace her and bring her back? I just don't understand what you are doing!' remarked Bhuvana Mahadevi in a genuinely amazed tone.

'That is what I meant when I said that my action is a punishment for being a descendant of the ancient Pallava clan. Not bringing Sivakami back will leave an indelible slur on the Pallava dynasty. Pulikesi will brag that he returned after defeating the Kanchi Pallavan. As long as Sivakami remains in Vatapi, the world will believe Pulikesi's claims. Sivakami's fame has spread far and wide, from Lanka to Kanyakubja. I myself sent a message to Harshavardhanar, inviting him to view the sculptures at Mamallapuram and to watch Sivakami dance. What will the world think if Sivakami is imprisoned in Vatapi? Can there be a greater ignominy for the Pallava dynasty?'

'Swami! Sometimes I have held the crown you wear in my hands. Its weight made me wonder how you bear this on your head. But in the last two to three years, I have realized that the burden you bear in your heart is a thousand times heavier than the one on your head. It is so true when people talk about the burden of ruling a kingdom!' pronounced the chakravarthini emotionally.

'At one time I bore that burden very enthusiastically. Now that burden is imposing an unbearable weight on my heart. Devi, I used to build castles in the air till three years ago. Yes; I ignored the Kanchi fort and built castles in the air. I thought that I could transform this world into heaven. I cursed all my ancestors in my heart. I regretted that they had unnecessarily spent their lives in warfare and bloodshed. I started building indestructible stone temples dedicated to all religions in Mamallapuram. I intended to invite Harshavardhanar and Pulikesi as soon as the construction of the temples was completed. That Chalukya demon dashed all the castles I built in the air to the ground. The fire he has set to the villages in Thondaimandalam is not going to be extinguished soon. The disgrace to the Pallava dynasty will not be erased till our forces invade Vatapi and defeat Pulikesi. If this is not achieved during my lifetime, it must be achieved during Mamallan's lifetime.'

'Prabhu! My brave son will definitely fulfil your wishes. He will erase the slur on the Pallava dynasty!' declared Bhuvana Mahadevi proudly.

Chapter 46

Vatapi

Most of the Chalukya forces marched in the northwest direction towards Vatapi from the banks of the North Pennai River. As Sivakami travelled with that army too, she was witness to incidents that were more horrific than the atrocities perpetrated in the villages of Thondaimandalam. She saw houses and haystacks being set on fire, elephants destroying verdant groves, crops being damaged, innocent villagers being murdered, sturdy youths and young women being imprisoned, and infants shrieking on being separated from their mothers.

An inferno was ablaze in Sivakami's heart. She wanted to meet the Vatapi emperor again and request him not to engage in such atrocities. She tried to meet him several times. She requested her guards to take her to Pulikesi. Those guards did not pay any heed to her. Every night, when she slept, she would hear eerie laughter. She would wake up with a start, thinking that she had heard a ghost laughing. She would see the Vatapi emperor walking away in the distance, his back towards her. By the time she sat up, that figure would disappear. She wondered whether she was hallucinating.

When Pulikesi was young, he had been tortured by his uncle, Mangalesan. This had made him hard-hearted and cruel. Ever since he had ascended the Vatapi throne with Naganandi's assistance, he had spent all his time decimating his foes within the country and waging wars with external adversaries. It was uncharacteristic of Pulikesi to empathize with others' sorrows. There were two reasons for Pulikesi becoming ten times more cruel than he used to be before.

First, he was furious that his invasion of Dakshina Bharata had ended in failure because of Mahendra Pallavar's ruses. Secondly, he was envious that Naganandi, who had thus far thought only about the glory of the Vatapi kingdom and his welfare, had now fallen for the charms of a maiden from Pallava Nadu. Emperor Pulikesi gave vent to his fury by torturing the innocent citizens on his way back to Vatapi. He also wondered how he could take revenge on Sivakami.

Sivakami, who was unaware of all this, was optimistic that she could convince the Vatapi emperor to command his forces not to commit atrocities should she have an opportunity to meet him face-to-face again. However, her desire to meet him was not fulfilled till they reached Vatapi.

Sivakami was taken to a large and beautiful palace in Vatapi. Two ladies-in-waiting were appointed to act as her escorts and to serve her. They spoke in a dialect that was a combination of Prakrit and Tamil. Sivakami was able to easily understand what the ladies-in-waiting said. They informed Sivakami that the emperor had commanded that she should be housed in the palace and that they should ensure that she was comfortable. This was what she had expected. Sivakami decided that Emperor Pulikesi would soon visit the palace to meet her. She incessantly thought about how she ought to behave and what she should say when he visited her.

Sivakami held two contradictory opinions about the emperor. Sometimes, she felt furious when she recollected the atrocities perpetrated by his army. At the same time, she felt proud that a helpless girl like her could wield so much influence over such a cruel king. Sivakami was frequently reminded of Sita, whom Ravanan had abducted and had imprisoned at Ashoka Vanam. Her situation was akin to Sita's. Rama defeated Ravanan, freed Sita, and took her along with him. Similarly, Mamallar would come one day and rescue her from that barbarian, Pulikesi.

Sivakami also pondered on the difference between herself and Sita. Ravanan had been captivated by Sita's beauty and had abducted her. But Pulikesi had been impressed by her dancing prowess and had imprisoned her (Sivakami's view was shaped by the firm belief that Pulikesi was the bikshu in disguise). So, Sita did not possess the kind of clout she, Sivakami, did with Pulikesi. Her art would give her the power to make Pulikesi dance to her tune. 'Ah! I am not going to spare that wicked bikshu! He will have to come to me anyway!'

Sivakami's wish was fulfilled on the eighth day of her arrival in Vatapi. The emperor visited her palace. When the lady-in-waiting rushed in and announced that the emperor had come, Sivakami hurried to welcome him and attack him with her sharp glances and speech. When the emperor entered the palace, surveyed her from top to bottom, and laughed in a ghastly manner, like he had in her dream, her intentions vanished into thin air. She felt an indescribable fear that rocked her body and soul. She felt tongue-tied.

When Pulikesi enquired, 'Sculptor's daughter! Queen of dancing! The artistic treasure of Mahendra Pallavan!

Are you well? Do you like your stay at Vatapi', Sivakami trembled. Was this the same bikshu who became ecstatic even over her ordinary dance movements? Was this the same Naganandi who was so overcome by emotion that he struggled to speak every time he approached her? He had not behaved in this manner when she had beseeched him to free the womenfolk of Thondaimandalam on the banks of the Ponnmugaliaru. Had his return to Vatapi transformed him?

As Sivakami's heart was in turmoil, she was unable to respond to Pulikesi. Observing this, Pulikesi asked, 'Lady! Why are you silent? Do you think it doesn't befit you to talk to Pulikesi, who is incapable of appreciating the arts? I don't completely lack artistic sensibility. If it were so, would I have housed you in this palace? Doesn't this beautiful mansion befit the peerless queen of dancing from Pallava Nadu? Are you comfortable here? Do the ladies-in-waiting serve you well? If you find anything lacking, say so!'

Though Sivakami found Pulikesi's speech repulsive, she decided that she ought not to keep quiet. She strengthened her resolve and replied, 'Prabhu, I am comfortable here. I have no complaints. Thank you very much.'

'Ah! It's you who spoke! Thank God! Seeing you stand silently, I was wondering if I had imprisoned a living being or one of the stone statues your father sculpted. I am very happy that you spoke. If you truly want to demonstrate the gratitude you just expressed, there is an opportunity . . .' Pulikesi hesitated before speaking further. Sivakami remained speechless, fearful of what he would say next.

'Lady, the foolish Mahendra Pallavan observed that I was incapable of appreciating the arts; you believed him. The difference between Mahendra Pallavan's and my ability to appreciate the arts is as stark as the difference between a jackal and a tiger, the difference between a pond and an ocean and the difference between the miniscule Thondaimandalam and the expansive Chalukya kingdom. You will soon realize this. Queen of arts, listen to me! The emperor of Persia has sent emissaries to my court. He has sent tribute and gifts and has sought my friendship in return. A large assembly will congregate at the coronation hall tomorrow to welcome the emissaries and accept their tribute. You must dance in that assembly.'

Sivakami, who had been scared and confused till then, gained uncharacteristic courage when she heard the word 'dance'. She looked at Pulikesi directly in the eye, without a trace of fear or hesitation, and replied in a firm tone, 'I will not dance.'

Pulikesi glowered angrily for an instant. He gritted his teeth to suppress his fury and stated, 'Lady, why do you stubbornly refuse to dance? I will give you three days to think about this!'

'There is no need to think, prabhu! You will make me dance in your court and then trumpet to the world that you have defeated Mahendra Pallavar. You will point at me and state, "She is a slave from Pallava Nadu"! Ah! I understand your intention well. You may be able to imprison me and enslave my mortal body, you may also control my soul, but you cannot enslave my art. I will not dance in subservience to your authority and fearing your command! I will never dance,' declared Sivakami.

When Sivakami uttered these words in an angry tone, Pulikesi's eyes reddened with fury. When Sivakami stopped talking, Pulikesi laughed in a ghastly manner as he had before. 'Lady, be patient! Why do you get so agitated? I have no intention of enchaining your body or your art. You don't have to dance if you don't want to. Don't think that you have been imprisoned in this palace. You may leave the palace whenever you wish. You may stroll around Vatapi and return. Though Vatapi is not as picturesque as Kanchi, there are interesting places to visit. The sentries stationed at the entrance are not here to detain you in this palace. They are here to serve you. They will fetch a palanquin for you whenever you desire to go out. If you wish to see me again, you may send me a message through them. Sculptor's daughter, you don't have to live in constant fear of my authority. You can live as you please, independently and comfortably!'

Once Emperor Pulikesi had finished speaking, he observed Sivakami keenly. Sivakami failed to observe the intense hatred and vengeance in Pulikesi's eyes. The helpless girl was staring at the ground. She was gloating over the fact that she had vanquished Pulikesi of Vatapi, who was renowned for his cruel and torturous ways.

That evening, Sivakami told the guards of her palace that she wished to look around Vatapi, and asked them to fetch a palanquin. She recalled Pulikesi telling her that she was not a prisoner and that she might stroll around outside the palace. She sat in the palanquin and ventured out to ascertain if she truly was free.

Chapter 47

Strolling around the Streets

One thousand three hundred years ago, Vatapi had been the capital of one of the three kingdoms that flourished in Bharata Kandam. Like Kanyakubja and Kanchi, Vatapi's fame had spread far and wide and even overseas. Every time Pulikesi's army returned from a military campaign, it brought back enormous wealth from the nations it had defeated. Hence, Vatapi was prosperous in those days. Trade flourished in that city. Traders of precious gems from far-flung countries used to visit Vatapi.

Travellers from several countries would visit the famous Jain temples and Buddhist monasteries in Vatapi. Therefore, the city was always vibrant. This was particularly true when the emperor was in the capital. Vassals used to come bearing tributes to gain an audience with the emperor. Ambassadors from far-off countries like China and Persia used to visit Vatapi. The streets of Vatapi, flanked by mansions and temple towers, were always teeming with people, and were reminiscent of a temple fair. The sounds of carts and chariots reverberated through the city incessantly.

Sivakami observed the sights and sounds of Vatapi while she was carried around in a palanquin. She mentally compared Kanchi and Vatapi. She very well understood the difference between a city whose affluence and culture had grown from ancient times and a new city that had suddenly been endowed with wealth. The clothes and ornaments worn by the affluent men and women of Kanchi were subdued and aesthetically conceived. The citizens of Vatapi were flashily dressed.

The people of Kanchi greeted each other with warmth and respect. The citizens of Vatapi laughed loudly and created a commotion when they met. In Kanchi, when masters commanded their servants, they did so with affection and consideration. The masters in Vatapi ordered their servants around harshly and used foul language.

Sivakami observed another difference between Kanchi and Vatapi. Bikshus, Digambar monks, orthodox sanyasis, mendicants, kabalikas and beggars flocked the streets of Kanchi and troubled passers-by. It seemed as though those who sought alms were found aplenty in a place inhabited by philanthropists. Not many bikshus and mendicants were seen in the streets of Vatapi. As the population was not charitable, not many beggars were there! As Sivakami passed through the streets of Vatapi, pondering over these issues and in awe of the city's wealth, she saw a sight she had not hitherto witnessed.

A group of men and women were standing at the junction of a street. Their hands were chained together. They stood with their heads lowered. They were surrounded by ruffians, who looked like Yama's messengers, holding long whips. Sivakami was distressed to see this sight. As the men and women who were thus imprisoned seemed to hail from Tamizhagam, her sorrow increased multi-fold.

Sivakami wondered for a moment if she should stop the palanquin and enquire about them. But she was unable to muster the courage to do so. Her palanquin went ahead. After the palanquin had moved some distance away from the street junction, Sivakami looked around, unable to suppress her curiosity. It seemed to her that some of the prisoners were pointing to her palanquin and that they were looking towards her with tear-filled eyes. Sivakami immediately looked away and commanded the palanquin-bearers to take her home.

When Sivakami returned home, she narrated the sight to a lady-in-waiting and asked her if she knew anything about it. As the lady-in-waiting claimed ignorance, Sivakami asked her to enquire into the matter. The lady-in-waiting complied. She returned with information that horrified Sivakami and caused her unbearable sorrow. Emperor Pulikesi had imprisoned several men and women at Pallava Nadu and had brought them to Vatapi. Some of them had tried to escape. Some others had refused to engage in slave labour. Certain others were obstinate and had refused to eat. Emperor Pulikesi had commanded that such rebels be taken to the street junction and publicly whipped as punishment. The whipping had begun only from that day. It was to continue for two months. Every evening, the citizens of Vatapi would be entertained in this manner.

Sleep evaded Sivakami that night. She felt a sorrow that was far more intense than what she had experienced in her grief-stricken and unhappy life till then. She felt as though someone was whipping her. She recollected pleading with Pulikesi on the banks of Ponnmugaliaru and securing the release of the women who had accompanied her. It seemed that those who were freed that day were only a fraction of the people the Chalukyas had imprisoned. The larger contingent of the army that had left ahead of Pulikesi must have imprisoned many more.

Sivakami now understood why the chakravarthy had spoken to her that morning and had asked her to look around Vatapi. The tyrant had acted in that manner to make Sivakami fall at his feet and beg him. But his desire was not going to be fulfilled. She decided that she would not plead with Pulikesi under any circumstance. She would never do so! That barbarian was trying to take revenge! Sivakami regretted her decision to look around Vatapi. She struggled all night, unable to sleep.

The following day dawned; the sun rose. As it traversed across the sky, Sivakami's distress intensified. As the sun continued to travel westwards, her body and soul trembled. By then, the men and women from Pallava Nadu would have been taken to the street junction! Their hands would have been chained behind their backs. The demonic guards must be standing behind them, holding long whips. They would soon start whipping the prisoners. The resolution Sivakami had made the previous night vanished. She hastily commanded the guards stationed at the entrance to fetch a palanquin. As soon as the palanquin was brought, she hurriedly sat in it and commanded the bearers to take her to the street junction they had passed the previous day.

When Sivakami's palanquin neared the street junction, the prisoners' faces exuded a joy not hitherto seen. They spoke amongst themselves. Several of them beseeched Sivakami, 'Amma! Thaye! Please rescue us!'

Sivakami was disconcerted by this unanticipated call for help. She wished that she indeed had the power to save these people. She asked the bearers to lower the palanquin, stepped out and approached the crowd. Once again the prisoners cried out, 'Amma! Thaye! Please rescue us!'

Sivakami approached the prisoners. Some of them bore marks of the whips' lashes. She observed blood oozing out of their wounds and staining the ground in several places. Sivakami felt dizzy; her stomach churned; she felt faint. She overcame these emotions and regained her composure. She then asked one of the female prisoners, 'Amma, why do you ask me to save you? I too am a helpless woman like you. I too have been imprisoned by the Chalukyas. I don't have the power to rescue you.'

The lady responded, 'You do possess the power to save us, thaye! The demon standing there told us so.'

Sivakami approached the chief of the warriors, who resembled a demon. In the mixed dialect spoken in Vatapi, she requested, 'Aiyya, why do you torture these people by whipping them? Please stop this sinful act!'

The chief of the warriors laughed heartily. He then paused to think and stated, 'We are powerless, thaye! It's the emperor's orders!'

'In that case, please wait for some time. I will intercede on their behalf with your emperor. Till then—'

That warrior interrupted Sivakami saying, 'Not necessary, amma! You don't have to approach the emperor. You have the authority to prevent them from being whipped. We will stop if you say so; but on one condition.'

Sivakami, who was filled with surprise and disbelief as the soldier spoke, became alert when she heard the word 'condition'. Sensing that there must be some treachery in the situation, she asked, 'What's the condition?'

The barbarian replied, 'You must dance at this very place, in our presence. We will not whip them. If you continue dancing until sunset, all of us will watch you dance. You may return to your house at sunset. We will take them back to the prison. If you wish that they should not be whipped tomorrow, you may dance here tomorrow too.'

Sivakami's heart at that moment was akin to a volcano emitting molten lava and black smoke. 'Ah! Is this what that tyrant had planned for me? Was he trying to seek revenge? Was this the reason for his pretending to appreciate my art when he was disguised as a bikshu? But that treacherous man's desire will never ever be fulfilled. I will never dance at a street junction of Vatapi under any circumstance.'

Sivakami stood rooted to the spot with fury writ large on her face and eyes. The chief of the warriors asked, 'What is your decision, thaye? Are you going to dance? Or may I ask them to proceed with their duty?'

That question pierced her heart. She resolutely looked at the soldier and declared, 'Ah! Are you asking me to dance at this street junction? No; I will never ever do that!'

Smiling, the chief of warriors told the men holding the whips, 'Fine, you may carry out your orders!'

Chapter 48

Performance at the Street Junction

If it is true that there is a God who is the embodiment of mercy, why did he create so much sorrow in this world? Why do human beings have to experience so much sadness? These questions have been asked since the days of yore. Enlightened souls have also responded to these questions. What humans regard as sorrow is not so in reality. Ignorance clouds our intellect like clouds that obscure the sun. So we perceive certain things as sorrowful. In truth, sorrow is a kind of happiness. Poet Subramania Bharathi sang in praise of Parasakthi as follows.

Love itself She is;
Yet miseries She inflicts
To make and break is Her play
In Her is happiness boundless.

But why does Jaganmatha Parasakthi, who is love personified and is the fount of joy, accord so much misery and difficulties to her children? When we examine issues

223

dispassionately we realize that sorrow is actually joy and what we regard as difficulty is pleasure.

But it is not easy to believe in this philosophy. People will incredulously ask, 'How can there be joy in sorrow and pleasure in difficulty?' But if we examine our life experiences, we will understand this philosophy.

We read sorrowful stories and epics. We watch sad plays. We sing and listen to plaintive melodies. Don't we seek and experience melancholy in this manner? Why? Because joy is inherent in all sorrow. We undergo several difficulties during our lifetimes. We believe that these hardships are unbearable, and life is not worth living. Yet, somehow, we endure all these difficulties. When we look back at them after a few years, we feel a strange kind of joy. We feel happy recollecting and talking about the difficulties we have experienced.

Sita devi experienced untold sorrow when she was in exile in the forest. No woman would have experienced as much sorrow as she had. And yet, when she was living at the palace in Ayodhya as Shri Rama's consort and was pregnant, and Rama asked her, 'What do you desire,' she responded, 'I want to return to the forest and visit all the places where I went through so many difficulties.' Doesn't Sita's desire prove the philosophy that what we perceive as sorrow is not truly so? It is our ignorance which prompts us to think in this manner. There is joy inherent in sorrow.

At the same time, it is not right to philosophize when Sivakami is in a difficult situation, except to understand Sivakami's behaviour. Commander Virupakshan had asked her to dance at the street junction to prevent the men and women of Tamizhagam from being whipped. Sivakami initially thought that acting in that manner would be demeaning to the divine art of Bharatanatyam and refused to dance.

But when the whipping commenced on Virupakshan's command, Sivakami's resolve vanished. The very next instant, Sivakami devi started dancing at the Vatapi street junction. Her performance was superb. She danced blissfully, as if to prove the philosophy that happiness is inherent in sorrow. While dancing, she lost all consciousness of herself, the outside world, time and location. The sight of Sivakami dancing was akin to the goddess of beauty dancing in an ecstatic rage.

When Sivakami was dancing at the Vatapi street junction, it seemed as though the earth and the sky had come to a standstill. The womenfolk of Vatapi who were walking down that street stood still and watched in appreciation. The imprisoned men and women from Tamizhagam stood motionless and watched. The demons who held whips were speechless. Their commander, Virupakshan, also stood still. All of them stood like statues. They were mesmerized, oblivious of time slipping by.

The sun had set, the fort gates were shut, and trumpets were blown to announce sunset. But this did not disturb Sivakami's ecstatic dancing. Finally, Sivakami stopped dancing and stood still. She looked around like someone who had been travelling all this time through a joyous world and had just returned to earth. She realized that she had been dancing at the street junction. Amidst the unbearable shame and sorrow, she also felt happiness and pride. The chained Pallava Nadu men and women looked towards Sivakami. She observed the gratitude in their eyes. She walked to the palanquin and sat in it without saying a word to anyone.

She returned to her palace.

Chapter 49

The Bikshu's Arrival

Sivakami had started dancing at the Vatapi street junction on the first day of shuklapaksham. She danced for the whole fortnight of the waxing moon and then krishnapaksham, the fortnight of the waning moon, set in. She danced through krishnapaksham and soon it was shuklapaksham again. Sivakami's performances at the street junction continued. Commander Virupakshan kept changing the performance venue. He produced the imprisoned men and women of Tamizhagam at the important street junctions of Vatapi, one after the other. Sivakami would go to where the prisoners were assembled and dance. Every day, crowds thronged the spot to watch this spectacle. Men, women and children came in large numbers.

Government officials arrived in chariots. Women from the royal family and their ladies-in-waiting came in palanquins. News of the danseuse imprisoned by Emperor Pulikesi dancing on the streets of Vatapi spread far and wide. People from the neighbouring areas came to watch the performances. People from far-flung locations also came to view the spectacle. The entire Chalukya nation was talking about this issue.

There was a gradual change in the attitude of the Vatapi citizens towards Sivakami. Initially, they were stunned watching her amazing performance. They marvelled at the wonderful art form. They felt love, solidarity and pity for the embodiment of art who had forsaken her native place, country and family and had come to a distant country. Several people in the audience were eager to converse with Sivakami. They wanted to express their wonder, regard and affection for her. They were desirous of visiting the palace in which she lived and of befriending her. They wanted to invite her to their homes. But Sivakami did not reciprocate the friendly overtures of the Vatapi citizens. The joy she experienced while dancing, coupled with the natural fatigue that followed her performance and her bitter state of mind, rendered her incapable of striking a conversation with the audience.

As days went by, she came to be seen as an arrogant person. The affection and solidarity the people had initially felt for her soon transformed into hate and mockery. People increasingly teased and laughed mockingly at Sivakami as she arrived at and left the dance venue. The very people who had appreciatively described Sivakami's dancing as 'wonderful' and 'divine' soon started calling it a 'mad woman's buffoonery'!

When Sivakami passed by seated in a palanquin, young children ran after her, hooting. Sometimes, they even flung mud at her. All this did not have an iota of impact on Sivakami. Her heart had hardened. She had developed unshakable resolve. Sivakami had developed the ability to treat fame, disrepute, praise and scorn alike. She cultivated the detachment of an enlightened soul, who, like water drops on a lotus leaf, was awaiting the divine call.

Sivakami had been dancing on the Vatapi streets for almost one-and-a-half months. Trumpets heralding sunset were heard. Sivakami stopped dancing; she paused to regain her breath, turned around, and started walking towards the palanquin. She was shocked and confused on seeing a figure, and stood rooted to the spot. It was Naganandi adigal.

Sivakami observed a wide-eyed Naganandi staring at her angrily, without even batting an eyelid. Naganandi's expression changed in an instant. The anger in his eyes was replaced by pity. His expression and the look in his eyes seemed to indicate that he was pleading for her forgiveness. Sivakami, whose confusion had heightened, slowly regained her composure, walked to the palanquin with her head lowered, and sat down in it.

As usual, the palanquin headed to the palace. But Sivakami's heart dwelt on Naganandi. 'Who was this bikshu? Was he the Vatapi emperor in disguise? He was identical in appearance, but the expression on his face and in his eyes was very different. The expressions of the hard-hearted Pulikesi, who was devoid of any emotion, and that of the kind, gentle and appreciative bikshu were so different.' The bikshu's appearance reminded Sivakami of Pallava Nadu and her forest residence. She recollected her life during the days gone by. Not even a year had passed, but it seemed as though several eons had gone by!

Even after returning to the palace, Sivakami's mind did not regain its usual calm. She was assailed by an indescribable sense of anticipation and a meaningless agitation. Whom did her heart seek? Whose arrival did her eyes expect as they frequently darted to the entrance? Was it Naganandi bikshu?

When Naganandi entered the palace one jaamam after the onset of night, the lighting up of Sivakami's eyes and her expression indicated that she had been expecting him. Naganandi and Sivakami faced each other. The sharpness of their looks indicated that each was trying to penetrate into the other's heart and understand the mysteries that lay within. Pin-drop silence prevailed in the palace for some time. The calm was disturbed when the bikshu appealed in a choked voice, 'Sivakami! Please forgive me!'

Chapter 50

Sivakami's Vow

Sivakami, who had been sitting till then, immediately stood up. Her lips twitched; her eyebrows were raised. Darts of anger that flew from her eyes assailed the bikshu. Sivakami angrily attacked the bikshu exclaiming, 'Fake bikshu! Why are you apologizing to me? What harm did you cause me?'

The bikshu was stunned. Thinking that he had said something wrong, he stammered as he spoke, 'Yes, Sivakami! I have caused you great harm. I need to explain everything in detail. This is not something that can be clarified in one or two words. Please sit down and listen to me patiently!'

'Aiyya! Before you explain everything, please tell me who you are? Are you a monk of the order established by Gautama Buddha, the embodiment of kindness, who renounced all worldly pleasures? Or are you the Chalukya emperor who has donned ochre robes with treacherous intentions? Are you a mendicant who is genuinely passionate about sculptures, painting and Bharatanatyam? Or, like Ravana, have you assumed the disguise of a sanyasi to molest a humble sculptor's daughter? Who are you? Are you Naganandi or Pulikesi?' When Sivakami paused after questioning him in this manner, the ensuing silence was akin to the quiet after a prolonged bout of lightning and thunder.

Despite Sivakami's enraged outburst, there was no change in Naganandi's expression. He replied with surprising composure, 'Amma Sivakami, your suspicions are not baseless. But I am a genuine bikshu who has renounced all worldly pleasures. Your talent in dancing captivated my heart. I am not the barbaric Pulikesi, who made you dance in the presence of prisoners on the streets of Vatapi. Unfortunately, I was born as his brother due to the sins I committed in my previous birth. Twenty-five years ago, I pretended to be my brother, Pulikesi, to rescue him from murderers. Now, after twenty-five years, I assumed his disguise to fulfil your wishes. Yes, Sivakami. You pleaded with me in the middle of the forest outside the Kanchi fort to save your father. To fulfil your wish, I cast away the robes of a monk and assumed the disguise of an emperor ...'

A disconcerted Sivakami ran to the bikshu. She genuflected, brought her palms together and cried, 'Swami! Please forgive the angry words uttered by this helpless girl. Did you save my father? Is he alive? Where is he? How is he?'

'Amma, I saved your father's life. I fulfilled my promise to you. If you sit down and listen patiently, I will relate all that transpired,' replied the bikshu.

Sivakami sat down. The bikshu narrated how he had disguised himself as Pulikesi and had prevented the Chalukya soldiers from amputating Aayanar's limbs, how Aayanar had fallen from the mountain, had fractured his leg and lost consciousness. He also told her how he had transported an unconscious Aayanar to his forest residence and taken leave of him after he had regained consciousness. Listening to this, Sivakami felt deeply indebted to the bikshu. She regretted having suspected him. She told the bikshu with tear-filled eyes, 'Swami, I am deeply indebted to you for having saved my dear father from amputation and for having saved his life. Why did you apologize to me when you came here? It is I who ought to apologize for having unfairly suspected you! I thought that the Chalukya emperor and you were one and the same. I was angry thinking that it was you who had made me dance on the streets after bringing me to Vatapi. Swami, please forgive me!' When Sivakami uttered these words, tears filled her eyes.

'Sivakami! There is no necessity for me to forgive you. In truth, it is you who should forgive me. I have betrayed you. I am the reason behind your being imprisoned all by yourself in this far-off country! Please forgive me!' When the bikshu spoke in this manner, in a voice choked with emotion, Sivakami wiped away her tears and looked at Naganandi with amazement.

'Yes, Sivakami! I'm stating the truth. It was I who incited the Vatapi army to invade Kanchi. Initially, my brother, Pulikesi, had no such intention. The Vatapi army was supposed to march towards Vengi. It was I who asked Pulikesi to divide the army into two and lead one contingent to Kanchi. It was I who wrote to Pulikesi, stating that it would suffice if our brother Vishnuvardhanan led the second contigent to Vengi . . . My decision had disastrous consequences. Vishnuvardhanan's wife is now a widow. I escorted her and her infant son to Vatapi only today . . .'

'Swami were you away from this city all these days?' asked Sivakami.

'I was not here, Sivakami. Had I been here, would I have allowed your divine dancing to be laughed at? The barbaric Pulikesi, who is devoid of any artistic sensibility, has acted in this manner! Had I known that he would behave like this, I would not have handed you over to him on the banks of the North Pennai River . . .'

When the bikshu mentioned the banks of the North Pennai River, Sivakami recollected the image that had appeared in her dream when she was there. 'When did you leave me on the banks of the North Pennai River? How is that possible? Didn't I meet you near Kanchi and seek a boon from you?' she asked.

'I continued with my disguise as Pulikesi even after rescuing your father, Sivakami. I waged war with Mahendra Pallavan, disguised as Pulikesi. I defeated him at Manimangalam and pursued you. You met me on the banks of Ponnmugaliaru and beseeched me to free the imprisoned women of Pallava Nadu. I agreed to do so if you came to Vatapi willingly; you consented. I ought to have freed you then and united you with your father. I did not do so. I deceived you and brought you to Vatapi! . . . But I never ever imagined that the savage Pulikesi would humiliate you in this manner. Do you understand now why I apologized to you, Sivakami?' asked the bikshu.

'I do, swami! I now understand several issues which confused me earlier. But I still cannot understand one thing. Why did you act in this manner? Why did you behave so treacherously, why did you bring this helpless girl here? Of what use is this poor girl to you, who have renounced this world? What do you gain by separating me from my helpless father who is now injured? What did you seek to achieve by imprisoning me and bringing me here?'

'Sivakami, I will tell you, listen! The brave Vatapi army, which invaded Kanchi as advised by me, is now reduced to half. Vishnuvardhanan, who conquered Vengi and crowned himself king last year, died before he could consolidate that victory. You were the reason behind all these disasters! I did all this keeping you in mind. I will tell you why, listen!'

With this introduction, Naganandi started relating his story. He told her about his childhood spent in the Ajantha caves. He spoke about the painting of the Bharatanatyam dancer on the wall of the Ajantha caves, and his fantasies. An emotional Naganandi also recounted how he had travelled across Dakshina Bharata to understand the environment there and how he had been stunned to see the painting in the Ajantha cave come to life and dance at Aayanar's residence.

'From that day, I became a new person. All the castles I had built in the air regarding the Chalukya empire attaining supremacy lay shattered. My aspiration to bring this widespread Bharata Kandam under the control of a Buddha sangam, which I would ultimately head, also vanished. I decided that kingdoms and sangams were no longer important to me and that I would spend the rest of my life watching you dance. Since then, I was obsessed with bringing you to Vatapi. To achieve this, I engaged in deceitful activities and employed several ruses . . .'

When the bikshu spoke in this manner, the dual emotions of pride and compassion that Sivakami simultaneously felt came to the fore. She arrogantly thought, 'Ah! Two large kingdoms waged a war on account of this humble sculptor's daughter!' Then the compassionate thought, 'Aiyyo! All the atrocities I witnessed on the way from Kanchi to Vatapi were on account of me,' also struck her.

'Sivakami, your artistry mesmerized me so much that I was responsible for the outbreak of a war. I put in monumental efforts to save you from that coward, Mamallan. But all that has come to naught. The barbarian Pulikesi insulted you and your art by making you dance on the streets. Forgive me. I will make good the ignominy you have faced and the sorrow you have experienced. I will make arrangements to send you to your father's house. I have argued with the emperor and have secured his consent for this.'

Shouldn't Sivakami have danced with joy on hearing these words? Either due to fate or on account of a woman's contrary perspective, Sivakami was not happy. She remained silent and immersed in her own thoughts.

'Sivakami! Why aren't you saying anything? Tell me when you want to leave, I will arrange for a palanquin and adequate security to take you back. I will arrange for ladies-in-waiting to serve you and soldiers to safeguard you during your return journey. They will escort you up to Ponnmugaliaru . . .'

Sivakami, who had been calmly sitting and listening to the bikshu till then, suddenly stood up like one possessed and uttered the following horrific words. 'Adigal, listen to me. Do you know when I will leave Vatapi? One day, the brave Mamallar, whom you maligned as a coward, will invade this city. He will decimate the Chalukya forces like a lion attacking a skulk of foxes. He will despatch the sinner Pulikesi, who made me dance on the Vatapi streets, to Yama Loka. Rivers of blood will flow down the roads along which the imprisoned men and women of Tamizhagam were taken in procession. The corpses of Vatapi citizens will lie abandoned at the street junctions where the prisoners of Tamizhagam were made to stand and were whipped. The mansions and towers of the capital city of Vatapi will be set ablaze and be reduced to ashes. This city will become a graveyard. I will leave this city only after seeing this sight with my own eyes. Mamallar will come to defeat the Chalukya savages, hold my hand and take me back. I will leave only then. I will not leave when you send me. Even if you were to send me in a palanquin or on an elephant, I will not leave!'

A smile appeared on Naganandi's face after listening to this fearful vow. It seemed as though the wicked bikshu was secretly happy that his ruse had worked yet again!

Chapter 51

Jayasthambam[*]

There stood a hill two kaadam to the east of Vatapi. Dense forests surrounded the hill. Two adjacent caves were carved out of one of the hill slopes. The process of carving out the two caves was incomplete. Either the Buddhists or the Samanars must have started carving out the caves. Then, for some reason, they must have stopped it mid-way. A tiny stream was trickling out from one of the caves. The stream took a meandering path downhill, finally disappearing amongst the verdant trees. But certain objects that lay scattered amongst the rocks by the stream and under the trees marred the scenic beauty of the place and evoked a feeling of disgust. They were the symbols of the kabalikas—human skulls and cattle horns. The bloodstains on some rocks indicated that they had recently been used as sacrificial altars.

---

* Pillar (sthambam) commemorating victory (jaya)

The greenery in the region assumed a golden hue in the yellow evening sun. At this time, four people were seated on a rock that lay a short distance away from the caves. As they had travelled a long distance, they appeared tired. Their clothes were soiled, their locks matted. They sported beards. Wrinkles, which were unusual for their age, were seen on their faces; their eyes appeared more sunken. Nevertheless, there was an unusual glint in their eyes; courage and the determination to achieve their goals shone on their faces.

One man was standing atop the hill, surveying the surrounding area. Those who were seated on the rock below often looked up at him. Suddenly the man who was standing on the hill enthusiastically exclaimed, 'There!' The voice was that of our old friend, Gundodharan. Hearing him, the four men seated on the rock below smiled. They eagerly looked in the direction he was pointing to. A man was making his way through the dense forest. He was the chief of the Pallava Nadu espionage force, Shatrugnan. Unlike the others, Shatrugnan was clean-shaven. It was evident that he was returning from the city.

The five men surrounded Shatrugnan, who had a cloth bag slung on his shoulder. They asked, 'Shatrugna! Tell us quickly if your visit was a success or failure!'

Shatrugnan replied, 'It was a success!', as he removed the bag from his shoulder. Fruits spilled out of the bag and rolled down. The manner in which everyone hurried to pick up the fruits indicated how hungry they were. But there was one person whose attention was focused on what Shatrugnan had to say rather than on the fruits. Needless to say, it was Mamallar.

'Shatrugna, you said that your visit was a success. What do you mean by that? Did you see Sivakami?'

Shatrugnan replied, 'Yes, prabhu. I saw her!' and lapsed into silence again.

'Why are you silent? Where did you see her? How is she?' asked Mamallar.

'Prabhu! I saw Sivakami ammai. Everyone sit down; I will tell you where and how I saw her,' remarked Shatrugnan.

Immediately everyone sat down and Shatrugnan started talking. 'Last evening, I entered Vatapi disguised as a bangle seller. There was no difficulty in entering the city through the fort gates. People enter and leave the city freely. They would tighten the security of the fort only if they were anticipating an enemy to attack, wouldn't they? When the brave Vatapi forces have conducted successful military campaigns in all four directions—'

At that point, Commander Paranjyothi interrupted asking, 'What are you blabbering about, Shatrugna? What is this nonsense about successful military campaigns? Weren't the Vatapi forces defeated in their invasion of Dakshina Bharata? It is also obvious that the Vatapi forces that invaded Vengi are also in danger. Then how can you call the campaigns of the Vatapi army successful?'

Shatrugnan politely remarked, 'Commander, it isn't my opinion that the Vatapi army emerged victorious in all its military campaigns. I saw a tall jayasthambam erected at the centre of the city. I read the Prakrit inscription on the pillar. I will try to recite the engraving to the best of my ability. "Maha Rajadhiraja Rajamarthanda Ranathunga Sura Chaluka Kulathilaka Sapta Loka Devendra Pulikesi chakravarthy invaded Dakshina Bharata and defeated Mahendra Pallavan on the banks of the North Pennai River. Mahendra Pallavan fled from the battlefield and hid inside the Kanchi fort. Emperor Pulikesi continued his victorious campaign further south and crossed the Kaveri River by forming an elephant bridge. The Chera, Chola, Kallapalla and Pandya kings were waiting to seek refuge. He placed his lotus feet on their heads and blessed them. He returned to intensify his attack on the Kanchi fort. Mahendra Pallavan surrendered and beseeched the emperor to spare him. The emperor acquiesced to Mahendra Pallavan's request, enjoyed his hospitality and accepted the tribute paid by him. After successfully completing his military campaign in the south, the emperor returned to Vatapi heralded by trumpets and conches that proclaimed his victory on this Monday of the Shalivahana era. May this jayasthambam proclaiming the successful military campaign and the Chalukya dynasty flourish as long as this world exists!"'

The others exclaimed, 'What perfidy! How arrogant! We should not rest till we raze that jayasthambam to the ground!'

When they paused, Shatrugnan continued: 'Prabhu, when I read the inscription on the jayasthambam, I forgot myself. I even raised a foot to kick the pillar. Fortunately, and by God's grace, I remembered the purpose of our visit to Vatapi. I pretended to have lost my balance and fell down. People were swarming the streets. The consequences would have been disastrous had someone observed me!'

'Shatrugna, I am glad you remember the purpose of our visit to Vatapi. But you have not said anything about that yet!' observed Mamallar angrily.

'Prabhu, please forgive me. I walked ahead of the jayasthambam, which is an excellent testimony to the ability of the Chalukyas to lie. As I walked, I observed the excessive wealth of Vatapi and its citizens' ostentatious lifestyle. I was wondering how to trace Sivakami ammai and whom to ask about her in this vast city that spanned at least a kaadam from east to west and from south to north. I fortuitously saw her at a street junction . . .'

Several voices exclaimed in unison, 'What? At a street junction?'

'Yes; I saw her at a street junction. You will be shocked when you come to know what ammai was doing there. I too was taken aback when I saw her; I was distressed. But when I enquired and understood the reason, I felt extremely proud. Prabhu, Sivakami ammai is a testimony to the greatness of the women of Tamizhagam. Despite living desolately like an orphan, a hundred kaadam away at the enemy fort, ammai has demonstrated the merciful nature of the women of Tamizhagam—'

'Shatrugna! Why are you beating around the bush? What was Sivakami doing when you saw her?' demanded Mamallar in a harsh tone.

'Prabhu, I will tell you. Sivakami ammai was dancing there on the Vatapi street—'

'Ah!', 'What's this?' 'Shame! Shame!' 'Is this what you described as the greatness of the women of Tamizhagam, Shatrugna!' exclaimed those present.

'Pardon me; please patiently listen to what I have to say. I too felt very ashamed when I saw Sivakami ammai dance amidst a big crowd. I felt enraged. My ears were unable to tolerate the crass words uttered by the Vatapi citizens assembled there. I was so angry that I wanted to run to ammai and tell her, "Stop this ignominy!" Fortunately, my glance fell on the people who were standing behind ammai. Ah! How will I say this? Several men and women from Tamizhagam were chained together and made to stand there. They were guarded by demons holding whips. I stood frozen with shock on seeing this sight. When I recovered, I overheard what those in the crowd were saying. I also enquired around without arousing suspicion, and understood the reason for the occurrence of this shocking scene ...'

Shatrugnan then related the circumstances that led to Sivakami dancing on the street, as he understood it. Mamallar and the others felt goose pimples when they came to know that Sivakami was dancing to prevent the men and women of Tamizhagam from being whipped. They eagerly listened to what happened after that. 'I stood mesmerized like a cobra enthralled by mellifluous music watching Sivakami ammai dance. Ammai paused to regain her breath after dancing and then turned around. As soon as she did so, indescribable shock was evident in her eyes for a few moments. I looked in the direction she was looking. Do you know who was standing there?'

'Who? Who?' 'Was it Pulikesi?' asked those present.

'No, it was our friend Naganandi!' announced Shatrugnan.

Chapter 52

Bangle Seller

When Shatrugnan uttered the name Naganandi, those present were taken aback. Mamallar looked at Gundodharan as he exclaimed, 'Ah! The bikshu? In that case, what Gundodharan said was not correct!'

'No, prabhu. Gundodharan was right. The bikshu did visit Vengi en route to Vatapi. Unfortunately, he returned to Vatapi yesterday. His arrival has made the achievement of our task ten times more difficult. If only we had come two days ago!' lamented Shatrugnan.

'Did the bikshu return just yesterday? How did you come to know that Shatrugna?' asked Commander Paranjyothi.

'The entire city is talking about this, commander. I gathered it from the people's conversations. Wasn't Pulikesi's brother, Vishnuvardhanan, crowned king of Vengi last year? He probably ascended the throne at an inauspicious time—he died a few days ago. It seems Naganandi returned yesterday,

243

escorting Vishnuvardhanan's wife and his six-month-old infant son,' replied Shatrugnan.

'The Pallavendrar's prediction of the imminent destruction of the Chalukya kingdom is not inaccurate. How did Vishnuvardhanan die?' asked Paranjyothi.

'Vishnuvardhanan was unable to completely annihilate the Vengi army. As advised by our chakravarthy, the Vengi forces had retreated and hidden themselves in the forests on the banks of the Krishna and Godavari rivers. After Vishnuvardhanan was coronated, revolts broke out across the country. The soldiers in hiding attacked unexpectedly. Vishnuvardhanan set forth proclaiming that he himself would quell the revolts. After he was grievously injured in combat, more revolts broke out in the country. Naganandi reached Vengi in this situation. He escorted Vishnuvardhanan's wife and son to Vatapi. Prabhu, aren't you aware that Vishnuvardhanan's wife is Durvineethan's daughter?'

'Why do we have to worry about that, Shatrugna? You're relating gossip instead of talking about the task at hand. Tell us what happened next!' ordered Mamallar.

'Sivakami ammai, who was shocked on seeing Naganandi bikshu, soon regained her composure and sat in the palanquin. I followed the palanquin for some distance. It came to a halt at the entrance of a beautiful palace located in a quiet street. Sivakami ammai got down from the palanquin and entered that palace. I stood at the street corner, wondering what to do next. Then I walked to the entrance of the palace. Two sentries were posted outside. I asked them, "Does the danseuse from Kanchi reside here?" They responded, "Yes, why are you asking?" I replied, "I'm a bangle seller. I have brought beautiful bangles. I want to show them to ammai." They stated, "No one is permitted to enter this house at night; you can come tomorrow morning." I gossiped with them for some time and gathered a lot of information. I found out that Sivakami ammai, along with a lady-in-waiting and a cook, reside in that house and that no one visits her. Emperor Pulikesi had come to the palace just once and had asked ammai to perform at the royal court. As she had refused to do so, he had punished her by forcing her to dance on the street daily. Hearing this, even I was furious. I left that place cursing that cruel demon. When I reached the street corner, I observed a retinue of guards holding torches accompanying a palanquin. I hid behind a pillar of a house and observed who was coming. As I had expected, Naganandi bikshu was seated in that palanquin ...'

Hearing this, Mamallar ground his teeth. Commander Paranjyothi interjected saying, 'Shatrugna! Why are you unnecessarily lengthening your narrative? Did you meet ammai and speak to her? Is there any news? Tell us about that!'

Mamallar shot a slightly annoyed glance at Paranjyothi and remarked, 'Shatrugna, don't omit anything. Where did Naganandi go? To Sivakami's house?'

'Yes, prabhu. He entered ammai's palace. He was there for a nazhigai and then left. I was strolling around that street that whole nazhigai. I approached one of the sentries in between and asked him if there was a rest house or market close by. It was then that I observed Sivakami ammai talking to the bikshu angrily. I was able to hear what she was saying. It gave me immense satisfaction ...'

'Everyone here shares your sentiment!' quipped Gundodharan.

'I slept peacefully that night at a rest house in that street. Soon after dawn today, I visited ammai's residence. Sivakami ammai was shocked to see me. She sent the lady-in-waiting on an errand and then asked, "Shatrugna! What is this?

Didn't you go to Kanchi? Did you follow me here?" I replied, "No, ammani! I went to Kanchi and related your message to Mamallar. He has come; so has the commander!"

'Hearing this, Ammai became excited and agitated. She asked, "Where has the army camped?" I informed her that the army had not marched to Vatapi, that the commander and Kannabiran had come along with Mamallar, and that they were now at the foothills outside the fort. I told her that all of us would visit her at night the next day, which was a new moon night. I also told her that she should send away her lady-in-waiting on an errand and be prepared to come with us.' Saying this, Shatrugnan concluded his narrative.

Mamallar asked, 'What did Sivakami say?'

'Ammai did not speak much, prabhu. She said that she would be waiting for us and gave me leave.'

Hearing this, Mamallar grew thoughtful.

Chapter 53

Suspicion

On that new moon night, Sivakami was sitting alone in her palace. As her lady-in-waiting had mentioned that her mother was unwell, Sivakami had used it as a pretext to send her away.

A lantern was Sivakami's sole companion. Several thoughts arose in her mind. Every time she thought of Mamallar's impending visit, she felt a choking sensation. On the one hand, she felt anger and pride; on the other, sorrow and eagerness overcame her.

She often felt that her love for Mamallar was the root cause of all her sorrow. Had she fallen in love with a sculptor's son and married him as was appropriate for her social stature, would she have faced this ignominy? Why did Mamallar have to captivate her, who had been living in a secluded house in the midst of a forest? Having done so, why did he leave her behind at Mandapapattu and go away? It was her love for Mamallar that had compelled her to visit Kanchi. Again, it was her love that had instigated her to leave the fort through the secret tunnel. Ah! He was the reason behind all her sorrow! Though thoughts such as these fuelled her anger towards Mamallar, her yearning for him intensified as time slipped by.

In the middle of the night, when Sivakami was immersed in thought, she was startled by the sudden appearance of two bearded men. She sat up. However, the faces of the two men did not cause any fear. They appeared familiar. She asked them boldly, 'Who are you? Why have you come here in the middle of the night?'

As soon as Mamallar replied, 'Sivakami, don't you recognize me?' a surprised smile broke out on her face.

The smile that appeared on Sivakami's face after a long time enhanced her beauty. But the smile did not make Mamallar happy. The thought that Sivakami was happy in Vatapi caused Mamallar to frown. Sivakami stood up and asked in a choked voice, 'Prabhu! Is that you?'

'When you're leading a luxurious life at the Vatapi emperor's palace, how is it possible to remember old friends?' asked Mamallar in a harsh tone.

Hearing those cruel words, Sivakami stood motionless out of shock. She wondered if the person standing in her presence was truly Mamallar or a masquerader.

As both of them stood staring at each other, Commander Paranjyothi realized that it was inappropriate for him to be there. Immediately, he whispered into Mamallar's ear, 'Prabhu, please do not delay! We do not have much time', and walked to the entrance of the palace.

After Paranjyothi had disappeared from sight, Mamallar remarked, 'Oh! It seems that you're unable to recollect who we are. That's all right. Do you at least remember your father Aayanar, Sivakami?'

Sivakami's eyebrows knotted, anger caused her eyes to redden and widen; her lips twitched. She suppressed her anger with great effort and asked, 'Prabhu, how is my father? Where is he?'

'Aayanar is fine. He is as well as a man who has fractured his leg and lost his only daughter can be. He keeps asking, "Where is Sivakami? Where is my dear daughter?" Sivakami, come. Let's leave!'

Tears filled Sivakami's eyes; yet she made no effort to leave with Mamallar. 'Sivakami! Why are you still standing? If you wish to see your father alive, let's leave immediately!' urged Mamallar. Sivakami continued to stand motionless. 'What is this, Sivakami? Don't you wish to return to Kanchi? Ah! What I had suspected is true!' accused Mamallar.

Sivakami broke her silence to enquire, 'Prabhu, what did you suspect?'

'Why talk about it now? I will tell you later.'

'What was your suspicion, prabhu?'

'Do I have to tell you now?'

'You certainly have to tell me.'

'I suspected that, after having lived lavishly at the Vatapi emperor's palace, you would be reluctant to return with me.'

Hearing this, Sivakami laughed! Sivakami's laughter in the middle of the night jarred on Mamallar's ears. When Sivakami stopped laughing, she unequivocally stated, 'Yes, Pallava kumara! What you suspected is true. I am unwilling to leave this opulent palace. I am also unwilling to leave Vatapi; you may leave!'

Hearing this, sparks of anger darted from Mamallar's eyes. He exclaimed, 'What the elders say is true!'

'What do the elders say?'

'They say that women are fickle!'

'Haven't you now realized the truth in that statement? You may leave, prabhu!'

Mamallar muttered to himself, 'Ah! I travelled a hundred kaadam in search of you. Who can be smarter than me?' He then reasoned, 'Sivakami; you don't have to come for my sake. Come for your father's sake! Come for your friend, Kamali's sake! I promised them that I would bring you back.'

'I too made a vow, prabhu!'

'What vow have you made?'

'Why should I tell you?'

'Tell me, Sivakami! Tell me quickly!'

'You will not believe me even if I were to tell you. After all, it's a helpless maiden's vow!'

'Tell me now. We're getting delayed!'

'I have sworn to leave Vatapi only when the city is set on fire, the houses are reduced to ashes, rivers of blood flow down the streets, and the city is transformed into a graveyard!'

'This is a gruesome vow! Why did you make such a vow, Sivakami?'

'Prabhu, had you seen the horrific sights I saw en route to Vatapi, you would not ask this question. Had you witnessed the imprisoned men and women of Thondaimandalam being whipped in public and the kalarani of Pallava Nadu dancing in their presence, you would not have asked why I made this vow.'

'Sivakami, though I did not witness these sights, I'm aware of all that transpired. Nevertheless, why did you make such a ghastly vow?'

'Prabhu, several years and eons ago, a prince claimed to be in love with me. He promised to make me his consort when he ascended the throne. He swore on a spear and told me that he would never forget me. On the banks of a lotus pond drenched in the full-moon light, he promised me that I would be his wife in this birth and in all subsequent births. I believed that he was a true warrior and that he would uphold his word. It was this belief that drove me to make this vow,' Sivakami stated regally and looked up at Mamallar. Her sharp glance that pierced Mamallar's heart like a spear unsettled him.

Chapter 54

Disaster

Mamallar composed his disconsolate heart and looked at Sivakami with a kind expression on his face.

'Sivakami, your trust is not misplaced! I have come here to fulfil the promise I made. I have travelled a hundred kaadam, crossing forests, mountains and rivers. I have tolerated hunger and thirst and have foregone sleep. I rode my horse so swiftly that it is now on the verge of death. Forget the harsh words I uttered some time ago. I directed the anger I bore towards someone else at you. I never imagined that our meeting, after so many days, would be filled with anger and sorrow. I came here out of affection, building castles in the air. Sivakami, come, let's leave!'

'Prabhu, please forgive me, I will not come; I will come only after my vow has been fulfilled.'

'Sivakami, why do you speak thus? Don't you wish to come with me? There is no time to waste.'

'Illavarasey, fulfil the vow I have made. Kill the barbarian Pulikesi, set Vatapi ablaze, and then hold your slave by her hand and take her away. Then I will follow you like your shadow.'

'Sivakami, I swear I will uphold your vow. But that is no mean task. I have to mobilize a massive army and equip it with sufficient arms. I need time for all this; it may take several years ...'

'Is this the Pallava kumarar speaking in this manner? Is it such a difficult task to slay Pulikesi and defeat Vatapi? Have I, a helpless maiden, made this vow without understanding this ...? Pallava kumara! Return to Kanchi and attend to the affairs of the state. Don't worry about this humble sculptor's daughter! I am neither the daughter of the Pandya king nor the Chola king. What happens to me is of no concern to you. The fulfillment of my vow is of no consequence to you!' remarked Sivakami bitterly.

'Sivakami, is it you who is speaking in this manner? Is this the Sivakami I knew?' asked Mamallar.

'No, prabhu! I am not the Sivakami you knew. I have transformed into a new Sivakami. I am disillusioned with life. I am suspicious. Forget this new Sivakami. I had once asked you to promise me that you would never forget me. Now I ask you to forget me!' retorted Sivakami.

'Sivakami, heed me! You may have changed; I have not. I did not forget you even for an instant when we were apart. Memories of you filled my heart day and night, when I was awake and in my dreams, when I was at the palace and in the battlefield, and no matter what I did and whom I spoke to. I swear by my pure love for you. I will fulfil the vow you have made. Come with me now!' insisted Mamallar in a voice choked with emotion.

His words, which would have softened even a stone, had no impact on Sivakami. The difficulties she had experienced and the atrocities she had witnessed had hardened her.

'Who wants love and marriage?' asked Sivakami.

'Are you telling the truth? Don't love and marriage matter to you?' asked Mamallar furiously.

'I am stating the truth. I don't want to be in love; nor do I want to get married. Seeking revenge is of utmost importance to me. Pulikesi must die. Vatapi must be set on fire. The fear-stricken citizens of Vatapi must run around in despair. I desire nothing else!'

Once again, Mamallar spoke gently. 'Sivakami, I have now come to know of your desire. The anger I feel exceeds yours multi-fold. I yearn to seek revenge on the savage who humiliated you by imprisoning you. I will definitely fulfil your vow. I request you to come with me right away!'

'I will not come, Illavarasey! Inform the sculptor Aayanar that his daughter is dead!'

'Sivakami! Why are you so stubborn? Listen to what I have to say in conclusion! I will definitely fulfil your vow. But I will be disillusioned if you don't accompany me now. You will lose my love forever!'

'I don't need your affection, swami! Just fulfil my vow.'

'Lady! The Pallavas do not renege on their promises.'

'Illavarasey! Neither does the daughter of the sculptor, Aayanar, act contrary to her words!'

'Ah! Why this arrogance?' asked Mamallar.

'Yes, Illavarasey! I am arrogant. Why shouldn't I be so? Is it only the birth-right of the Pandya princess and the Chera princess to be arrogant? I may be a mere sculptor's daughter, but I belong to a tribe of valorous women from the ancient Tamizhagam. I am from the lineage of women who garland their lovers and send them to the battlefield. I was born in the same country where the Goddess Kannagi* was born. Why shouldn't I be arrogant, prabhu?'

Before Mamallar could think of saying something to convince Sivakami, Commander Paranjyothi came rushing inside. He whispered something into Mamallar's ears.

For an instant, Mamallar appeared dismayed. 'Commander, it seems as though all our plans will come to naught because of this obstinate girl!' Mamallar angrily turned to Sivakami and asked, 'Lady! Will you come with me, or won't you? I have no time to argue with you.'

Then Commander Paranjyothi interjected saying, 'Ammani, please understand our situation. Four of us have entered our foe's fort. Kannan and his father are waiting for us on the ramparts with a rope ladder. As we speak, the kabalikas are searching for us outside the fort. That fake bikshu has come to know of our arrival and is now at the street corner. Devi, in this situation, you shouldn't be unnecessarily stubborn . . .'

Elders have opined that a woman's mind is benighted. What Sivakami said then supported this view. 'Aiyya, I never realized that the Pallava kumarar and his dear friend would flee from mere kabalikas, who seek alms using skulls as bowls, and ochre-robe clad bikshus. Please forgive my ignorance. I never prevented you from escaping! You may leave,' she stated.

The Pallava kumarar felt a black fury. 'You obdurate woman! You will bear the consequences for this!' he fumed. He then told Paranjyothi, 'Commander! I now understand

---

* The protagonist of Illango Adigal's Tamil epic *Silapathikaram*, who opposed the Pandya king for wrongfully sentencing her husband to death and proved his innocence.

this treacherous woman's motives. She wants to betray us to that fake bikshu; come, let's go!'

Paranjyothi pleaded, 'Prabhu, please forgive me. I was listening to your conversation. Aayanar's daughter is incapable of such treachery. She is refusing to come due to the vow she has made—'

Mamallar interrupted. 'Commander! You are ignorant of the treacherous nature of women. All her claims of a vow are perfidy. She is unwilling to leave the Vatapi emperor's palace. Let's go!' So saying, Mamallar dragged the commander away by his arm.

Commander Paranjyothi stood firm and remonstrated, 'Prabhu! This is unfair. Leaving Sivakami ammai behind is a Himalayan blunder! If she refuses to come of her own accord, we must abduct her!'

When Sivakami heard these words, she trembled. She recollected Mamallar confiding in her that he had once dreamt that he had saved her from a venomous snake. She wondered, 'Will that dream come true now?' She hoped that Mamallar would carry her away, as Commander Paranjyothi had suggested. Ah! If only Mamallar had acted in that manner, all the disasters that were to occur in the future could have been avoided!

Fate deigned that Mamallar acted otherwise. 'No need, commander! No need! We need not abduct an unwilling maiden. I will fulfil my promise to her one day. She can then come if she so desires; till then her lot is with the fake bikshu ...'

As Mamallar was speaking, Shatrugnan and Gundodharan came running inside. 'Prabhu, the bikshu is walking around the street corner. Half the warriors who accompanied him are headed to the backyard of this house!' stammered Shatrugnan.

Again, Paranjyothi turned to Sivakami and frantically pleaded, 'Amma—'

'No, commander! No! This malicious woman is trying to get us captured by the bikshu! Come, let's go!' roared Mamallar. He then dragged Paranjyothi by his hand to the backyard of that palace. The next instant, the four of them disappeared from Sivakami's sight.

Chapter 55

A Dagger Was Wielded!

For a moment, Sivakami stared in the direction in which Mamallar and his companions had left. Then she fell in a heap on the floor. It seemed as though an invisible demon had contorted her body. All her bones seemed to be breaking. She felt as if she was being crushed by a mountain placed on her. Darkness enveloped her. The next moment, flashes of lightning passed through her mind. The house and the lantern seemed to revolve around her. Sivakami felt as though she was falling deeper and deeper into the netherworld. Ah! Would she never cease falling? Would she sink deeper and deeper forever?

Someone was calling, 'Sivakami! Sivakami!' in the distance. It was definitely not Mamallar's voice. She heard a noise that resembled a cobra's hiss close to her face. She also felt warm breath. She opened her eyes. Aiyyo! She saw a snake with its fiery eyes and raised hood! No; no! It wasn't really a snake, it was Naganandi. She had felt his poisonous breath on her face.

Sivakami exercised great effort to sit up and moved away from the bikshu. She was trembling. Naganandi looked at her and gently asked, 'My girl! What happened to you? What danger befell you? Why were you lying unconscious on the floor? Poor you! It must be difficult residing all alone in this large house. Where is your lady-in waiting? Where has she disappeared to . . . ?' As Naganandi spoke, he looked around.

Sivakami too looked in the same direction and noticed the turban and angavastram left behind by Mamallar who had rushed out in a hurry. She was disconcerted. Naganandi, not having noticed these, approached Sivakami and remarked, 'My girl, listen to me. I am saying this for your good!' His cold hand held Sivakami's. Immediately, Sivakami began trembling again. She fantasized for a moment that a cruel cobra was about to bite her. She composed herself and swiftly extricated her hand from his grip.

'Ah! Sivakami! Why do you tremble at the sight of me? What harm did I cause you? All I did was to shower genuine affection on you! What did I do to you except save your father's life? Why do you hate me?' asked the bikshu in a gentle voice.

'Swami, I am neither scared of you nor do I hate you. You did not harm me in any manner for me to hate you. You have done a lot of good for me!' replied Sivakami.

'I'm happy, Sivakami! It suffices that you acknowledge this. Why are you shivering still? Are you unwell?' he enquired.

'Yes, adigal. I'm unwell!' stated Sivakami.

'Is that so? I will send for a good physician tomorrow. But where did your lady-in-waiting disappear to when you are unwell? Is she fast asleep in some corner of this house?' Enquiring thus, the bikshu looked around. The turban and angavastram that lay behind a pillar caught his eye. 'Ah! What's this? It seems as if someone has been here.' He went to the pillar and studied the things lying there. He turned around and asked Sivakami in a mocking tone, 'Well done, Sivakami! You have found lovers here too, so soon? Are they from Vatapi or are they outsiders?'

Sivakami continued to stand silently. He stated, 'You will not reply. I will find out myself!' He then walked towards the entrance.

Sivakami immediately recollected Mamallar's words. 'She is trying to betray us to the bikshu!' The disastrous consequences of the bikshu tracing them occurred to her in a flash. A flustered Sivakami looked around. She saw a glittering object lying under the prince's angavastram. Sivakami's eyes then glowed with an unnatural light. She leapt forward and picked up that object. It was a dagger, as she had expected. The next moment, Sivakami threw the dagger at the bikshu's back. The bikshu fell down shrieking. Blood oozed out of the spot on his back where the knife had pierced him. The bikshu turned around, looked at Sivakami, and divulged in a compassionate voice, 'My girl! What have you done? I rushed here only to unite you with your lover, Mamallan!'

Chapter 56

Mahendrar's Request

By the time Mamallar, Paranjyothi and the others returned to Kanchi, Mahendra Pallavar's health had deteriorated. When he heard that they had not brought Sivakami back, he became weaker. Though Thiruvengadu Namasivaya vaidhyar treated him very skilfully, his health did not improve. One day, Mahendra Pallavar summoned his son, Mamallar, the ministers' council, army commanders and the chiefs of kottams. The chakravarthy looked around at everyone as he lay on the bed. He observed everyone's eyes brimming with tears and their devotion and loyalty evident in their faces.

Those who had heard Mahendra Pallavar's leonine voice previously were taken aback when they listened to his feeble speech. They tried to suppress their emotions. Mahendra Pallavar confessed, 'It is twenty-five years since I ascended the famed throne of the Pallavas. The devotion and loyalty you have demonstrated thus far is incomparable. When Kanchi's eminence spread across Bharata, you were devoted and loyal to me. You treated my wishes as commands and my words as law. That's not surprising. When I committed one mistake after another, when Kanchi's fame was on the wane, when we had to retreat in the face of an invasion and when we had to hide inside the Kanchi fort, you remained unflinching in your loyalty to me. You demonstrated your unswerving devotion to me. I disregarded your wishes and invited the Chalukya king Pulikesi to Kanchi. Despite this, you tolerated the devastating consequences of that visit. Now that I am approaching the last days of my life, I would like to convey the immense gratitude I feel for you. I humbly request you to forgive me for the mistakes I've committed and for the hardships you had to undergo on account of those mistakes . . .'

When Mahendra Pallavar spoke in this manner, some of those assembled wept copiously.

The prime minister stepped forward and requested, 'Prabhu, I beseech you not to speak in this manner. When you ask for our forgiveness, it is akin to punishing us. Don't cause us distress by assuming responsibility for mistakes you did not commit. All that occurred was fated to happen. There is no use in dwelling on bygones!'

Mahendra chakravarthy continued: 'Sarangadeva Bhattar's words further increase my debt of gratitude to you. I will state the reason for my summoning all of you here. These are the last days of my life. My soul will leave this weak and sick body in a few days. My dear son, Narasimhan, will perform the last rites for his deceased father in accordance with Vedic traditions . . .'

When the chakravarthy uttered these words, Mamallar, unable to control his sorrow and rage, cried out, 'Appa! Appa!'

Mahendra Pallavar affectionately embraced his son, looked up, and remarked, 'My child, I must say what I have to say. If you feel distraught listening to me, you may step out for some time and then return!' But Mamallar did not leave the chamber. The chakravarthy addressed the ministers' council again: 'My dear son will perform my last rites. You will also pay your respects to the deceased chakravarthy. But my soul will never rest in peace until you fulfil the request I am about to make. Otherwise it will not be in peace even if it were to reside in heaven.'

'Prabhu, please tell us. All those assembled here are ready to swear to abide by your command, whatever it is!' beseeched the prime minister.

'You are aware of the great slur cast on the Pallava dynasty on account of my recklessness and the Chalukya king's treachery. I am unable to obliterate that insult. I am taking leave of you without restoring the lost glory of the Pallava dynasty. You must achieve the task I am unable to. The Pallava army must invade the Chalukya kingdom, decimate the Chalukyas, defeat Pulikesi, raze Vatapi to the ground and set it ablaze. The Pallava jayasthambam must stand tall and proud amidst the ruins of Vatapi. Only then will the slur cast on the Pallava dynasty and Tamizhagam's valour be erased. This is my request. Will you fulfil this?'

'We will! We will!' echoed several voices in unison. Those assembled raised the following victory slogans. 'Long live Mahendra Pallavendrar! Long live the brave Mamallar!'

Once again, Mahendra Pallavar looked at everyone and remarked, 'I again convey my heartfelt gratitude to you.'

Then the prime minister observed, 'Prabhu, when you articulated your request, all of us consented to fulfil it. But the two people who are key to fulfilling your request kept quiet. I am referring to the kumara chakravarthy and Commander Paranjyothi. I am unable to comprehend their silence.'

'Mamallar and Paranjyothi have already sworn to do so. That's why they are silent now. Courtiers, you must support them in fulfilling their promise! I need to discuss an important matter with Mamallan. I need to communicate the outcome of that discussion to you. Please give us some time,' he requested.

Chapter 57

Royal Canon

The ministers and the courtiers who had surrounded Mahendra Pallavar understood his desire and stepped away. They were waiting to congregate once again when the chakravarthy summoned them. Mamallar stood next to the chakravarthy and Paranjyothi stood some distance away, with their arms folded. The entrance to the anthapuram was located beside the mandapam in which Mahendra Pallavar lay. When Mahendra Pallavar looked towards the anthapuram, a lady-in-waiting hurried towards him. The Pallava emperor instructed her, 'Fetch the maharani!'

Then he told Mamallar, 'My child, I had decided to complete two tasks before I close my eyes forever. One of them is now complete. To ensure that the minsters' council poses no obstacles to your fulfilling Sivakami's vow and bringing her back from Vatapi, I have secured their commitment in your presence. They will not renege on their promise. They will extend their full support to your invasion of Vatapi.'

Mamallar did not respond.

'Mamalla, I depend on you to complete the second task. You will have to fulfil it. The ministers' council immediately acceded to the request of the chakravarthy, who is on his death bed. Won't you, my dear son, also comply with my last wish?' asked Mahendrar.

'Appa! I will obey your command, whatever it may be. Please don't utter words like request and beseech!' pleaded Mamallar.

'Kumara, the responsibility of ruling this vast kingdom is soon going to rest on you. The time for you to ascend the Kanchi throne, with a renowned ancestry of over a thousand years, is nearing . . .'

'Appa, if you intend on speaking in this manner, I wish to leave this place. I seek neither the throne nor the kingdom. All I want is you. You must lead a long and healthy life . . .'

'Mamalla! It is futile to close our eyes and refuse to acknowledge what lies ahead. I will not be alive for long. Even if I were to live, I am unlikely to be healthy. I cannot bear the burden of ruling the kingdom anymore. You must assume that responsibility . . .'

'I never refused to assume responsibility, did I? You can sit on the Kanchi throne and command me. If I fail to uphold your command, you can question me.'

'That's good, my son! If you have to assume the responsibility of ruling this kingdom, there is an important prerequisite. You must fulfil that prerequisite!'

'State the condition, appa!' pleaded Mamallar. His sorrow was beyond words.

'My child, I do not want to be evasive. You're my only son. The ancient Pallava dynasty should not come to an end with you. To be eligible to ascend the Kanchi throne, you must get married. Mamalla, marry the Pandya princess. I want to see you married before I die. If not, my soul will not be in peace!' insisted the chakravarthy.

These words increased the sorrow in Mamallar's heart. Even if a sword had pierced his heart, it would not have caused so much pain. He kept quiet for some time and then asked, 'Appa, why do you test me thus? Don't you understand my mind? Aren't you aware that my love for Sivakami is indestructible? When I have lost my heart to one maiden, how can I marry someone else? Wouldn't such an action spell doom to all three of us? Are you commanding me to perform such a task?' Every word of his reflected the agony he was going through.

Mahendra Pallavar patted his son with love and affection. Then he counselled in a gentle tone, 'Yes, Narasimha, I am commanding you to perform such a task. I understand the nature of the task. Listen, Narasimha. In this world, civilians and royalty are bound by different codes of conduct. Civilians may act in a manner that reflects their personal preferences. But royalty cannot act in that manner. They must forget about their happiness. The personal lives of royalty are to be conducted in a manner that is conducive to the nation's welfare. Narasimha, think about it. Is it still possible for you to marry Sivakami? You are not going to invade Vatapi today or tomorrow. You would have to prepare for the invasion for several years. Then, who can predict for how long the war will be waged? Will you remain unmarried for so long? Will the citizens of Pallava Nadu consent to this?'

Mamallar heaved a deep sigh; he felt overwhelming anger towards Sivakami. The refusal of that unfeeling woman to accompany him had put him in a quandary! Understanding his train of thought, Mahendrar asked,

'Kumara, didn't I advise you that royalty must ignore their personal preferences and that their actions must be guided by the welfare of the nation? Even in this situation, I had decided to perform an unusual task for the good of the nation. Do you know what that is?' Mahendrar paused.

A puzzled Mamallar looked alternatively at his mother and father. 'Yes, kumara! I had decided to marry again at this age. Had you brought Sivakami back from Vatapi, I would have married her . . .'

When Mahendrar said this, Mamallar cried out, 'Appa!'

'Narasimha, please forgive me! It was for the sake of the kingdom that I had decided to undertake such an unpleasant task. I wanted to act in that manner to stop you from marrying Sivakami. I explained this to your mother and secured her consent. But Sivakami refused to leave Vatapi and saved me from committing the sin!'

Mamallar's heart went out to Sivakami, who was living all alone in the Vatapi palace. 'Ah! Her refusal to accompany me was for the good.'

'Kumara, think about it now. Is the task I am asking you to perform in the interest of the kingdom more difficult than what I was about to do? Think about how much stronger the Pallava kingdom will become by your marrying the Pandya princess. You have great heights to scale. Is invading Vatapi and decimating the Chalukya dynasty a mean task? You require a lot of support. This task may be achieved only through the concerted efforts of all the kings in Dakshina Bharata. Even if you have one foe here, will you be able to march northwards and invade Vatapi? Narasimha, from all perspectives, it is essential for you to marry the Pandya princess . . .'

After Mahendrar spoke continuously in this manner, he felt breathless. Seeing his pain, Bhuvana Mahadevi asked,

'Prabhu, should you speak for so long? Hasn't the vaidhyar instructed you not to speak for too long?' She then looked at Mamallar and muttered, 'My child! Your father . . .' Mamallar did not want his mother to speak further.

'Appa, please don't speak too much. I will marry the Pandya princess,' he acquiesced, gritting his teeth.

Mahendra chakravarthy's face brightened. But Bhuvana Mahadevi looked away to hide her tears. As soon as Mahendra Pallavar gestured, Commander Paranjyothi and the ministers stepped forward. 'Leaders! I have made you wait for a long time. To compensate for this, I am now going to announce a bit of joyous news. The wedding between the kumara chakravarthy and the Pandya princess has been fixed. In that very hall and at that very muhurtham, Commander Paranjyothi's marriage will also be solemnized.'

When Mahendra Pallavar made this announcement, those assembled joyfully cheered, 'Long live Mamallar! Long live the commander!

* * *

To be continued . . .

Glossary

Tamil Months	
Cittirai	mid-April to mid-May
Vaikasi	mid-May to mid-June
Ani	mid-June to mid-July
Aṭi	mid-July to mid-August
Avaṇi	mid-August to mid-September
Puraṭṭasi	mid-September to mid-October
Aippasi	mid-October to mid-November
Karthikai	mid-November to mid-December
Markazhi	mid-December to mid-January
Thai	mid-January to mid-February
Masi	mid-February to mid-March
Pankuni	mid-March to mid-April
Distances	
1 kaadam	Approximately 10 miles or 16 kilometres

Units of Time	
1 nazhigai	24 minutes
1 muhurtham	48 minutes
1 jaamam	2 hours 24 minutes
10 jaamams	1 day